STAGES

Also By Whitney Amazeen

Meadow Hills Series

A Summer of Dandelions

Carefree Series

One Carefree Day

One Day Too Late

Something Bright and Burning

LITTLE BIRDIE BOOK 1

STAGES

Whitney Amazeen

Published by Swan Pages Publishing LLC.

This book is a work of fiction. The characters and events in this book are fictitious. Any similarity to real persons, living or dead, is purely coincidental and not intended by the author.

Cover Illustration & Design: Andra Murarasu
Editor: Wendy Higgins at Pink Pen Editing

ISBN: 978-1-961559-86-8 (ebook), 978-1-961559-85-1 (paperback)

First Edition: November 2024

10 9 8 7 6 5 4 3 2

Zach—this one's for you, little brother.

Playlist

1. *Hunnybee* — Unknown Mortal Orchestra
2. *Cool Kids* — Echosmith
3. *Stuck* — The Aces
4. *When Am I Gonna Lose You* — Local Natives
5. *Hollywood* — RAC, Penguin Prison
6. *Brooklyn* — Fickle Friends
7. *Elevate* — St. Lucia
8. *hold on* — flor
9. *Something Has to Change* — The Japanese House
10. *Cinema* — Harry Styles
11. *We Fell in Love in October* — Ricky Jamaraz
12. *Illin'* — Black Kids
13. *Enjoy the Silence* — Depeche Mode
14. *Nonsense* — Sabrina Carpenter
15. *restless soul* — flor
16. *Rose Colored Lenses* — Miley Cyrus
17. *Hurricane Jane* — Black Kids
18. *Autumn Leaves* — Ed Sheeran
19. *Fake Nice* — The Aces
20. *Adore You* — Harry Styles

"I have dreamt in my life, dreams that have stayed
with me ever after, and changed my ideas; they have
gone through and through me, like wine through
water, and altered the color of my mind."

— Emily Bronte, *Wuthering Heights*

Chapter One

My heart thunders in my chest as I stare at the door to the audition room. It feels like I stood up too fast or maybe ate something bad. The last thing I want to do right now is walk through that door and read cheesy lines to a drama teacher who will probably laugh at me. "Remind me again why I'm doing this."

Carlton chuckles. He places his hands on my shoulders and squeezes. "You tell me." His voice tickles my neck as he speaks against the collar of my uniform shirt, the sweet, minty scent sending pleasant shivers down my spine. "I've been wondering the same thing."

His presence is the only reminder I need. *He's the reason you're doing this, Dot. You need to impress him so he'll finally ask you to be his girlfriend.*

I paste a smile on and face him, my eyes fluttering as his gaze meets mine. "I'm just kidding. I'm interested, remember? The way you talk about how much you love this stuff has me curious is all. And I have no other extracurriculars at the moment. This should help my college applications a lot."

When he grins again, the sight of his bright smile and endearing, golden-brown eyes taking me in practically makes me melt. He taps my nose with his thumb. "You're adorable."

And just like that, my heart restarts.

Carlton is the whole package—smart, sweet, Black, and even more boujee than I am. So I lead us through the doors of the classroom.

The brightly-lit room is set up with a heavy, oak podium at the head and groups of seating sprinkled throughout the space. The hum of conversation dims a little when we enter, and I notice several inquisitive gazes on my face, noting me and Carlton standing so close together. I feel a swell of pride at the idea that they might assume we're together. Carlton cocks his head at an empty cluster of seats, and we sit. Our wood desks creak beneath our weight, and I wonder if they, like the rest of this prep school, are old enough to belong in a history book.

More students enter the room one by one, filling the remaining empty seats. When the rest of Carlton's friends arrive—the offensively pretty Evans twins and Rue Sullivan, they have to lean against the wall because there are no more seats available.

"There are so many people here," I whisper to Carlton. "Do they all want to audition?"

He nods. "The drama club here is fire. Everyone and their mom wants to be part of the play."

I frown, struggling to remember some of the details he shared with me this summer before term began. "Because of that gossip columnist, right? Everyone wants to be featured by her?"

He nods, holding my gaze like it's a shared secret between us. "Yeah. And Little Birdie only talks about the drama students for some reason. It's wild."

I'm about to ask more questions, but I'm interrupted by the appearance of the drama teacher, a tall, balding gentleman with pink cheeks who looks fifty-something. When he makes his way to the blackboard, some of the chatter in the room dies down. He writes his name, Mr. Saltzman, at the top of the board and turns to stand at the podium, straightening his stack of papers on the surface.

"Hi there, everyone. My name is Mr. Saltzman, and I'm thrilled to be leading this year's auditions for Fallbrook Christian Prep's winter performance of the beloved Wuthering Heights."

There's a smattering of claps.

"Before we begin," he continues, straightening the square glasses on his nose, "I just want to stress something. There is no small part in any production. Every role in this play is as important as the lead, and I mean that. With that being said, if you don't receive a callback, it's not necessarily a bad thing. That could mean that I know exactly what role will best suit you and that's that."

A few people snort.

"Callbacks are almost always a good thing," Carlton whispers. "At least, if you want a main part."

I shrug. "And I don't want that, obviously. I'm just wetting my feet here."

"Our first audition today will be Meredith Evans and Nicolas Saffron," Mr. Saltzman continues. "Please follow me to the adjoining room next door."

Meredith, the green-eyed Evans twin, blinks in surprise. Her sister, Mabel gently nudges her forward, and Meredith follows another classmate to the door where the teacher is waiting.

The three of them disappear, and the chatter resumes full force. A few students crowd around Carlton, firing off questions for him about last year's play and asking if he thinks he'll get the lead this year.

"I really, really hope so," he says. As he describes his role in last year's production, he idly traces shapes on my panty-hosed knee with his pinkie, making heat travel through my body.

"It will either be you or Zayne," someone tells Carlton. "That's my guess."

His finger briefly stills on my tights, and then resumes. "I guess we'll find out," he murmurs.

After what seems like fifteen minutes, the door opens at the front of the classroom, and Meredith and Nicolas exit, followed by the instructor. Meredith is grinning, practically oozing confidence, but Nicolas is wearing a grim, sullen expression.

Without preamble, Mr. Saltzman returns to the podium and picks up his list. "Up next is Zayne Silverman." He scans the page with intensity. "Zayne, let's have you read with Bardot Bennett."

Oh, crap. My heart beats like a drum as I stand from my desk, painfully aware of all the curious eyes watching me. As the new girl at Fallbrook Christian Prep, it's only expected I'll stand out. I've been mentally preparing for random glances and questioning gazes all month. But with the classroom full of attentive stares currently on my face, I feel like a giant spotlight is permanently fixed above me. "It's Dot, actually," I tell Mr. Saltzman, and clear my throat when my voice comes out too quiet. "I just go by Dot."

"Dot," he repeats, making note of it on the paper.

A boy—Zayne, I presume—stands. All I can see is the back of his head, his undercut topped with short dreads as he makes his way toward Mr. Saltzman.

Carlton offers my knee a final comforting squeeze like a sendoff, and I make my way forward, following Zayne. We stop in front of the door that leads to the classroom adjoining ours. The audition room.

Mr. Saltzman smiles warmly at me. "You must be new here, Dot. Welcome." He extends his hand and I shake it. His friendly gray eyes, framed by those stylish square glasses, do little to ease my nerves.

"Hi." I try not to glance behind me at the classroom full of theater students still waiting their turn to audition. I can practically feel the heat of Carlton's gaze on my back. After the summer we had together before school began, the feeling of it has become somewhat familiar.

Unable to resist, I look over my shoulder.

Just as I expect, he meets my stare. The corner of his full mouth lifts, and I can't help but smile in return.

"If you'll both follow me next door, we can begin the

audition," says Mr. Saltzman, holding the door open for us. The boy standing next to me nods. I take a peek at him, and my eyes almost fall out of my face. He's tall, with velvety brown skin and strong cheekbones. Lean muscle stretches the arms of his grey v-neck sweater. Long lashes frame his warm, deep eyes, and there's a hint of sweetness in the air surrounding him. I look away before he can notice me ogling him and follow Mr. Saltzman to the classroom next door.

The room is empty, save for the three of us. As we walk in, dust particles stir in the air, catching the light filtering in through the tall, narrow windows. Mr. Saltzman leans against one of the heavy, wooden desks, crosses his ankles, and hands each of us a script. "We'll be reading a scene from the middle of the play," he says. "Dot, I'll have you read for the character Catherine at the top of page twenty-six. Zayne, you read for Heathcliff."

Zayne walks to the front of the classroom, so I follow him. We stand before the whiteboard, which is covered in a half-erased chemistry formula. I flip through the Wuthering Heights script to the correct page, my stomach a bundle of nerves. Why am I even doing this, again? I'm not an actor. I've never acted in anything before. Yet, here I am, standing in front of the acting teacher, auditioning for a play at a new school where I hardly know anyone.

Just get through this audition, I tell myself, *and you'll fit right in with Carlton and his theater friends. Besides, you'll probably get cast as a tree or something.* No biggie.

When my family first moved to Cambridge from our small, rural Massachusetts town, I'd been worried about starting over at a completely new school and having no friends. So, when the cute guy in my new neighborhood told me we'd be going to the same school, I latched onto him immediately. Anything to avoid being a loner, which is why I couldn't resist when he invited me to check out the drama club to see what he and his friends were all about.

But now that I'm actually here, it's more nerve-wracking than I was prepared for. I take a deep breath.

The boy—Zayne—reads his lines with concentration, sounding dark and broody. I want to laugh for some reason, even though I'm kinda impressed.

When it's my turn, I blink myself back to attention and fumble with my script. "Don't you know...uh." I clear my throat, scanning the words on the paper for where I'm supposed to speak. "Don't you know I'll always come back?"

Zayne stares at me with narrowed brows, and I feel my cheeks get hot. "Sorry," I say. "I'm new at this."

He ignores me, reading the rest of his lines. Shoot. Wasn't supposed to break character yet.

Zayne takes my hand, and I jolt in surprise. Is this part of the scene? "Come away with me then, as we planned," he murmurs, staring deep into my eyes. His expression is entirely focused on my next words.

My heart pounds in my chest. Wow, this guy is good. I glance at my lines on the paper in my other hand. Something about how seriously he's taking this makes me want to try a little harder. "I can't," I read. "I'm frightened."

"Of what?" Zayne's frown deepens and he leans in so our faces are almost touching. *Oh, wow...*"Of poverty?"

I blank again because he makes the question sound like he's asking it, not his character. But then I remember all my lines are written down, so I check what my character says next. "You're asking me to risk my reputation." I crack a smile when Zayne's lips turn down at my response because this is actually kinda...fun. "Once a woman loses her reputation, she has nothing."

He scowls. "The old Cathy would never have said such a thing." He forms a fake grip around my arms and pretends to shake them. I swallow down a giggle. From Mr. Saltzman's view, it probably looks like Zayne has an iron grip on my arms, when really he's barely touching me.

"The old Cathy didn't know any better." I turn my nose up in the air.

Zayne searches my face. "If you've become indifferent to me, at least do me the favor of releasing me." The words are anguished. Tortured. I almost believe him.

Line...what was my next line? I scan the page and meet his stare again. "I'm as trapped as you are."

As we continue going back and forth, the weirdest thing happens. I stop bumbling my lines and let myself really fall into the whole thing. It's like everything else melts away and I can't deny how good it feels to stop being Dot, just for a moment.

This is the most at ease I've felt in ages, going back and forth with Zayne like this, throwing myself into the dialogue, the face expressions, the hand gestures.

And when we're finished, Mr. Saltzman looks... impressed. He claps for us. "Outstanding, you two."

It's because of Zayne. Not you, Dot. He carried that entire audition.

But it feels good to pretend anyway—just for the moment—that Mr. Saltzman is also impressed by me, too.

I drive home after my audition. As much as I wish I could have waited with Carlton till his turn was over, Dad wouldn't like me missing dinner.

Or tonight's phone call.

Still, I'm excited to hear Carlton tell me how his audition went when I call him tonight.

The weather is warm, the last remnants of summer barely in the air, so I roll down the windows of my yellow sedan and let my long braids whip out behind me. There's so much traffic here, it almost makes more sense not to own a car. But, coming from a town like Stockbridge, which is full of vast expanses of nothing, I'm used to driving. It's not a bad thing either; being stuck in New England traffic. The trees have already begun to shift from lush green to orange and maple. The stunning scenery of Boston passes me by as I arrive in East Cambridge, my new neighborhood. Tour boats float along the twinkling Charles River that separates Boston from Cambridge. The bulbs in the green iron streetlights lining the road illuminate as the day starts to dim, and the brownstone I now call home comes into view.

This is the life.

Or, it will be once I impress Carlton with my ability to fit in. Then his impression of me might finally shift from "that cute, new girl who doesn't have anything in common with me and my friends" to "girlfriend material." After today's audition, though, I'm a little doubtful. Zayne's performance definitely put mine to shame. I'll be amazed if I get a part at all.

I park on the street and grab my leather backpack from the passenger seat. From the outside, the average person walking by would take one look at our elegant home right on the Charles River and think we're living a dream.

But from the outside, my life is a lie.

When I open the front door, Dad's favorite jazz station greets my ears, floating down the hall from the TV. I plop my bag on the entryway table and make my way down the hall. I stop in front of the first door, knocking. "Beau?"

The door opens and my younger brother peeps his head out. "When did you get here?"

"Just now." I ruffle his curly hair. "What do you want for dinner?"

He shrugs. "I don't really care."

I roll my eyes. "Of course not. Because you're a middle schooler now, and everyone knows middle schoolers don't care about anything."

"Whatever."

I know he's annoyed by my teasing, but I can't resist. Ever since we moved to the city, Beau has been on a mission to *reinvent* himself, meaning he's now too cool for everyone. If I can get away with making fun of him while Dad is working, I'm obviously going to.

I turn on the stove and make us some mac and cheese,

covering the pot with a lid so it stays warm until Beau will inevitably creep from his room to the kitchen to secretly eat. I take my bowl to my room when I'm done so I can call Carlton.

I have to admit, my new bedroom is amazing. The walls are painted a soft, buttery yellow, and my bed is adorned with plush pillows and a cozy comforter in shades of sunny gold and pale lemon. Near the window, gauzy yellow curtains allow sunlight to stream in, illuminating the space. I sit on my bed and take a few bites before tapping Carlton's contact photo on my phone. The phone rings a few times, but he doesn't answer.

I frown. Try again. Still no answer.

I can't help the pang of disappointment that shoots through me. I go on Instagram and find his page. He posted a photo this morning before school. In it, he's got his back to the camera, hands in the pockets of his beige uniform pants, his shoulders relaxed. He's standing in front of the drama room, and the caption reads, "Happy to be back home."

I scroll through the comments. There are over fifty of them. Some are from random people complimenting him, and others are from profiles I recognize—his friends, talking about how excited they are for the next play. But one comment makes me pause.

lilo_thestagegirl: Wonder what Little Birdie will have to say. Either way, this better be the year that gets you into Underwood.

I try to remember more of what Carlton told me over the summer about Little Birdie, the anonymous gossiper from Fallbrook. We were at the beach when he first brought it up, waiting in line for cotton candy. "You won't have to worry about her posting about you," he told me. "Not unless you join the drama club. We're the only students who get talked about for some reason." He snaked his hand around my waist. "And even if you do join, I bet there will be nothing but nice things to say about you."

I laughed, not really caring about the chance I might get posted about on some random app that only the kids at my new school cared about. It was probably some loner who didn't have any friends, with nothing better to do than talk about other people.

I look at the Instagram comment again, focusing on the second part of it.

Either way, this better be the year that gets you into Underwood.

I expand the comment and see that Carlton replied.

carlton_peters: Oh, it will be.

My heart sinks at his response. Since the day I met Carlton, he's gone on and on about getting into Underwood Academy, Boston's most prestigious acting school for high school and college students. Probably in the same way that I've incessantly talked about getting into Harvard or Yale.

But if Carlton gets into Underwood, he'll spend the rest of high school there, leaving me behind senior year.

With a sigh, I navigate away from his page and allow myself a few moments of stalking my favorite fashion influencers. I screenshot a few outfits I'd love to put my own spin on.

"Dot?" Beau says from my bedroom doorway.

I shut off my phone screen. "What?"

"Some of your new friends were at the door, so I let them in."

"What?" I screech. I'm about to get out of bed when I hear their footsteps coming down the hall. My hopes lift momentarily. *Maybe Carlton is with them.* But I'm disappointed when Carlton isn't with his friends, who are now my friends, too. Kind of.

"Hey, Dot," says Rue. She smiles at me and sits on my bed. The twins, Mabel and Meredith linger in the doorway. They're wearing matching white sweat-suits, but their hair is different. Mabel's is out and curly, and Meredith's is in a straightened ponytail. I recently discovered that they used to be baby models for a kids' clothing company, and I can see why. They're both not only beautiful, but also interesting to look at, especially since they would be identical if it weren't for Mabel having two different colored eyes, one brown and the other green.

"How was your audition?" Meredith asks. "Who did you read with besides Zayne?"

I frown. "Uh, no one. Was I supposed to?"

"Usually you read with a few people," shrugs Mabel.

"Well, that makes sense." I blush. "I did horrible. I bet

Mr. Saltzman didn't want to put anyone else through my acting. It was cringe."

Rue laughs. "Stop it."

"Yeah," Mabel says. "I bet you weren't that bad."

"Whatever you're imagining," I tell them, "I promise you it's worse."

"I did pretty great," states Meredith. "Mabel and I will probably get the lead roles this year. Again."

Mabel offers a shy, dimpled smile.

"I don't care about getting a big part. As long as I have some lines this time," says Rue.

I'm about to tell them I don't even care about getting lines at all, when all three of their phones go off at the exact same time. The notification is a seductive whistle in a distinct tune.

Meredith rips her phone from her pocket. "Little Birdie."

I'm left staring as they check their phones, my expression hopefully not as confused as I feel. "Little Birdie posted something? How can you tell?"

"The app alerted us," says Meredith, as if it should be obvious.

Mabel's mouth rounds into a giant O. "You haven't downloaded it, yet?"

"I'll send you the link, Dot," says Rue, eyes still glued to her cell. "Guys, look at this. It says that Zayne and Carlton had to read together for the audition."

"How does Little Birdie even know?" I ask, feeling like a complete moron. "And so what? Why is that newsworthy?"

"Um, anyone can send information to Little Birdie through the app." Meredith's eyes narrow. "And I thought you knew...Zayne and Carlton *hate* each other."

Before I can ask why, Mabel says, "Ask Carlton about it. I'm sure he'll tell you."

I try to keep up with the conversation as best I can, but I have to admit that I'm lost. I've only been at this school for a week, and all the names I'm still learning are starting to blend together.

Just when I'm about to give up trying to follow along, my brother knocks on the door. "Hey, Dot?"

"What is it, Beau?"

His expression is solemn. He's silent for a beat, like he wants me to guess what he's thinking so he doesn't have to say it. The climate in my room shifts, the laughter and chatter of Mabel, Meredith, and Rue dying down and sizzling into nothing. Beau holds up his phone. "It's Mom."

My lips part. How could I have forgotten? Mom only calls one night a week, and tonight is that night. I glance at my friends. I'm not sure what the proper etiquette is for this type of situation. Do I ask everyone to wait here while I talk on the phone? Do I skip the call altogether because there's company over? It's been a while since I was last in school, which means it's been a while since I've had any friends. And it's starting to show.

But I'm saved from having to do anything because Mabel stretches her arms. "It's probably time to get going, Mere," she says softly.

"Me, too." Rue stands up. "See you tomorrow, D."

I wave to their backs as they leave, grateful they took

the hint. When it's only me and my brother left, he puts the call on speaker. "Hi, Mom," I say.

"Is that my Bardot?" Her voice sounds so sweet. So loving. "How are you, baby?"

"Good, and you? How's Aunt Lucille?"

"She's good." She hesitates. "And I'm about the same."

I nod, though she can't see me.

"Dot had friends over today," Beau blurts.

"Yeah, I heard their voices. I'm real happy for you, baby." A pause. "But you're still studying real hard, aren't you?"

"Of course," I tell her. "I'm practically a model student for Harvard." The familiar twinge of dread trickles down my spine the same way it always does when I talk about my future to Mom or Dad. The weight of the lie I've been living for years feels heavy enough to crush me.

"That's good, sweetie."

I close my eyes, reveling in the sound of her voice. I don't think about the textbooks I've been dreading cracking open, or the list of assignments that never seems to end. I forget about the fact that if I disappoint my parents, all their hard work to help me succeed will be for nothing. Just for the moment, I forget the fact that I might be smart enough to go Ivy, but I don't even want to.

If I could go back in time to when naive, ten-year-old Dot announced her ambitions, I'd shake her and tell her to shut up. I'd tell her that being jealous of Beau for learning his third language, and the attention he was rewarded from our parents as a result, isn't worth *this*. All the studying, the feeling dead inside with no time for hobbies. The boredom.

Going to an Ivy League college will only make make things worse because the endless loop of academics will only get more intense.

I wish I could just hug my mom, cry into her shirt and tell her how much I hate reading textbooks, or stuffing precious corners of my spare time with researching the extracurriculars I should be participating in, but simply don't have the drive to.

"Is it helping, Mom? You being there?" I have to know. It's the question I'm always desperate to ask, but also afraid of the answer. Because if she can't be here, it better at least be worth it.

She's silent, pondering. Beau and I wait patiently, holding the phone between us.

"It's hard to tell so soon," she finally says. "But I think so. I hope so."

"Can I tell you about my day?" Beau asks, taking the phone from me to clutch it in both hands.

"Sure, baby."

"Bring the phone back to me when you're done," I tell him." When he leaves my room, I fall back onto my bed and stare up at the ceiling, swallowing back the knot in my throat. I try to think back to the moments I used to stare at my mother with admiration, noting the differences between us, admiring her ability to march into a burning building with the full expectation of reemerging. But it's hard to remember what life used to be like when she was home and still working. When she was still a firefighter, out there saving lives every day.

Now she can hardly manage to save her own.

Chapter Two

The next morning at lunch, I walk through Fallbrook's ancient, crowded stone halls to the newer cafeteria. Fallbrook used to be an orphanage before it was converted to a prep school in the early 1900s. I can't help but sometimes feel like I've gone back in time when I walk through the narrow, creaky corridors, but I'm not complaining. It's a total vibe.

I squint through the masses of upper and middle-class students, my stomach uneasy at the thought of not finding my friends and having to sit with strangers. Or worse, alone.

I release my breath when I find Carlton sitting at our table, his face down and resting in his folded arms. I relax as I approach the table, but frown when he doesn't look up. Why is he sitting alone? Where are the rest of our friends? I place my tray on the table. The soft thud it makes doesn't seem to catch Carlton's attention, so I clear my throat.

He glances up. "Oh. Hey, Dot."

"Hey." I study him. There's a glean of sweat dripping from the place where his short hair meets his forehead. His eyes have bags under them, and his mouth is set in a scowl I'm not used to seeing. "You good?"

"No," he says, his scowl somehow deepening even more. "No, I'm not."

My stomach grows uneasy when I note his biting tone. I've never heard him sound like this before. "Any particular reason why?"

Carlton sits up, balling one of his hands into a fist. He finally meets my searching gaze with his own, and I have to stop myself from looking away from the fierce expression on his face. He could be made of stone. "Zayne," he spits. "Zayne Silverman."

"Oh. Seriously?" I tilt my head. I don't know what I was expecting him to say, but it definitely wasn't that.

Carlton looks murderous in an adorable way. To someone else, he might look scary, but I know the soft, charismatic Carlton. The one who laughs uncontrollably when I tickle his face with my braids, and who would rather study the art of vocal cadence than ever have a physical altercation with someone who offended him.

"Yes, seriously. Dude has been pissing me off since we were kids. It was all over Little Birdie yesterday. Why are you acting surprised?"

I bite my lip, fighting a sudden, irrational urge to laugh. Zayne just seemed so harmless when I met him yesterday. "I heard about you having to run lines with him, but I haven't downloaded the Little Birdie app yet. I keep forgetting."

Carlton continues to glare at his balled-up fists on the table. The unease in my stomach returns. Gone is the funny and easygoing guy I spent the summer with. The one who made my cheeks hurt from smiling and my knees weak. Who briefly took my mind off Mom's absence. It's such a shift in demeanor, he seems like a different person.

"Hey." I touch his shoulder. "What could he possibly have done to get you this worked up? I've never seen you like this before."

"Dot." Carlton squares his shoulders. "You know how badly I want to get into Underwood Academy. Nigel Weathers is going to be at this season's performance, and there's no way he's going to be able to see my potential if I get stuck playing a supporting character."

"So, the part you play really matters, then?"

"Of course it does." He shakes his head. "Nigel Weathers is the admissions director for Underwood Academy. He comes to our school every year to hand-select two students, Dot. Only two. And he always chooses the lead actors."

"Okay. I can see why you're so worried, but what does Zayne Silverman have to do with it?"

"The jerk messed with my script, Dot. My *script*. And I stumbled on my lines."

My mouth falls open. "What? What do you mean?"

Carlton sighs. "All I know is that one moment, I'm running lines with Meredith, and the next, I'm reading with Zayne for the audition, and my lines are crossed out with Sharpie, and different lines are added in with pen. It's like he took my script and messed with it, so my audition would be ruined."

I wrinkle my nose. "But that doesn't make any sense."

"So...I'm lying, then?" Carlton's tone is stiff, and my stomach sinks. I don't want him to get the wrong idea, and I don't know why I'm sort of defending some boy I barely met yesterday.

"Of course not. I just mean that I can't see why he would do something like that, or why you wouldn't just tell Mr. Saltzman and ask him for a new script."

"I'd never give Silverman that satisfaction." Carlton shakes his head. "He obviously wants to play the lead, too. Don't be stupid."

Stung, I flinch at his words. But he's right. I have no reason not to believe him. If Zayne's as bad as Carlton says, it's him I should be interrogating.

"I didn't mean that." He touches my chin, bringing my gaze back to his. "I'm so sorry. I'm just stressed."

My heart softens, but before I can respond, two lunch trays plop down on our table. I squint up through the fluorescent lights at Meredith and Mabel. They both have their hair up in buns and are donning denim jackets over their uniforms. "You two are matching," I tell them. "It's like I'm seeing double."

Meredith laughs. "What good is being a twin if you aren't allowed to match?"

Mabel glances from me to Carlton. "Everything okay?" Her tone is uneasy, like she can sense the tension between us. Or maybe she's referring to the Little Birdie post from yesterday.

I shrug. To be honest, I'm not sure if Carlton is alright. He's never acted like this before, not in the three months I've known him. Hopefully, once he gets the lead role in the play like he's hoping, he'll be able to relax.

When no one answers her question, Mabel crosses her arms. "I need to use the bathroom." She raises her eyebrows at me pointedly.

I catch on, acknowledging the classic code for needing girl-talk. I may have been homeschooled for the majority of my life, but I'm not clueless. At least, I hope I'm not. I stand from my spot next to Carlton. "Me too."

We leave the table and walk through the halls to the nearest bathroom. The chatter from hoards of students surrounding us drowns out my thoughts as we make our way through the sea of white button-ups beneath navy vests and cardigans, pleated skirts, and beige trousers. The halls of this school are narrow, paneled in smooth dark wood, with the occasional nick in it that makes me wonder who left it and *when*. The historical architecture at every corner makes me feel like I'm in a castle. Except the bathrooms. They're a much newer addition to the building, and I find it jarring every time I step into the modern, cool-toned area.

We wordlessly stop in front of the sinks. It's clear that neither of us needs to use the restroom. Mabel fixes her hair in the mirror and darts her eyes to mine through our reflections. "What was that about?"

I frown. "What was what about?"

"Carlton. He looked like he was ready to rip someone's head off."

"Ah." So, it was obvious. "Yeah, he's really upset about Zayne Silverman."

Mabel winces. "It was awful, Dot. I know I didn't go into much detail yesterday, but you should have seen him after his audition. I thought he was going to cry. And C never cries."

"Really?" My eyebrows narrow. "It was that bad?"

She sighs. "I don't know what happened in that audition room, but whatever Zayne did to Carlton was pretty messed up. In fact, he's been a jerk to him since they were really young. I've watched them fight, like, our entire lives."

My frown deepens. I feel a surge of protectiveness shoot through me for Carlton. Who does Zayne think he is, anyway? What gives him the right to think he can treat Carlton so badly?

"We should probably get back," says Mabel. "I want to ask Rue about the chem test before the bell rings."

I nod. "Okay."

We exit the bathroom and walk back down the hall. I clutch my backpack as someone passes me too closely, knocking it off my shoulder, and then someone else bumps into me, sending the papers they're carrying flying across the floor. I squat down to help retrieve them. "Sorry."

"It's fine," a deep voice says, and I look up into large brown eyes on a handsome face I recognize from yesterday.

Zayne Silverman.

His short dreads are in a bun today, revealing his

undercut. He sighs deeply as he picks up his scattered papers.

The anger I experienced in the bathroom returns full force. "*You.*" I snatch one of his papers off the ground and stand, crossing my arms. "You should watch where you're going."

"Dot," Mabel says, sounding torn between shocked and amused.

"I know," Zayne admits, standing up as well. He brushes off his jeans and glances up at me with a faint smile. "My bad."

I purse my lips. I didn't expect him to agree, so now I have no reason to keep being rude. Other than because he messed with Carlton's script. But there isn't enough time for the things I want to say to him, so I shoulder past him and keep walking.

"Uh, Dot?" he calls from behind me. "Can I have my math homework, please?"

Without turning around, I toss the paper I'm still holding over my shoulder. Mabel catches up with me. "Ouch, Dot. I didn't realize you could be so harsh." But she's smiling as she says it, like it's a compliment.

Good job, Dot. This may be your first time at school, but you're doing okay so far. Her approval lifts my spirits so much, I add, "If he doesn't leave Carlton alone, what you just saw will seem like nothing by comparison." I have no idea what I'm going to do to him, but she doesn't need to know that.

All I can hope for is that Zayne minds his own business so I can continue to win over Carlton and his friends.

"How was school, honey?" Dad says across the dinner table.

I spear a piece of overcooked, instant lasagna with my fork before answering. "Fine." I don't mention Carlton's recent bad mood or the reason behind it. Or *person*, rather. Dad is of the firm belief that a mature individual should never take their frustrations out on those they care about. If I tell him Carlton got mad at me today, he'll probably overreact.

"Find out if you got a decent part in that play yet?"

"No. I only auditioned in the first place to fit in, remember?"

"There's nothing wrong with liking different things as your friends, Bardot," he tells me, "A real friend wouldn't care if you fit in or not."

Beau wipes his mouth. "Can I be excused?"

"Only if you promise to run a comb through that hair before bed," he says. Dad is good at many things, but our hair isn't one of them. It's why he keeps his own short and low-maintenance. Lucky for all of us, Mom taught me well enough to handle the thick curls Beau and I were gifted.

Beau pushes his chair in and goes to his room. Dad lowers his voice and asks me, "How do you think he's doing?"

"Probably fine." I shrug one shoulder. "His grades are up, and he hasn't been having anymore nightmares lately. But you already know that."

Dad looks lost in thought. "And what about your mom?

How was the phone call?" His eyes are far away, and I realize, with a start, that the stubble on his face is starting to look more gray than black. It's only been four months since we've begun operating without Mom, but it feels like it's been much longer. Especially when I look at my dad.

"She says she's doing well." I try not to wince. "Sorry you missed the call again."

"Nothing to be done about it. I had work."

Beau walks back into the kitchen, silencing us. He holds my cell phone out to me. "Carlton called."

I glance at Dad. "May I leave the table?"

He nods, and I scramble up from my seat, reining in my urge to sprint to my room. We aren't allowed to bring our phones to the table. My parents are old-school that way. I'll never admit it to them, but I actually kinda like the rule. It feels nice to take a break from social media and my friends at least once a day to chat with Dad and pray before dinner.

The only downside is missing a phone call or message from Carlton.

Beau follows me to my room. I raise my eyebrows at him. I can't help but feel impatient for him to leave so I talk to Carlton.

"I answered the call," Beau admits. "And Carlton didn't say so, but it seemed like he was in a really bad mood."

"Seriously? You answered my phone?" I cross my arms.

He fidgets and looks down at his shoes. "Just to tell him you were still eating dinner."

"Okay." I shake my head, irritated. "Thanks, I guess."

"He seems kind of mean," he adds with a cringe.

"He's not." I wave my hand to brush off his statement,

but he's already leaving, making me angrier than I would have thought possible. "You don't even know him," I mutter as I shut the door, though I know he doesn't hear me. It's not fair for Beau to judge Carlton based on today's bad mood, when he has no idea what happened with Zayne at the audition. I don't think my brother realizes that Carlton came into my life at a time when I really needed someone.

Right when Mom left.

I was destroyed at the start of summer, like an expensive silk blouse cut down the center, then carelessly stitched back together for display despite my raw, fraying edges. And no matter how much thread was used to sew me back up, I knew deep down the stitching didn't match what was there before. It was too bold, too contrasting, and not fooling anyone.

But Carlton had been there. He was nice enough to take me into his circle before school even started. And he might not know it, but having him, Mabel, Meredith, and Rue to talk to about lighthearted things that have nothing to do with my mom makes me feel like I'm finally whole again.

I check my messages before I call Carlton back. Rue texted me.

RUE

Here's the link to Little Birdie's app. Make sure you turn the notifications on so you don't miss anything.

ME

Thanks.

As indifferent as I am to the whole "Little Birdie" thing, I should probably stay in the loop. Shaking my head, I call Carlton. I bring the phone to my ear and pace back and forth while I wait for him to answer.

"Hey," he says.

"Hey."

He sighs into the phone. "I'm sorry about being such a jerk today. I didn't even get a chance to ask you how your audition went."

I breathe a sigh of relief. This, *this*, is the real Carlton. The one with the kind voice, who makes me feel like I'm the only person on his mind.

"It went well." It didn't go well, of course, but now that I'm an "actor," I should probably start practicing stretching the truth. "At least I think it did. I hardly tried, to be honest."

"Don't worry. You hardly need to. You're not the one trying to get into Underwood. It won't matter if you end up being cast as a singing tree on the moors."

Even though it's him who lives and breathes theater, I'd be lying if I said I wouldn't be embarrassed to be cast as an actual tree. That would be the opposite of impressive. "You don't think that will happen, though, do you?" I ask.

"Why does it matter?" There's a smile in his voice.

"I mean, I'm obviously not auditioning for the lead or anything, but I'm still hoping to be cast as something other than a singing tree on the moors."

"Dot," he chuckles, "you're still new at this. Everyone else in the drama club has been doing theater for years.

And a lot of them end up being part of the ensemble. That's not a bad thing."

"Great," I mutter. "I wish you'd told me that before I tried out. Now I feel stupid for hoping for something more." *Like impressing you.*

"Well, like you said," he states. "You hardly tried. Maybe put in some effort next time."

My heart sinks. He's right. Why didn't I try harder? Why did I think I wouldn't have to? "Everyone else makes it seem so *easy*," I explain. "Acting, I mean. But it's harder than I thought."

"That's your problem, Dot. You're capable of so much, but you never really apply yourself." He lowers his voice, and the bitter note is impossible to miss. "Some of us actually do try, and it doesn't work out."

Could he be referring to my lack of extracurriculars, when I've told him about my plans to apply to such prestigious universities? Or the way I groan aloud every time I have to study? How I willingly fall asleep in classes that bore me?

Carlton is lucky he doesn't have my problem. At least he's passionate about the path he's pursuing.

And then the last part of his sentence registers with me for the first time. *Some of us actually do try, and it doesn't work out.*

"That's right," I say, feeling like the most selfish person alive. "I forgot what happened with Zayne."

"Of course you did," he mutters. Almost like he doesn't want me to hear it. And then louder, he says, "It's fine. Hey, I gotta go. See you at school tomorrow?"

My lips part. I hurt his feelings. "Carlton—" But he hangs up.

He's just stressed about his bad audition, at the possibility of losing his chance of being noticed by Nigel Weathers, I tell myself. *That's all this is.*

I stare at my pastel yellow bedroom walls. At my fuzzy white rug. At my cozy, amber bedding. At anything, I realize, other than my round vanity mirror, so I won't have to look at myself.

This is all Zayne Silverman's fault. If it weren't for him meddling with Carlton's script, none of this would be happening. Carlton's chances of getting into his dream school wouldn't even be a question. He wouldn't be so angry and he wouldn't be lashing out at me.

I can't help but feel like I must have done something wrong. Maybe it's my lack of socialization, all those years spent with no one but Beau, and Dad as our teacher, instead of learning how to navigate tricky social situations like these.

I'll have to fix this somehow. I'll find a way to prove to Carlton I'm not as self-centered as he thinks.

I click the link Rue sent me and download Little Birdie's app. And I don't forget to turn the notification alert on.

Chapter Three

School doesn't disappoint the next day—it passes quickly and uneventfully. That is, until I get to the drama room after sixth period. Rue is poised outside the door, ankles crossed and texting. When she sees me, she waves. "Hey, Dot."

I smile. "Hi." My senses are a bundle of nerves because this is technically my first official theater meeting. *Is that what they're called? Meetings?* "Who are you waiting for?"

"Anyone." Rue flicks her fingers at the air vaguely. "Whoever gets here first. And that's you." She pushes off the side of the corridor, pleated skirt swooshing with the movement. "Shall we enter?" She waggles her brows dramatically, earning a laugh from me.

When we walk through the heavy door, there are two rows of chairs lined up at the front of the classroom.

"Oh, no," Rue mutters.

I wait for her to elaborate, but she just hangs her head

and leads us to a group of empty desks. Soon after, Carlton and the twins shuffle in and sit next to us. Carlton sits on my other side, and I note the way he smiles at me. Like I'm the only one in the room he notices. Like our conversation last night never happened. Some of the tension in my shoulders eases.

The room buzzes with conversation until Mr. Saltzman emerges from the room with the adjoining door.

"We're doing the character bus today, everyone." He claps his hands together to hush the collective mix of squeals and groans that follow. "Who wants to be the driver?"

"I will," says a short, blond girl near the front of the classroom. She practically beelines from where she's sitting and plops into the first chair in the line of seats Mr. Saltzman has arranged. There's a gleam in her eyes and her full cheeks lift in excitement.

Mr. Saltzman nods at her. "Thank you for volunteering, Joy." Turning back to the class, he adds, "I want Hayden, Danielle, Carlton, Leighton, and Rue to be the passengers."

Carlton straightens his spine and Rue mutters, "Wonderful." She and Carlton stand up and head to the front of the class to line up with the other chosen students.

"For those of you who are new," Mr. Saltzman continues, "the driver of the bus will take on the personality of each new passenger, and so will any passengers on the bus. So, get ready." Turning to Joy, he asks, "Where is the bus headed?"

"To Manchester," she replies with a grin.

"Then let the show begin." Mr. Saltzman cracks his

knuckles and backs away, a pleased smile on his face. A short boy wearing a leather jacket over his uniform is first in line. He approaches Joy.

"I hear this bus is headed to Manchester." The boy emphasizes his words with a heavy, clearly fake southern drawl. He yodels a laugh at the end of his statement, and Joy yodels a laugh right back.

"You're darn tootin'," she says.

The boy skips to the first available seat behind Joy. "Well cut my cake and call me biscuit. That's where I'm headed."

I stifle a giggle, along with several others in the class.

Joy leans back in her chair and pretends to drive with one hand.

The next person in line walks over to Joy, a girl with dark curls and bright red lipstick. She's crying, actual tears pouring down her cheeks as she wails, "I need to get to Manchester. Is this the bus that can take me? Please."

Joy doesn't even hesitate as she, too, begins crying. "I need to get to Manchester, too but I don't know how to drive." She covers her mouth with both hands as sobs wrack through her and the passenger who started out with a southern accent wails, "We're all going to die."

Then it's Carlton's turn. He sings the words, "Hi, I need to ride the bus," to the tune of the ABCs.

Joy sings back, "Could you take a seat for us?"

Southern Boy sings, "Let us stare up at the sky."

And Crying Girl sings, "Waving as the birds fly by."

It's incredibly impressive. So much so, that I can't help

but feel out of my element. I'm nowhere near as skilled as anyone on the character bus. Not even close.

I sink down in my chair.

The next girl laughs uncontrollably as she speaks, and so does everyone and the bus—and the class, for that matter. Laughter bounces around the room until it's Rue's turn. She's the last passenger on the bus, and she whispers everything she says so quietly, the class can barely hear her. Everyone else on the bus does the same, and when all the seats are filled, the class erupts with a round of applause.

"And that's how it's done," Mr. Saltzman beams.

My gaze sweeps the room, noting all the fellow students who pat Carlton on the back as he makes his way back over, Rue trailing behind him. In fact, almost every gaze in the room is glued to Carlton.

Except one.

I can't help but stare because, once again, I'm struck by his beauty. His long lashes framing those incredibly warm brown eyes. The way his full lips are downturned into a scowl, making him look like an enraged statue, or a model for a frowning ad, perhaps. Either way, I can't help but watch Zayne Silverman not watch Carlton. His graceful jaw works as his eyes land on mine from the other side of the classroom.

I look away instantly, cheeks burning.

Carlton doesn't seem to notice. He returns to his spot next to me and grins, his half-smile lazy and seductive. "What did you think?"

I clear my throat. "That was amazing." And it's true. Watching that mini performance was nothing short of inspiring. I tell him the parts that made me laugh. I tell him how impressive his singing voice is, even when matching the tune of a children's song. I even compliment Rue. "I can't believe your voice can even get that quiet," I say.

But what I don't mention is how insecure I feel now that I've seen what improv looks like. I don't talk about how scary it will be when I inevitably have to perform in front of the class. And I definitely don't bring up how worried I am that by trying to fit in, all I've done is highlight how unlikely that is to ever, ever happen.

"Cast list is posted," Meredith tells me at school the next day. I'm walking through the hallway to my locker when she practically collides with me. There's a huge smile plastered across her face.

I grin. "Who did you get cast as?"

"Well, I haven't checked yet." She blushes a little and tosses her curly hair over her shoulder. "There weren't even any callbacks, which is unusual, but a good sign. It just means that Mr. Saltzman knew exactly who he wanted to play each part. I better have gotten the lead."

"I'm sure you did. Don't worry."

"Me and Mabel auditioned for Catherine Earnshaw and her daughter, Catherine Linton," continues Meredith. She claps her hands. "Since we're twins, we'll look crazy alike as mother and daughter, just like in the book. Golden opportunity, you know? Mr. Saltzman won't be able to resist."

I nod along, but I've never read *Wuthering Heights* so I'm not sure what she's talking about. That part wasn't mentioned in the detailed summary I skimmed before the audition.

Some Ivy-bound student I am. A surge of dread seizes me at the thought.

Rue finds us by the lockers. "Hey, y'all." Her hair is in space buns, making her look slightly childish, but in a cute way.

"Cast list is posted," Meredith tells her.

"I know. I saw it." Rue brightens. "Congrats Dot!"

Congrats? I frown. "Congrats on what?"

"You got the lead female role. I'm playing your sister-in-law, Isabella." Rue scrunches her nose. "Wait, why don't you look more excited?"

Lead female role? What is she talking about? My stomach feels heavy, like I got stuck on a roller coaster with a drop I wasn't prepared for. It's like a nightmare about accidentally going to school in nothing but your underwear. That moment, looking down and realizing you have nothing else on. That's how my stomach feels. *There's no way. There must be some mistake.*

"But she didn't even audition for the part of Catherine!" Meredith's voice is frazzled, nearly a screech. "*I* did!"

"Oh," says Rue. She bites her lip. It takes her a moment to think of something else to say. "Well, at least you're playing Nelly. Hers is arguably one of the most important roles." She places a careful hand on Meredith's shoulder, but Meredith shakes her off.

"I don't want to play freaking Nelly!" she shouts. Her voice attracts the attention of a few students around us. I want to get in my locker and hide from their stares, but Meredith doesn't even seem to notice. She turns to glare at me, her gaze filled with more venom than I ever thought possible.

Great. Now she's mad at me. I hold up my hands. "I'm sorry! You know I didn't try out for the lead. In fact, I'm pretty sure my audition sucked."

She scowls. "Fantastic. Like that's supposed to make me feel better, Dot."

"Yeah, why would you even say that?" Rue side-eyes me.

My cheeks burn at her expression. This is exactly what I was worried about. I can't help but recall what I overheard Mom telling Dad before she left, while they were discussing me possibly attending Fallbrook. "It would be good for her," Mom said. "Bardot is smart, but sometimes that girl lacks self-awareness."

Meredith storms off down the hall, just as Mabel approaches. Her lips are turned up into an impossible grin. "Guess what?" Mabel jumps up and down and then hugs me. It's a bit jarring after speaking with Meredith, especially since they look so much alike. "I'm playing Catherine Linton!"

She pulls away, still grinning, and then takes in Rue's round eyes and my shoulders, still bunched up to my ears after our encounter with Meredith. Mabel's face falls. "Oh, no. Mere's upset, isn't she? I saw that she got cast as Nelly."

Instead of answering, I push past them both and head to the main office of Fallbrook, where the bulletin board with the cast list is posted. Whispers echo through the halls as I march through them, and it takes me a moment to realize they're about *me*. I'm the one being talked about. Fragmented phrases like, "Dot playing Cathy" and "Meredith is upset" and "wonder what Little Birdie will say" ring in my ears.

Mistake. This is all just one big mistake. It has to be.

I have to see it for myself. Maybe my name and Meredith's name are right on top of one another, and she somehow got our roles reversed. That would make so much more sense.

I make my way through the halls, my footsteps echoing on the floor now that almost everyone else has cleared out to make it to first period. Luckily, mine isn't too far from the office, so I'm not worried about missing the first bell.

I round the corner, expecting to find the list open and free from prying eyes, but instead find Carlton standing there, alone in the dim corridor. There's a beam of light illuminating his symmetrical face through a high stained-glass window, like a spotlight shining on a stage. For a moment, I'm struck with longing, remembering our summer together. I miss the feeling of his warm hand in mine, his twinkling eyes telling me stories without a word. The gentle caress of his lips against mine, like a shared secret between us.

He scans the list, frozen in place. His shoulders are

taut, and I realize what he must be seeing: my name under "Catherine Earnshaw," next to his under "Heathcliff." Despite everything, I can't contain my flutter of excitement at the idea of playing his romantic interest, even though if it's true, I'll be in way over my head.

"Hey," I say as I approach him, causing him to stiffen. He must not have heard me walk up, though I don't know how he could miss it, since we're practically alone in the corridor now that the bell is about to ring.

He points to the bulletin board. "Did you see this yet?"

I bite my lip. "No. But Meredith told me."

Carlton stares at the ground, eyes shining. For a moment, I think he might cry, but then his eyebrows pull together and his mouth twists into a scowl. In one rapid movement, he turns and throws something hard against one of the lockers behind him, and I jump.

"What was that?" I stare at the object he threw, now lying on the ground. Carlton's phone is face up with thin lines now cutting across the screen in different directions. My lips part. "Carlton, what's wrong?"

His hands clench into fists. "What do you mean, 'what's wrong,' Dot? How can you even ask me that right now?"

My stomach ties itself in a knot. I know how much he cares about this play, but would it really be such a bad thing to have me as his costar? I can't deny that I'm more than a little stung at his reaction. "Look, I know I'm inexperienced," I begin, "but is it really so bad that I'm playing Catherine? Aren't you a little proud that I got the biggest role, first try?"

His eyes widen as he stares at me. He's looking at me like he can't believe he's really seeing me, or something. It makes me feel like I'm on display. "Is that why you think I'm upset?" He exhales through his mouth. "Of course you would think that. Why am I even surprised? You're always thinking about yourself first."

My throat clogs with trepidation.

"I didn't get the part, Dot!" Carlton's voice is so loud, it echoes as it bounces around the walls and lockers surrounding us. "I didn't get the lead role. I'm not playing Heathcliff." His eyes have me locked in the tight grip of his angry stare. I can't glance away from him, much as I want to.

"Who is, then?" My voice sounds like a whisper.

"*He* is," Carlton seethes. "Zayne Silverman. And I'm stuck playing the main supporting character, Edgar Linton."

"Carlton...I'm so, so sorry—"

He breaks away from me as soon as I speak, turning on his heel and marching down the long stairway toward the wing of his first class.

I stare after him, my heart sinking as he leaves.

What have I done?

It may not be my fault that Carlton didn't get the role he wanted. But if I hadn't been so focused on my own situation, I would have realized how much he needs me right now. Meredith being mad at me for stealing her role feels like nothing compared to Carlton being mad at me.

I walk up to the cast list, my eyes scanning the names

of the drama club and the characters we'll be playing this winter. I stop when I reach the name at the top.

Zayne Silverman.

If he hadn't changed Carlton's script in the first place, he wouldn't have gotten away with taking the lead role. In fact, he only won by playing dirty. It isn't fair.

Zayne isn't fair. And the worst part is now that we're co-stars, we'll probably be spending a lot more time together, rehearsing as the main couple in the play.

My eyes burn with unshed tears, but I won't let them fall. And I will not let Zayne get the best of me or get in the way of me having a relationship with Carlton.

Latest on the *Little Birdie* gossip feed:

> There's been quite a stir among Fallbrook's most interesting students. Have you heard the news?
>
> I'm sure you've noticed the new girl by now. If not, her name is Bardot Bennett. Apparently, she goes by "Dot." A drab nickname, in my opinion, but to each their own. It looks like Dot has found her way into the circle of none other than Carlton Peters himself. And who can blame her? With a knack for theater and a jawline like his, she was bound to be interested.
>
> Carlton and Dot are both playing leads in

Fallbrook's adaptation of the classic love-story *Wuthering Heights*. Only, it looks like Carlton won't be playing the Heathcliff to Bardot's Cathy! No! Heartthrob Zayne Silverman snagged the role of the ruggedly handsome Heathcliff, and I can't complain that he doesn't fit the bill. If anything, Carlton was made to play the passive and polite Edgar Linton.

But the question is: Who will truly play the part of stealing Bardot's heart?

Yours truly,

Little Birdie

Chapter Four

The rest of the day, everyone continues to stare at me. Only now, I've officially gone from quietly being the new girl to being the girl who was blasted about by Little Birdie. And not even for having the highest grades or the best chances of getting into a school like Harvard or Yale. Of course not. It's about me starring in the stupid play.

Part of me wishes I never downloaded the app, but I'm also glad I did, because otherwise all these whispers would have me thinking I sat in gum or something.

At lunch, I pretend to need help with tonight's algebra homework and eat in Mrs. Lane's classroom, so I don't have to show my face in the hallways. I don't have Carlton on my side right now. Not after the way I acted earlier. Even if he did want to see me, I doubt Meredith would appreciate me showing my face in their circle at the moment.

It's bad enough being new and having no one know you.

It's even worse having everyone know you, and not having anyone to turn to.

I can hide now, but there's nothing I can do about the drama club meeting after school. They'll both be there, and I'll have to face them, along with the rest of the theater crew.

My phone rumbles and my heart races when I see that Mabel texted me.

MABEL

Where are you???

ME

Hiding.

MABEL

Why?

ME

Meredith and Carlton are mad at me. Little Birdie posted about me and now everyone keeps staring.

MABEL

LOL. Get used to it. You're in theater now. LB is obsessed with us, which means the rest of the school is too.

ME

Great.

MABEL

Give Mere & C time. They'll stop being mad soon.

I put my phone away. My heart feels a little bit warmer now that I know Meredith being mad doesn't mean Mabel is also mad by default. I hope she's right about them cooling off sooner rather than later.

By the time I walk into the drama room after school, Meredith is already present, sitting with her back to me and engrossed in a conversation with her twin. Mabel sees me when I walk in and brightens. "Hey, Dot," she says, making Meredith look over her shoulder at me.

"Hey," I say. I'm shocked by how many people have turned to look at me now, even among the theater students. It's not that I necessarily have a problem with being looked at—it's more the reason they're all looking at me. I, the newbie, landed the lead role without deserving it. Little Birdie alerted every single student at Fallbrook Prep of my presence because of it.

I'm already contemplating quitting.

I glance around the room at the faces pointed in my direction. Many of them drop their glances when I look their way, but others just keep studying me. I wonder if someone in this room could be Little Birdie. It's likely, since everyone here heard me tell Mr. Saltzman I go by the name Dot, which was mentioned in the blast. I squint at all the different faces as if doing so will somehow help me uncover the anonymous blogger's identity.

Carlton walks in and I watch as his thick frame passes right by me. I'm guessing that means he's still not happy with me, so I look around for a different place to sit. The desks in the drama room are all pushed against the back wall to make room for rehearsing and improv, so everyone has formed small groups and found crannies of the room to sit on the hardwood floor. I briefly consider sitting with Mabel and Meredith anyway, especially since Carlton has just joined them, because it's not like I know anyone else in this room. I am the outsider. Ironically, joining the play was supposed to eliminate that label of mine. But now that I'm supposed to play the lead, it looks like I've alienated myself even more.

Rue joins the group, and I make my way over, swallowing my apprehension. I try to make eye contact with Meredith, but she turns her head away as I approach. Rue and Mabel scoot over, so I plop down next to them on the floor. I offer Carlton a small smile, hoping he'll return it. He meets my eyes briefly and then faces the front of the classroom.

Mr. Saltzman is passing out the full script to everyone, and when he reaches us, Mabel offers me some highlighters. "It's so you can highlight all your lines," she whispers.

"Thanks." I pick a yellow one and find my first set of lines to run the marker over. Turn the page. More places to highlight text. Turn the page again. More lines. My stomach drops as I flip through, the full weight of my part finally settling in. It looks like I have the most lines of almost any character, with the possible exceptions of Meredith's character, Nelly, and Heathcliff, played by Zayne.

Zayne.

I sit up straighter and look around the classroom, trying to spot him. I peer over the clusters of groups, trying to find his hair, since his face isn't in my line of sight.

"Who are you looking for?" Mabel asks curiously.

"Zayne Silverman."

Carlton makes an incredulous sound, breaking my concentration. "You mean your new boyfriend?"

An awkward silence falls over the five of us. Is he really going to act like this in front of our friends? Rue examines her nails, and Meredith's mouth lifts into a smirk.

"Knock it off, Carlton," Mabel says in an even tone. "You know it's not her fault."

He sighs. It's deep, heavy. An angry sigh. He walks to the front of the classroom to sharpen his pencil. I shoot Mabel a grateful look. "Thank you," I mouth. She smiles back, her brown left eye and green right eye twinkling.

Mr. Saltzman clears his throat, straightening the beret on his balding head. The class falls into a hushed silence. "Let's have the crew and ensemble head over to the auditorium to take notes on the first scene, and then I want all the main roles except Dot and Zayne, my Cathy and Heathcliff, to head next door where I'll join you shortly."

My stomach tangles with nerves, hearing myself spoken of as Cathy.

Rue, Mabel, and Carlton all turn to look at me. Meredith pays me no attention, already starting out the classroom door without a word. Rue squeezes my hand. "Break a leg," she says with a nervous grin. She gets up, and so does Mabel, to follow behind Meredith.

But Carlton remains next to me, seated on the floor. I

open my mouth to say something, but he speaks first. "Have fun," he says flatly. "I know I won't."

He stands up and leaves. "Wait, Carlton," I say, but he doesn't turn back around. The cold fury in the set of his shoulders is impossible to miss as he makes his way to the next classroom over with the rest of our friends.

"Looks like it's just us," a deep voice says. I glance up and see Zayne standing next to me. This close, I catch a whiff of his scent. He smells like coffee, and possibly cake, too. His dreads are in a neat bun, and he smiles warily, a closed-lipped, lopsided grin.

I want to punch him.

If it weren't for his need to cheat his way to the top of the play, poor Carlton wouldn't have had his chances at getting into Underwood jeopardized. And he wouldn't be mad at me, either.

"Yes, unfortunately, it *is* just us," I mutter.

Zayne's brows draw together. "Uh, okay."

Mr. Saltzman approaches us. "You two start reading over the first scene of Act One," he says. "I'll be next door and you can ask any questions you have when I get back." He looks at me through his square spectacles. "But from your auditions, I doubt you'll need much help at all," he says. "You two had great chemistry."

Chemistry? What is this? A joke?

When he leaves, I grit my teeth. "Great. Now I'm stuck with you," I tell Zayne.

He holds up his hands. "Okay, I'm sorry, but what is going on? Why are you acting like I personally insulted you or something?"

I look at Zayne, at his genuinely baffled expression, at the script in his hands, and I see red. It's like every bad moment I've spent with Carlton since my audition has weighed too heavily on me and now that I'm standing in front of the reason for all of it, I'm ready to explode.

"You have!" I yell at him. "You insulted Carlton, and now he'll barely even speak to me!"

Zayne tilts his head to the side. "Carlton?"

"Yes! Carlton!" I swat his arm with my script.

Zayne's mouth twitches. I swear, if he's about to smile, I hold no responsibility for what I will do next. "How did I insult Carlton, Dot?"

I narrow my eyes at him. Doing what he did is one thing, but now he has the gall to pretend he doesn't know what I'm talking about?

"You sabotaged Carlton's script, so he'd fumble during his audition. All so you could get the lead role. And you succeeded. Now he's the angriest I've ever seen him."

Zayne stares at me like I've grown two heads. "Wait a minute. He said what?" Then his expression changes. His lips form a straight line, and the set of his shoulders stiffens. "Of course he would say that."

"Don't even try to deny it. I know exactly what kind of person you are."

He pinpoints me with his glare, his taut body towering over me. "And what kind of person might that be?"

"A liar and a cheat, according to Carlton. And if that's what he says, then I believe him." I cross my arms.

"Why doesn't that surprise me?"

I laugh humorlessly. "What's that supposed to mean?"

It's not like anything he says will sway my opinion. Especially if it's his word against Carlton's.

Zayne throws up his hands. "You know what? Never mind. You're going to believe what you want and it's not my job to stop you."

I briefly consider his words before shaking them off. I have every reason to be mad at Zayne for messing with Carlton. And part of me is also a little mad at Carlton for taking it out on me. But most of all, I'm mad at myself. If I'd never joined the stupid drama club to begin with, I wouldn't be stuck in this situation. "This was a terrible idea," I say.

Zayne raises his eyebrows. "What was? Auditioning? Because if you're having second thoughts, please just drop out now. The last thing I need is a flake ruining my chances of getting into Underwood."

The mention of that stupid school right now makes my blood boil. "Ugh. Not you, too."

He glares at me. "I mean it. This isn't a joke. In fact, if you're serious about staying in the play, we really should start running lines together today."

"Relax. All this fuss is ridiculous. I doubt Underwood is actually *that* hard to get into. It's not like it's Yale or Harvard."

"Well, literally every theater student at this school wants to get in, and to stay there through college." The lines of Zayne's forehead seem to become even more prominent. "Considering only two high school students get accepted every year—and on scholarship, I might add—the odds aren't exactly in your favor."

"Ha!" I laugh without humor. I don't know why I'm letting him get to me, but something about his tone irks me. I should just go tell Mr. Saltzman I quit and be done with all this, but for some reason, I can't let his jab go. "I landed the role of this Catherine character easily enough," I tell him. "I bet I could get into Underwood, too."

Apparently, my comment doesn't amuse Zayne. "Please, just drop out," he deadpans.

"No." If he thinks he's going to get rid of me that easily, after everything he's done, he's got another thing coming. "Not after all that. I might have before you suggested my acting skills are lacking. But now? No way. Once I've set my mind on something, there's no talking me out of it."

I'm not sure where my sudden bravado is coming from, since I've felt nothing but insecure about my acting since the audition, but I roll with it. Maybe it's the stupid smirk on Zayne's face making me want to defend myself, or maybe it's something else. Either way, the words are spoken now and it's too late to take them back.

Zayne's grip on his script tightens. He looks like he's fighting for control. Good. Let him see how it feels to have his hopes and dreams possibly ripped away, like Carlton's might be. If I were to actually get into Underwood, there would only be one more spot left. Him, or Carlton, but not both. Obviously, I have no desire to actually attend Underwood Academy. But just the idea of seeing Zayne's face if I got accepted over him is too delicious to pass up.

"Whatever," he finally says, and storms toward the classroom door, leaving me standing alone in the center of the room.

"Where are you going?"

"To have a word with Mr. Saltzman."

"I thought you wanted to run lines?" I'm goading him now. Truly trying to infuriate him. And I can tell it's working. I smile.

As he's leaving, he practically spits his answer over his shoulder. "My house. Tomorrow. Five o' clock."

Latest on the *Little Birdie* gossip feed:

> *Rumor has it that Dot's got a thing for Carlton, but her acting says otherwise! Apparently, the chemistry between her and Zayne Silverman was too hot for Mr. Saltzman to handle. Why else would he cast an undeserving new girl like Dot Bennet to play the romantic lead alongside Zayne?*
>
> *Let's just hope Carlton can handle the heat. I, on the other hand, am melting for this love triangle.*
>
> *My prediction is that Carlton and his rival will have something new to fight over.*
>
> *As if they needed anything else!*
>
> *Yours truly,*
> *Little Birdie*

Today, my presence has only produced half the amount of whispers as yesterday, but a freshman asked me to sign her drama class syllabus, so that was new, at least.

When the lunch bell rings, I keep my head ducked down and make for our table as fast as I can. Voices float around me, and I hear my name a few times. I resist the urge to cover my ears.

Someone grabs my arm. "Dot?"

I glance up at the unfamiliar face. "Yeah?"

"Congrats on getting the lead," they say. "I remember the Evans twins got it their freshman and sophomore year, and they were really good. So, you must be good, too."

"Thanks." I walk away before they can say anything else. What good would it do to admit that, actually, I'm not talented enough? That I'm nothing but an imposter, but somehow my "chemistry" with Zayne Silverman was enough.

I ascend the long staircase leading from my classroom wing to the cafeteria. A cluster of girls stares at me from the top, resting their elbows on the railing. One of them pretends to adjust her knee-high sock when I catch her watching me, and another whispers in her friend's ear. When I get to the cafeteria, I spot Carlton sitting with Rue, Mabel, and Meredith. I sit down and they all turn to look at me.

There's a beat of awkward silence until Rue waggles her eyebrows. "So...you and Zayne Silverman, eh?" Her joking tone seems to ease the tension at our table. Even Carlton rolls his eyes, his mouth twisting into an almost smile.

My shoulders relax. "Please tell me Little Birdie isn't as big of a deal as you guys are making her out to be."

Carlton clenches his jaw, but his eyes are soft. "Sorry, Dot."

"It will get better." Mabel touches my hand. "Probably. And how do we know it's a her?"

"We don't, I guess. It just feels more natural to say, so until further notice, it's a she." I sigh. "And honestly, the nerve of that Little Birdie. It's like she's desperate for news. And if you're going to post something, like, at least make it *true*. Am I right?"

"Relax," Rue says. "*I* don't believe anything Little Birdie says. I never have."

A weight disappears from my stomach. "Really?"

"Of course not." She takes a bite of her salad, swallows, and dabs her mouth with a napkin. "One time, in middle school, she said I let my pet rat loose in the hallways. I've never owned a pet rat in my life."

I laugh. A group of freshmen passes by our lunch table. A few of them walk extra slow so they can get a good look at us, and one of them takes out his phone and points it at me.

"Are you...taking a picture of me?" I sputter.

Carlton swats the hand holding the camera away. "Get lost."

They disappear, but I'm still gaping in my seat. Being featured by Little Birdie feels how I'd imagine being a celebrity in tabloids feels. Like a violation of privacy. It would probably be worse, though, if Little Birdie was actually writing the truth.

Under our table, Carlton reaches for my hand. "I can't help but wonder, though," he murmurs, playing with my fingers, "Why *did* you get the lead role? You know. If what Little Birdie said about you and Zayne having sizzling chemistry isn't true?"

"Um," I stammer. I look at Mabel for help, but she shrugs. "I have no idea." I'm about to say something that will hopefully change the subject, but Zayne Silverman chooses that precise moment to walk by, place a small piece of paper in my other hand on the table, and say to me in passing, "Don't forget. My house, after school at five." I stare at my hand. The paper he handed me has his address written on it. I shove it in my pocket, face burning.

Carlton stares at me. And so does Rue. And Mabel. And Meredith.

"That was really bad timing," I tell them with a nervous chuckle. "He just wants to run lines after school. But I'm not going." I don't know why I add that last part. It isn't true.

Carlton slowly drops my hand and stares at me for a long moment. There's a hardness to his expression that wasn't there a minute ago. "Right."

The group falls into an awkward silence. This is all becoming too much. I need to get away for a moment to clear my head. "I'll be right back," I say to none of them in particular. I'd rather be anywhere but here at the moment, under their scrutiny. If only Mom were here. It's her I need to talk to right now. I break away from the three of them and head to the parking lot. On my way, I attract the attention of a group of girls I've never seen before.

"Hi, Dot!" One of them waves at me.

I wave back. The fake smile I'm wearing feels much too heavy.

I burst through the giant oak doors leading outside. The crisp, autumn air stings my bare knees. The transition from summer to fall in Massachusetts has practically been nonexistent. I rub my arms, the friction from my skin against my cardigan warming me.

When I reach my car, I grab the handle, but don't open the door right away. I catch sight of my reflection in the car window, and I can't help but stare. My eyes are shining with unshed tears, my mouth curved downward, little puffs of air visible when I exhale.

If I'd known what kind of pressure joining the play would put me under, I never would have auditioned. All I wanted to do was fit in with my new friends and get Carlton to like me as much as I like him. But now, it feels like everything is blowing up in my face. I'm more tempted to quit than ever, but I *have* to stay in the play to prove everyone wrong. Especially Zayne. The whole school watching me now is just the cherry on top. I'm living every new kid's nightmare.

I just hope I wake up soon.

Chapter Five

I decide to skip the rest of the day. What good will it do me to stay at school if I can't even focus? I need to get my head on straight before I have to run lines with Zayne this evening.

When I get home, I go straight to my room. Beau is still at school and Dad is at work, so I could sit in the living room and watch TV. I could heat up a frozen chicken pot pie and stuff my face while I stare at the pretty flower arrangement in the center of our dining table, freshly picked by Dad.

But to be honest, I just feel like hiding.

From no one. From everyone. From myself.

At least until five, when I'll inevitably have to see Zayne.

There's got to be a way for me to somehow pull all this off: getting Carlton to like me again. Staying in his circle. Getting the attention of that admissions director, Nigel

Weathers, to prove Zayne wrong. Not making a complete fool of myself in front of the entire school now that Little Birdie has it out for me.

All of this may have been plopped into my lap, but it doesn't seem like it's going anywhere, so I better get started.

I open my script and flip through it, testing some of my lines aloud. I can't ignore the dread in my stomach when I hear myself talk, when I hear myself act. I just don't have the emotion my friends so easily deliver. My voice sounds stiff and...scripted.

Still, I continue, throwing in some hand gestures and facial expressions for better effect. I scoot over on my bed until I can see myself in the round mirror attached to my vanity, and then I keep reading. I watch my expressions as I utter my lines and adjust them to match the tone of my dialogue.

Better. Still not great, but better, and dare I say...fun? I'm having fun. It's liberating to pretend to be someone else for a little while, and the more enthusiasm I put into my lines, the more I enjoy speaking them. Catherine Earnshaw is entertaining to read because she has a tough choice to make: she can be with Heathcliff, the poor orphaned boy who would bring down her rank in society, or she can marry Edgar Linton, who is higher status and kind of a snob. In her high society lifestyle, her choice should be obvious. Who wouldn't want to advance their social status? The only problem is that she loves Heathcliff.

The next time I glance at my clock, it's four-thirty. I peek out my bedroom door. "Beau?" He should have been dropped off by the bus two hours ago. I check my phone and see a message from him.

BEAU

At an ASL club meeting.

Relief floods my chest. Relief, and then envy because Beau is now learning his fourth language. I can't help but wish I had something that lights me up inside the way learning new languages lights up Beau.

And instead of figuring out what might excite you, Dot, you decided to blurt that you want to go Ivy to impress your parents.

My stomach knots itself as I text Beau back.

ME

Would have been nice to know.

Somehow, my little brother has found his place here faster than me. I can't remember ever struggling so hard to fit in when we lived in Stockbridge, but then again, when you live in a small town with no homeschooling co-ops nearby, there's not much to fit into.

Another text comes through, this time from Mabel.

MABEL

You okay???

ME

Yes. Just needed some space.

I pause, then add,

ME

On my way to Zayne's house...

Her response is practically instant.

MABEL

Zayne Silverman?!?!

ME

Yeah

MABEL

Why?

ME

To run lines. Duh.

MABEL

OMG. Does Carlton know you changed your mind? I thought you said you weren't going!

I stare at my phone, biting my lip. I did say that, didn't I? I wonder if I should bother saying anything to him. It's not like he's my boyfriend, even if I want him to be. I could just send him a quick text. Or I could ignore Mabel's question.

I opt for the latter. There's no need to start even more unnecessary drama. Carlton might not like him, but it doesn't change the fact that Zayne is my co-star.

I slip into some leggings and a hoodie, not wanting to be in my pristine school uniform a moment longer. I gather the top strands of my braids into a bun, brush my teeth, and splash some blush on my cheeks before heading out the door.

According to my GPS, Zayne Silverman lives in Kendall Square—only an eight-minute walk away from me, and only eleven minutes from Carlton, who could possibly drive by and see my car parked in front of Zayne's, so walking is the safer choice.

My hoodie keeps me warm, protecting me from the New England air. The smell of a pumpkin spice latte makes my mouth water when I pass a cafe along the way. My boots crunch the brown and orange leaves that have fallen from the trees lining the sidewalk as I approach Zayne's two-story condominium.

It's a bright, cheery neighborhood. Some kids are riding bikes down the street, and several cats lounge on the front steps of surrounding porches. I dodge the sprinklers stretching over from his neighbor's front yard as I walk up, pausing before I knock on the door.

Am I really doing this? If Carlton finds out, I won't be winning myself any points with him. I should probably just go back home. But deep down, there's a part of me that doesn't want to admit how much fun I had in my audition with Zayne, unbearable as he is. I kind of want to see if it happens again, or if it was just a one-time thing.

A boy who looks a few years younger than Zayne answers the door when I knock, and he has the same velvety skin, the same dreads and undercut, and the same warm brown eyes. His mouth forms a lopsided grin when he takes me in.

"Hi." He holds out his hand. "The name's Lenny."

"Bardot. But I go by Dot." I shake his hand. "I'm here to run lines with Zayne. Is he here?"

"Zayne!" Lenny shouts, not taking his eyes off me. "Bardot, who goes by Dot, is here to run lines with you!" Lenny leans against the door frame. His grin widens. "You know, I'm learning to drive this year."

"That's fantastic." I shift my feet, feeling like a fool still standing on the porch.

Zayne appears behind Lenny, shuffling down the staircase. His dreads aren't in a bun anymore, and they fall to the side of his forehead. He's wearing jeans and a plain blue T-shirt. With a start, I realize I've never seen him in regular clothes before. I don't understand how he makes such a basic outfit look just as good as our preppy Fallbrook uniform.

When he reaches the door, he scowls at Lenny. "Aren't you going to invite her in?"

Lenny shrugs. "I don't know, man. I've been rewatching *The Vampire Diaries* lately, and you should never just invite anyone in. She could be a vampire. You never know."

Zayne blinks several times and turns to me. "Please excuse him."

I can't help but laugh. "I like that show," I tell Lenny. "And I promise I'm not a vampire."

"That's what a vampire would say." He grins, seeming pleased that I'm playing along, and steps aside so I can enter. "If you bite me, you're in for a nasty surprise."

Zayne runs a hand down his face. "I don't even want to

know what that means." He turns to me. "Did you bring your script?"

I nod.

"Good. We can practice in my room, upstairs." He turns around and starts heading toward the stairwell.

In his room? I plant my feet in the ground. "Where are your parents? Wouldn't they rather us practice down here?" I know from experience how parents can get about teenagers being alone together. Every time I go to Carlton's house, we remain under the dutiful supervision of his dad at all times.

Not to mention, Carlton would flip out if he knew I was here to begin with. If he found out I was alone with Zayne in his room, I might as well bury our future relationship in a cemetery right here and now.

"My mom and my grandma are at work," Zayne says. "They won't be back till late. Why?"

"It's just..." I glance around the living room helplessly.

Realization finally dawns on his face. "If you feel more comfortable down here, it's fine with me. Just know you'll have Lenny for an audience."

I glance at Lenny, who actually licks his hand and uses it to slick his hair back, and then waggles his eyebrows like some kind of cartoon character.

I burst into laughter. "On second thought, upstairs sounds good to me."

I follow him to his room, leaving Lenny pouting in the entryway. There are a few family portraits on the wall, and one catches my eye with a young Zayne and Lenny wearing matching cowboy outfits, back-to-back and blowing fake smoke off their toy guns. Lenny looks proud in his cowboy hat, but Zayne looks embarrassed. An impatient frown is on his face. I bite my reluctant grin away before it can form.

We reach Zayne's room and I take in my surroundings. The walls are painted dark blue, and there's an iron-frame bed against the wall, neatly made up with a simple plaid comforter. There's a large bookcase on the other side of the room filled with novels, and a comfy looking leather chair positioned in front of it. I scan the titles of the books. There's some sci-fi, fantasy, and plenty of classics. "You read?" I ask him.

He frowns. "Don't you?"

"Not much."

"Well, if you ever need any recommendations, let me know." He grabs his script off the bed and starts flipping through it. "Let's get started."

I take mine out of my bag, and then notice three missed calls from Carlton. Another one comes through as I pick up my phone, so I answer. "Hello?"

"Where are you?" Carlton asks. "Why haven't you been answering?"

"Sorry." I contemplate telling him the truth but blurt something else out on a whim. "I've been helping Beau with math homework. My dad is still at work."

He pauses. "Oh. Alright. Well, call me when you're done, then."

"I will." I hang up and look at Zayne.

He looks right back at me. "Why did you lie?"

"Nosiness is a very unattractive quality, you know."

"It's because of me, isn't it?" he guesses easily. "Your boyfriend hates my guts, doesn't he?" And then he does something that makes heat spark in my veins. He *smiles*. He actually *smiles*.

"You seem very pleased by that sentiment."

Zayne just rolls his shoulders. "I don't like your boyfriend much either."

"He's not technically my boyfriend. And of course you don't like him, because he's so much more talented and... intimidating than you."

Zayne looks appalled. "Intimidating? *Carlton?*"

His disbelief sounds so genuine that it irritates me. "You're just jealous."

"Not really. Why would I be? I got the part I auditioned for. Can't say the same for him."

"Only because you tampered with his script!" It takes more effort than I'd like to admit to keep my voice level. "You stole the part from him. You made him stumble to make yourself look better."

Zayne glares at me with his eyebrows pulled together. "You still believe that?"

I cross my arms. "Don't even try to deny it."

"You know what?" He shakes his head. "I'm not surprised it was so easy for you to get cast as someone as cold and heartless as Catherine Earnshaw. It's perfect for you." He takes a step closer to me and lowers his voice. "It's no wonder Mr. Saltzman asked me to run lines with you on top of rehearsals. He probably realized he mistook your real personality for acting and thought you had talent. "

I gape at him, at a complete loss for words. I hate to

admit it, but his insult stings. I can't let him know that, though, so I scramble for a retaliation. "Funny. I was thinking about the irony of you playing Heathcliff. It's completely unrealistic that you'd be considered a love-interest by anyone with even half a brain." I gather up my materials, stuffing them back into my bag with harsh, jerky movements.

"Don't forget this." Zayne retrieves my phone from his bed and holds it out to me.

As I snatch it from him, our fingers brush and a thrill goes through me. It's like by accidentally touching me, he zapped me with dopamine. I stuff my phone in my open bag. "I don't know why I thought running lines with you was a good idea."

"Apparently, we have *chemistry*." Zayne says it like it's a foreign concept without meaning.

"Well, whoever decided that is an idiot." I sling my bag over my shoulder and glare at him one last time as a farewell. As I rush downstairs and out the front door, I can't help but wonder why I didn't just quit the play and save myself all this trouble. Doing so would make my life a thousand times easier. I wouldn't have to learn how to act. Little Birdie would leave me alone. And best of all, I wouldn't have to practice with Zayne ever again.

Mr. Saltzman would have to search for a new actress to replace me with. That wasted time could potentially hurt Zayne's chances at getting into Underwood.

I imagine it all as I walk home. It's a tempting outcome. One I could easily make happen.

One I *should* make happen.

But I can't ignore the tiny seed of interest newly planted within me. The thought of simply returning to my linear plan of studying topics that don't excite me, stressing over my grades and attendance, and joining the ocean of sterile individuals desperate to achieve the exact same thing makes my spirits deflate.

Acting is different. Acting is straying from the plan I've been promising to accomplish since I was seven. I know that should terrify me, but it does the complete opposite.

And deep down, quitting would feel too much like proving Zayne right. Not about me being talentless, or incapable of getting into Underwood, like he implied at our first rehearsal, but about me being perfect for the role I was selected for.

About me being cold and heartless, just like Catherine Earnshaw.

Chapter Six

Dad makes it home in time to serve dinner. This is a rarity, considering he works two jobs. I can't blame him though. He's basically forced to shoulder the costs of our household all alone. Mom's medical bills combined with Fallbrook's tuition is practically the amount of a second mortgage.

Sometimes I feel guilty that he works so hard, but I couldn't stop him if I tried. When we lost Mom's income, he had to make the tough decision to stop homeschooling me and Beau so he could reenter the workforce. But because my brother and I were ahead academically, he wouldn't send Beau anywhere but his advanced, private middle school, and he wouldn't send me anywhere but Fallbrook. Even if it meant him working nonstop and hardly seeing us.

"You don't have to waste money on sending me to a fancy prep school, Dad," I remember telling him.

But he just shook his head, determined. "An education is never a waste of money."

As soon as I got accepted, his role in my life shifted from warm and fun homeschool teacher to overworked TSA employee and food delivery driver. For him to make the same high salary mom did as a firefighter, he had to take the jobs in Boston. I know he misses our massive, sprawling colonial in Stockbridge, because sometimes, I can practically feel how unsatisfied he is by our modern but overpriced townhome in the heart of the city.

He works so hard, all to make sure Beau and I have the same privileged life we had when Mom was still here.

It's part of the reason I'm so determined not to let him down. Going to an Ivy League college is the dream I said I wanted, after all, no matter how young and naive I was when I announced it to my family. The least I can do is stick to my word, even if doing so makes me feel like a bird with clipped wings.

I give him a kiss on the cheek before I sit down at the table. When we're done saying grace, I ask, "How was work?"

He hands me a plate of green beans and half-burned meatloaf. "I'm just happy to be home."

"I wish Mom could come home," Beau murmurs.

My dad pats his shoulder before sitting down at the table himself, plate in hand. "Me too." His shoulders sag. "But she's doing the responsible thing. She's getting better so she can keep being the mom you know and love."

Beau uses his fork to carve patterns in his meatloaf. "I just don't see why she couldn't get better from home."

"Addiction is ugly, son. And withdrawals are physical proof of it."

I take a bite, chewing slowly through the solemn silence at the table. "I got the lead role in the school play."

He removes his glasses so he can look at me. "You pulling my leg?"

I laugh. "No. I swear."

"Whoever cast you should get their head checked," Beau teases.

"Shut up."

"I'm real proud of you, Bardot." Dad tries to bite his smile back. "I'm going to have to see this play."

"Don't worry," I say, more to myself than to either of them. "I'm sure you will. Along with everyone else." My stomach swims at the thought.

The next day goes according to plan: I don't fail my calculus quiz, I take diligent notes in Bible class, Carlton and I make it through lunch without talking about Zayne Silverman, and I fall asleep in history.

When school ends, Carlton walks with me to rehearsal. The rest of our group is already there, waiting in a seated circle on the floor. "Hi guys," I say as we approach them.

"Hey, Dot." Rue waves a paper in her hand. "Mr. Saltzman is making us learn some weird choreography."

"Really?" I glance at the paper she's holding.

"Well, not you," she amends, "or even Zayne. But the rest of us, yeah."

"What about me?" Carlton grabs the paper out of Rue's hand. "And what is this, anyway?"

She shrugs. "The written form of the choreography. We're supposed to be wuthering on the heights, as trees or something."

Carlton snorts. "Who wrote this lame script?"

"And what does wuthering even mean, anyway?" Mabel mutters.

"Roaring," someone says. We all glance up to find Zayne looming over us. "It means roaring. Basically." He's looking at me, which makes me shift my gaze to the floor. I hope he doesn't bring up me going to his house last night to run lines. Especially since I insulted him before I all but stormed out and wasted both our time. He knows I lied to Carlton about being there, too. Talking about it now would be excellent revenge on his part.

Carlton crosses his arms as he regards Zayne. "What do you want?"

I stiffen, prepared for him to bring up last night. But he just points over his shoulder. "Mr. Saltzman wants us next door while everyone else learns the next scene."

Carlton's face reddens. "What about me? I'm playing the other love interest to Catherine. Shouldn't I be there too?"

Zayne squints at him. "Like I said. He only wants me and Dot. Everyone else stays here."

I glance at Carlton, but he won't meet my gaze. With a sigh, I get up and follow Zayne, who is now walking away. Speed-walking, in fact. When I finally reach him, I snap, "You could have been nicer to him."

Zayne stops walking to shoot me an incredulous look. "Because he's the pinnacle of delight. Right?" He resumes pace.

"That's not fair." I catch up to him so he's no longer walking ahead of me. "He's going through a lot, what with you stealing his part."

He snorts. "Right."

"Besides, I've decided to offer you a truce."

We're back in the classroom we auditioned in. It's dark inside, all the blinds shut, and Zayne walks around to open them. "A truce?"

"Yes." It bothers me that he's not totally paying attention to what I'm saying for some reason, and instead is more focused on opening all the windows. "A truce." I wait until he's done, until he's standing right in front of me.

"What kind of truce, Dot?" He's standing close enough that I can see my reflection in his eyes, flecked with hints of gold. I can smell the peppermint on his breath as he speaks. It makes me dizzy.

"I'll stop wasting time and commit to the play once and for all on one condition."

He arches a brow. "And what is that?"

"You have to promise to stop trying to sabotage Carlton. He really wants to get into Underwood Academy, and I can't have you screwing things up for him."

Zayne crosses his arms and scowls. "It's not me you have to worry about."

"I don't know what you're insinuating, but I've had enough of it." It's bad enough Carlton's been in a bad mood because of Zayne. The last thing I need is for him to try to pit me and Carlton against each other.

Zayne sighs, rolling his shoulders to ease some of the tension. "If you say so." He grabs his script from the desk he placed it on before he started opening the windows. Light streams into the classroom now in long rectangles, illuminating our faces. "Let's get started." He flips through his book until he finds our first scene together. He pauses on it, reading the first line to himself in a muted tone. Then to me, he explains, "You're playing a ghost here, and you're haunting me. So, I'm calling out to you for you to continue."

Anticipation flutters in my stomach. "Okay." And then I pause. "To continue? Why would you want me to keep haunting you?"

He blinks. "You're the ghost of Cathy, Heathcliff's love. Haven't you read *Wuthering Heights*?"

I shrug. "I've read the summary."

"Alright." Zayne sighs. "Just do like it says on the script then."

I nod. He begins acting out the scene, and since I don't have any lines yet, I just watch him.

"*Delightful company,*" he mutters, as Heathcliff, to a character named Lockwood, even though he isn't in the room with us. "*Take the candle, and go where you please. Away with you! I'll come in two minutes!*

I watch as he kneels and pantomimes opening a window. It's pretty impressive, actually. Zayne arranges his features into that of pure, unadulterated anguish, and his eyes gloss over. For a moment, I'm alarmed, thinking he hurt himself when he kneeled down or something.

"Come in! Come in! Cathy, do come," he sobs, and with a jolt, I realize he's still in character.

He's still acting, and I'm still staring, when I should be flitting across the room in front of him like a ghost.

"Sorry," I stammer. "From the top?"

Zayne blinks several times. "What do you mean, 'from the top?' You don't even have any lines in this scene!"

My cheeks burn. "I got distracted. I'm sorry." Distracted by how good he is. By his ability to cry on command and then shut it off like it's nothing. By how terrible I'm going to look in comparison while acting with him.

He searches my face before returning to his starting point. "Fine. From the top."

He says his lines again, and this time, I remember to come in when I'm supposed to. And the more the scene goes on, the more impressed I am by Zayne's ability to act so well. When we auditioned together, it was just a lighthearted scene from the middle of the play that we read. Nothing like the intense, emotional sequence I'm currently witnessing.

It bothers me that I'm so impressed.

It bothers me because I'm starting to see why Zayne got the part over Carlton.

He deserves it.

And if Mr. Saltzman deemed me worthy enough to be cast alongside him, there must be something in me that knows what I'm doing.

Knowing that feels good. Really good.

We run through the scene a few more times, until it starts to feel natural. Until my participation starts to feel less robotic, and more enthusiastic. Until I have the whole thing close to memorized and Mr. Saltzman comes in to witness it, looking more than impressed.

And all the while I'm overwhelmed, intimidated, and even a little inspired by Zayne Silverman.

Chapter Seven

I was starting to think Little Birdie was done gossiping about me. After days of no news on the app, things were beginning to feel closer to how they were before I auditioned for the play. Normal. Sort of. I stopped getting random waves in the halls, stopped being photographed like I was suddenly doing something spectacular.

Until today.

As Meredith is complaining to Mabel about the costume design for her role as Nelly, a *Little Birdie* alert goes off. The sound of the familiar whistle echoes throughout the crowded corridor, both eerie and exciting. Where there are no whistles, there are phones vibrating. Every single person in view grabs their phone, some with both hands, and stares into the screen.

I can't help but follow.

At last, fledglings! I have emerged. After a week of being good, I can't stay silent any longer.

It appears Dot Bennett just couldn't keep away. Though the new girl seems to be smitten over Carlton Peters while in the public eye, she leads a very different life in private.

Dot was seen at the house of none other than Zayne Silverman last Friday at 5:20pm! And better yet, alone with him—in his bedroom! How very risqué!

I just wonder what Carlton thinks of all this. Let's hope he's made of tougher stuff than thread, because it appears the new girl may, in fact, be stringing him along!

Yours truly,
Little Birdie

I lower my phone slowly. My face feels like it's burning. My heart is beating at a rapid pace. How could this have gotten out? No one stopped by Zayne's house while I was there, at least not that I know of. Who would have told Little Birdie? The only person it could have been is Lenny, but somehow I can't imagine him doing such a thing.

I don't know what I'm more upset about—the clear invasion of my privacy or being caught in a blatant lie. I told Carlton I was helping Beau with homework when he called me that night. But now, there's no way I'm getting around this.

I glance up at him, but he's not looking at me. Carlton is staring down the wall of lockers at Zayne Silverman, past the classmates in the hall watching us.

Without a word, he marches over to him. Zayne crosses his arms as Carlton approaches. I'm on Carlton's heels in an instant. "What are you doing?"

But he's ignoring me as he leads the way. I glance helplessly over his shoulder at Zayne, who meets my eyes ever so briefly before returning his gaze to Carlton.

I belatedly realize a crowd has formed around us. There are, like, three phones out and recording already. Great.

Carlton shows Zayne the *Little Birdie* post. "What's this about, man?"

He shrugs. "What does it look like to you?"

"It's nothing," I chime in, hoping Zayne will go along with me. "A lie."

But Zayne gives me a blatant look and I can practically hear him thinking, *Really? Drop the act.*

"Don't look at her," Carlton says. "I'm the one talking to you. Back off of Dot. You hear me?"

Zayne turns his sarcastic gaze onto Carlton. "Might be hard, considering we're playing opposite each other onstage."

"Just stay away from her."

Zayne laughs. "Why? Afraid your little secret will spill?"

"Secret?" I ask. "What's he talking about?"

"No idea." Carlton's voice is low.

Zayne crosses his arms. "Whatever. Look, I know you're trying to be all macho-tough-guy in front of Dot, but you can relax. I'm not trying to, like, steal her away from you or anything. We were just running lines. You know, for the play we're both in? And last time I checked, Dot is fully capable of making her own choices. That includes choosing who she wants to hang out with." Zayne slams his locker closed and walks away.

Carlton and I are left watching him leave. Slowly, he turns to face me, and realizes we're still being watched. "Get lost!" he yells at everyone around us. I jump at his tone. It's so unexpected, but it works. No one is staring at us anymore, instead scurrying toward wherever they were going before, or at least pretending not to be eavesdropping. Carlton's face is tight. It feels like it's been so long since I've seen him look relaxed. He's so different from the guy I was first drawn to. I bet he's given himself premature wrinkles already. "I don't like this," he says.

"You don't like what?"

"You and *him*. Zayne. It's too much. That should have been me. We should have been the ones rehearsing together."

"We will be." I reach out and touch his hand. "We have plenty of scenes together."

"It just doesn't make sense," he continues as if I hadn't spoken. "Why would Mr. Saltzman choose him to play Heathcliff? I'm obviously better than him."

"It's not your fault. Zayne ruined your script, remember?" But as the words leave my lips, I can't help but think back to Zayne's performance at rehearsal. How impressed I was. How, if I'd been Mr. Saltzman, I probably would have done the same. Because I've seen Carlton's acting, and it's good. But—as ashamed as I am to admit, even if only to myself—Zayne might possibly be just a teeny bit *better.*

A flash of memory comes to my mind—the time Carlton demonstrated his skills to me at his house during the summer. I was impressed at his rendition of a scene from a role he played last year, but I couldn't help but notice the way his cheeks would flush, how his voice would waver, as if his self-awareness was a hurdle too high for him to overcome to truly become the role. Zayne has never made mistakes like that in front of me.

But there's no way I can tell Carlton that.

"Mr. Saltzman will realize how wrong he was. Your performance as Linton will blow everyone away, including Nigel Weathers." I grin. "You got this."

He rolls his eyes. "Easy for you to say. You're playing Catherine and you hardly deserve it."

"Oh." I flinch, stung by his tone. His words. "You—you don't think I deserve it?"

"Come on, Dot. Be real. Meredith should be playing the lead and everyone knows it. My audition with her was... *amazing,* and she's been practicing all summer. You literally just started."

My chest feels suddenly tight. I need to be alone. Away from him and his hostility. "I need to get to class."

He grabs my arm. His grip is firm, but not painful. "Wait. I didn't mean that. I'm just stressed about everything. I'm sorry." He pins me in place with a softer gaze. Pulls me into a hug. "I'm so sorry."

I shut my eyes, enjoying the warmth of his skin on

mine. Breathing in his minty scent until my bones thaw. "It's okay," I whisper.

"Will you come over for lunch tomorrow?" he murmurs into my braids. "My parents are dying for an excuse to break out the charcuterie board and I'd really love to see you outside of all this garbage."

My body practically trembles with excitement. Lunch with his parents? This seems...big. Special. But then I remember my previous engagement. "I'm taking Beau to breakfast tomorrow, so let's make it Sunday."

"Ok, sure."

"Great. It's *official*," I hint.

He smiles, and I smile back, but as I walk away, I can't help but think that it felt a little forced.

Taking Beau to breakfast on Saturday mornings has become a tradition of mine. Since Dad starts work super early, I have no other choice. It's not like I can let my little brother starve. And if the only other option is to actually *cook*, then diners here we come.

"Are we going to a new restaurant every time?" Beau asks as we walk up to *Mama & Mimi's*, the place we're eating today. It's a cozy-looking maroon building with white stripes on the awning. There's writing on the window, advertising a free slice of cake when you order the special.

"No harm in trying new things," I tell him. Since moving to the city, we've been to a total of twelve new restaurants, with no repeat visits yet.

He scoffs. "What, you mean like the play? You literally try *one new thing* and suddenly you're an expert?"

"That's right!" We make our way through the entrance to the restaurant. Checkered tile covers most of the entryway, leading to the kitchen on the left, and the dining area is on the right, separated by wood floors. The majority of the walls on the dining side are windows, but near the kitchen, an eclectic assortment of wall hangings cover teal and purple accent walls.

There's an elderly couple in front of us with two teenagers and a younger kid. The host returns to the podium to take the couple's names down, and instantly, I recognize his lean frame, his undercut and dreads that match his older brother's. "Lenny?"

Lenny searches around and then looks up. When he sees me, he beams. "Hey, Dot!"

Beau glances back and forth between the two of us. "You know the host? How? We just moved here!"

"Come on over, I'll seat you," says Lenny. "We have a table for two available against the window."

I nudge Beau forward. He sighs deeply, like I've just asked him to run a marathon. I take the lead and we follow Lenny to a small table near—as promised—the front window overlooking the downtown strip. I sidestep a waitress holding a hot pot of coffee and sit across from Beau. Lenny places two laminated menus on the table. The person sitting behind Beau hums delightfully as he crunches a slice of bacon into his mouth.

"I didn't know you worked here," I tell Lenny.

"It gets better," he says. "I'll tell Zayne that he'll be your server today."

I blink several times. "*What?* Zayne works here, too?" And then I realize what he just said. That he's going to make Zayne be our server. "Wait! You don't have to—"

Lenny holds up a hand like he's doing me a favor or something. "I'll personally make sure of it." Then he bows until his face is parallel to the ground before returning to his podium.

"You know," I tell Beau, "maybe you were right about the harm in trying new things after all."

He picks up his menu from the table. "You should really start listening to me." He looks over the breakfast items on the page. "What are you going to order?"

Food. Right. I pick up my menu, too. "Uh, probably pancakes." And then I see the type of pancakes they have. Blueberry banana and cream cakes. "Did I say maybe? I meant definitely."

"Actually, I'll take your drink orders first." It's not Beau's voice that says it, though, and I glance up to find Zayne standing next to us wearing a deep purple apron, notebook and pen in hand.

"Zayne," I mutter by way of greeting.

"Dot."

The events of what happened yesterday at school play behind my vision, and by the look Zayne is giving me, I think he might be remembering, too.

Beau glances back and forth between the two of us. "Am I missing something?"

Zayne narrows his eyes at me. "I was thinking the same

thing. Last time I checked, it's hard to stay away from someone if they keep following you."

"I'll take a diet soda," says Beau slowly. "And Dot will take an iced tea. Right, Dot?"

I scoff. "I am *not* following you. I didn't even know you worked here."

"Right. I'll be back with your drinks." He turns and walks away before I can protest, leaving me flustered in my seat.

Beau's eyes widen. "What was that all about?"

"*That* is what happens when you give someone the benefit of doubt for a tiny second. He's unbearable."

"Whoa, whoa, whoa." Beau holds up his hands, like I'm a caged lion trying to escape. "You're going to have to fill me in. I don't even know this dude. Why are you so angry at him?"

I lean over the table to keep anyone else from hearing. I'm not sure why I even bother, considering Little Birdie has made it her new mission to create a public display of my life. In fact, I can't help but worry that Little Birdie is somehow watching me right now. I resist the urge to check over my shoulder. "*He's* the reason Carlton and I are having problems."

Beau frowns. "Since when are you having problems?"

"Don't you read *Little Birdie*?" I huff impatiently. "Actually, never mind. You're only thirteen. Too young for all this drama. Do not read *Little Birdie*. All you need to know is that Zayne, our waiter, stole Carlton's spot as the lead in the school play, and now everyone thinks I like him because we were in his room alone together to run lines!"

"But..." Beau pauses. "You like Carlton, right? Not Zayne?"

"That's right." I remember Carlton's angry expression at lunch yesterday when he looked at Zayne after Little Birdie's latest blast was sent out to the entire school. "And because he's so mad, he's been acting...different. He's been saying things I know he doesn't mean."

"Like what?" Beau is no longer just an interested, but protective brother now. He leans forward, eyebrows furrowed. "What did he say?"

I shrug, attempting indifference. But deep down, what Carlton said bothered me, no matter how hard I try to pretend otherwise. "He said that Meredith should have gotten the part I was cast as. That I don't deserve to play the lead."

He crosses his arms. "Well, that's not right. He needs to keep his mouth shut."

I swallow back the knot in my throat. If I don't blink, maybe the moisture in my eyes will dry out instead of spilling over.

Beau shifts in his seat. "I, uh, have to go to the bathroom." As my brother, he cares. But I know how much others crying makes him uncomfortable. "I'll be right back."

I nod, grateful he's giving me a moment to recollect myself. As soon as he's gone, I cover my face with my hands. I take a deep breath and hold it.

"Did Carlton really tell you that?"

I peek through my hands. Zayne is holding mine and Beau's drinks, and he's frowning. "Tell me what?"

"That you don't deserve your part in the play?"

I throw my hands into my lap, no longer caring if anyone sees me cry. "What? Like you don't think I know it's true? Of course, I don't deserve my role. What Carlton said is the truth. That's the worst part." I release a frustrated sigh. "It wouldn't be so bad if I was the only one who thought it. But now the whole school has eyes on me, and *they all know it too!*" The last part sounds hysterical as it comes out of my mouth. A few angry tears trickle down my face, and Zayne looks around with a scowl, as if contemplating how he ended up in this situation, or hoping someone else might magically step in. But it's just him. With a low sigh, he sits down in Beau's seat.

I remain silent, aside from a few reluctant sniffles.

"Why do you care what Carlton thinks?" His voice is flat. Serious.

I shake my head. "What are you talking about? Of course, I care what he thinks. The whole reason I joined the drama club in the first place was to impress him. I just want him to like me." *Ugh, Dot. Why on earth did you just admit that to Zayne of all people? He's never going to let you live it down.*

Zayne looks at my hands, balled up and fidgeting in my lap, and his eyes travel up until they collide with mine. "If he doesn't already like you, then he's a fool. Drama club or not." The hardness in his tone makes me stare. At the firm set of his downturned lips, and his gentle eyes, in contrast with the rest of his demeanor. I'm momentarily locked in his gaze.

"That's possibly the nicest thing you've ever said to me," I tell him.

He doesn't say anything smart back like I expect him to, instead offering me a half-smile. "You're worth more to the play than you think."

I swallow, ignoring the thudding in my chest. Ignoring the way our eyes linking makes me feel like I gulped down caffeine.

"Am I interrupting something?" Beau asks. He lingers next to where Zayne is still sitting in his seat.

Zayne ascends from the chair like it burned him. He brushes off his purple apron, though I don't see anything on it. "Sorry." He takes a notebook out of his front pocket. "What can I get you?"

Beau sits and orders something to eat, and I numbly tell Zayne I want the pancakes. But I'm hardly paying attention. My mind is still stuck in the conversation we were having, and the lingering, unexpected warmth I'm still experiencing.

I stare blankly past Beau at a nearby table. There's a cluster of adults seated, and with a jolt, I realize I recognize some of them. "Is that..." I squint, cutting off Zayne from answering whatever question Beau asked him about the food. "Is that Mr. Saltzman? And Ms. Powers?"

"Among other teachers from Fallbrook," Zayne confirms with dismay. "They're all regulars here."

"What kind of place is this?" I ask aloud. "Everyone seems to bump into each other like it's nothing." Coming from such a small rural town, where I often bumped into people I knew, I expected the opposite to happen in the city.

"You get used to it after a while," says Zayne. He clears his throat. "If that's all, I'll be putting your order in now."

"Yeah," says Beau. "I'm good. Dot?"

I nod, unable to meet Zayne's eyes again at first. But then I force myself to, because his little pep talk actually might have helped. A little. Maybe, when he's not too busy torturing Carlton, Zayne Silverman isn't so bad after all.

Chapter Eight

On Sunday after church, my GPS helps me navigate from Cambridge to Boston. It's embarrassing to rely so heavily on my phone for directions, but I literally still don't know the streets of Boston, and city drivers scare me.

Still, it's worth it if I get to see Carlton.

The excursion takes a grand total of ten minutes, and when I arrive, my eyes widen at the mini feast his parents have prepared for us, complete with a colorful charcuterie board, hot apple cider, fresh fruit, a vegetable platter, and caviar. Yes...*caviar*.

This has to be the day he asks me to be his girlfriend. The day he finally makes things official between us.

We're seated in the heavily windowed dining room in stiff, beautifully upholstered provincial chairs. My legs tingle with numbness, so I swing them back and forth to keep my blood moving. The dining room, much like the rest of Carlton's house, is overwhelming to look at, with grand, double-height ceilings, extravagant light fixtures, custom wainscoting, and Renaissance-style paintings and sculptures nearly everywhere I turn.

The lunch meat his mom sliced is fanned out on a thick wooden board like a deck of cards, topped with paper-thin lemon wedges and a sprinkle of parsley. I'm afraid to mess it up.

"Nigel Weathers reposted Fallbrook's performance announcement. I saw it last night." Mrs. Peters beams. Her eyes are full of warmth as she smiles at Carlton. "This is the year. I just know it."

Carlton's cheeks lift in response, but the smile is too tight for his face. "You would think so."

"You're not going to let us down this time, son," his dad says. He says it like it's a simple truth. Like he's commenting on the fact that it's foggy outside with a twenty percent chance of rain.

The words aren't even directed me, but they send dread and sadness rocketing through me. When I glance at Carlton to see his response, his face is neutral. The only thing that gives him away is the way his hands are balled into fists on his legs.

"Even if he doesn't get into Underwood Academy," I say, ignoring Mrs. Peters's eyes landing on me sharply, "I know he'll give a great performance. And he could always just apply after high school, right?"

I'm not sure why I say it. Maybe because of the unbearable pressure his parents are putting him under. I can practically feel the tangible weight of it, and it's not even directed at me.

"He *will* get into Underwood Academy." Mr. Peters takes a sip of his hot cider. "It will be better for his future if he completes his high school education there while simultaneously earning college credits." His statement indicates the subject is now closed, so I drop it.

"I just hope Nigel realizes his mistake from last year. He's got a chance now to remedy it," Mrs. Peters says. "Carlton was the best sophomore in the whole play."

"Sophomore? I thought only juniors and seniors could get accepted to Underwood." I sound exasperated, even to my own ears. How long has Carlton been trying to get into this school, anyway?

"Sophomores and even freshmen can get accepted," says Mr. Peters. "But it's pretty rare. Usually, the two lead actors are the ones chosen, and those roles are always given to upperclassmen." He purses his lips. "But Carlton was better than both of them last year, even as a supporting role."

Carlton's shoulders relax. "Thanks, Dad."

"It's true. And if things get serious after you graduate from Underwood," his mom says, "we'll have to either move to Los Angeles or New York, depending on the path you want to take in your career." She pats Carlton's hand.

My brows draw together. "Path?"

Mrs. Peters glances at me. "Film or Broadway. LA for film, New York for stage." She scrunches her nose. "But so much filming is done in New York, it's the best of both worlds, in my opinion."

"Right." I nod, like I knew that already, of course I did. "That makes sense."

Carlton's parents continue planning what he'll do after he gets into Underwood. They discuss where he'll stay, helping him with rent or even getting a second home there, and what kind of roles would best suit him. If this is what he wants, and he's not just trying to please his parents like I am, then I'm happy for him. But one thing is clear: the future they're discussing does not include me. And why should it? I'm not Carlton's girlfriend. For all his parents know, I'm just another friend of his, like Rue, Meredith, or Mabel. Carlton fidgets in his seat as his parents go on, his eyes downcast beneath his furrowed brows.

After lunch, his parents announce they're going to the club for a round of golf.

Carlton stretches his shoulders. "Dot and I should probably run lines together." He's not wrong. Carlton and I have plenty of scenes together, but we still haven't taken the time to rehearse alone yet.

"Hm. I don't know." Mr. Peters lingers, like he's not sure if they should leave us in the house alone together, yet, but Mrs. Peters hurries him along. "They're children, not criminals. Goodness."

When they shut and lock the door behind them, silence echoes around the house. I hadn't realized how much of the talking had been coming from them. Now it's just me and Carlton, and I'm not sure what to say.

We get up from the table and he finally breaks the silence. "That was intense." He rubs the back of his neck.

"Yeah. All that talk about film and Broadway..." I trail off, searching for the right way to phrase my thoughts.

"What about it?"

"I guess I'm just trying to figure out where I fit into all of it." I don't know how to hint any longer, so I'm just going to finally ask the question. "What are we, exactly?"

"Well, I'm Carlton. And you're Dot." The corner of his mouth lifts. "So, I guess that makes us Carlton and Dot."

I fold my arms. "You know what I mean."

"Last I checked things were going well. Why the sudden need for all this heavy talk?"

"It's not that heavy," I mutter. But at the same time, I know he's probably right. I'm just feeling insecure because of all these plans being made about Carlton's future. Last I checked, none of the eight Ivy League colleges are in Los Angeles, so him moving there would probably mean goodbye for good.

Unless you don't get into an Ivy, Dot. I try to ignore how light inside I feel at the concept of not going Ivy. Of possibly going to an unconventional school like Underwood.

I try to tell myself that's not what I really want, that I'm only thinking like this because I miss the impulsive structure of homeschool and still haven't adjusted to the linear setup of Fallbrook.

"Hey," Carlton says, lifting my chin with his finger. "Let's just start over. Come here."

We both get out of our chairs, and he gives me a light hug, patting my back a few times. I don't know why, but the gesture irritates me. Being patted on the back reminds me of how I would pat a dog for behaving well. Not how I would comfort someone I care about.

But then Carlton kisses me lightly on the lips, and all

negativity drains from my mind. I shut my eyes, enjoying the soft warmth of his lips.

You're overthinking things, Dot, I tell myself. *Just relax. Be cool.*

When the kiss stretches out and becomes deeper, the remaining insecure thoughts I've been harboring evaporate. If only I could just stay here in this moment, never returning to reality. Just stay here, feeling Carlton's lips on mine, and letting my arms wind gently around his neck.

A whistle sounds in the room, followed by another. I belatedly realize that the noise is not a person, but our phones going off.

A Little Birdie blast.

Carlton breaks apart from me, eager to read whatever the anonymous blogger has to say. A prick of annoyance stabs me.

Seriously? Little Birdie is more important than this moment we're sharing right now?

I heave a dramatic sigh, not hiding my irritation, but otherwise take out my phone to check the blast as well.

And I read:

Fledglings!
My goodness, do I have a scoop of something yummy for you to snack on until I return next!
How could I, after all, keep something this delicious to myself? It wouldn't be fair.
Just yesterday, none other than Dot Bennett, arguably Fallbrook's new It Girl, was spotted in a

*restaurant sitting across from—you guessed it—
Zayne Silverman! But what could easily be
mistaken as a friendly rendezvous in fact appeared
to be much more! See from the photo—snapped by
an anonymous bystander—the look in Dot's eyes,
the way she stares longingly at Zayne, who is
obviously just as enraptured by Dot's beauty as she
is by his appeal.*

   *Now the question is only what Carlton, her
original beau, will do in response.*

   *Eagerly awaiting some action is Yours Truly,
Little Birdie*

When I look up from my screen, cheeks burning in rage, Carlton is already done reading. His lips are pressed together in a tight line, and he's staring not at me, but past me, like I'm not right in front of him. Like I don't even exist.

"Carlton—" I start, but he holds up a hand, silencing me.

"I don't want to hear it, Dot."

My heart hammers against my ribcage. Caught. I've been caught, and I wasn't even doing anything wrong, but how can I explain that to Carlton? If I were in his shoes, this would all cut me so deep, I wouldn't be sure who or what to believe. I'd like to think I'd believe *him*, trust *him*, but how do you deny what's right in front of you, picture evidence?

"It's not what it looks like," I try again.

He finally looks at me. "Oh, it isn't?" He holds up his phone, showing me the photo of me sitting across from Zayne at the restaurant, our intimate shared moment that would have been lost in time, now forever recorded by one finger tapping a camera button on a phone. It looks like whoever snapped the photo was near the exit, as if they took it on their way out.

"Because what it looks like," he says, bringing me back to the present, "is that you failed to mention you met up with Zayne, who happens to hate my guts." He doesn't drop the phone, though his point has been made. Just keeps holding it up to my face. "So please, Dot, tell me how this is not what it looks like."

I grasp for words, my mind in fragments. Finally, I remember how to speak. "I didn't *meet up* with him. It's not like I specifically sought him out or something. I just took Beau out to eat, and Zayne was our waiter."

He nods, but his grimace only deepens. "Right. Like you didn't know he works there."

"I didn't!" The words come out helplessly.

Carlton grits his teeth. "Everyone knows that restaurant is his family's. Come on, Dot. I know you're not actually that stupid."

My heart clenches. Just moments ago, Carlton's arms were around me. We were kissing. How did those sweet moments turn into this? Just thinking about it gives me whiplash. "Maybe I should go."

"Maybe you should. We can rehearse at school."

We stare at each other wordlessly. I will him with my eyes to take it back, tell me he didn't mean any of it. To laugh and brush this argument off as a result of stress from trying to get into Underwood Academy.

But he doesn't.

He just stares at me, his eyes like a curtain, closed against the blinding, unwelcome sun on a lazy morning.

So, I have no other choice but to turn around and leave.

Chapter Nine

It's been a week since my argument with Carlton. In that time, I haven't spoken to him, and he's been pretending I don't exist. I have to admit, his efforts are impressive. During play rehearsal, I accidentally trip over him when I go to sit at the stool where I'm supposed to pretend to play piano. He barely blinks.

Maybe if he put all this acting effort into the play instead of giving me the cold shoulder, he wouldn't be so worried about getting accepted into his drama school.

Rue says her line in a perfect, British accent. *"There's a person here from Gimmerton who wishes to see you, Cathy."* Her face betrays no nerves at having the entire class watch us perform the scene. Behind us, a collection of tall, half-painted boards form a makeshift backdrop, but it's still hard for me to pretend I'm on stage rather than in the drama classroom.

"What does he want?" I ask.

"I did not question him," she replies.

Carlton's voice comes out purposefully bored as he asks, *"And why ever not?"*

Zayne enters the scene then, appearing from behind one of the boards. I try my best to portray the right amount of shock and tension as I'm supposed to, and then throw my arms around Carlton's neck, pulling him into a tight hug. He stiffens. It's the last thing I want to do since we aren't on the best terms right now, but it's in the script. *"Heathcliff has returned!"*

"Well, don't strangle me for that." I note the slight gruffness in his voice that isn't supposed to be there. *"And try to be glad without being so absurd in front of the household. Heathcliff is nothing more than a runaway servant."* His gaze seems to land past me rather than directly on me.

We turn to Zayne in unison, and he fixes me with an intense, Heathcliff-y stare. My stomach does a little flip. I break away from Carlton's embrace and go to him. He takes my hands. I take one of Zayne's hands and place it into Carlton's, like the blocking says to do. I pause for a moment too long, struggling to remember my line, and then say, *"The two of you must be friends for my sake."* This is so awkward.

Zayne rips his hand out of Carlton's and Carlton says, *"Sit down, sir."*

"Cut," Mr. Saltzman says.

My shoulders sag in relief. We all unconsciously take a step backwards, away from each other.

Mr. Saltzman makes a note on his clipboard. "That was excellent. But Carlton, try to show less disdain for Cathy, and make it clear your animosity is aimed toward Heathcliff."

I glance at Carlton, trying not to let the hurt show on my face. *Even the teacher noticed he's mad at me.*

Mr. Saltzman scratches his shiny head with the pen he's holding. "Carlton, let's go over some notes and then we'll do it again, from the top."

Carlton crosses the room to where Mr. Saltzman is sitting and the rest of us go back to our starting places. I return to my piano stool. Rue leans against one of the painted boards behind us. "Thank God we don't have to make these sets ourselves," she whispers to me. "It's enough work just trying to memorize lines."

I tilt my head. "Who *does* make the sets?"

"The crew."

Carlton returns to his position, standing next to my seat when he's done talking with the teacher. He avoids meeting my gaze, and my stomach ties itself in a knot.

And Mr. Saltzman claps. "All right, everyone. From the top!"

At lunch time, I try to swallow down my irritation when Carlton storms out of the drama room without me. Only Mabel hangs behind to wait for me while he, Meredith, and Rue sprint away, and we end up near the end of the lunch line.

"I wish we could find someone who would let us cut," Mabel says, biting her lip and scanning the line ahead of us for a familiar face. She brightens. "Hey, what about Zayne? He's up pretty far."

My heart beats rapidly at the mention of his name. "No!" I practically shout. "Are you crazy?"

The mischief in her grin is unmistakable. "Why not? Aren't you two like, buddy-buddy now? According to Little Birdie anyway."

"No. We are *not* buddy-buddy. In fact, what Little Birdie says couldn't be farther from the truth."

But Mabel is already heading his direction, halfway up the line, and leaving me to look like an idiot talking to myself. I scurry after her, my beating heart now thundering. What is her problem? If Carlton catches me anywhere near Zayne outside of drama club, I might as well put a stake in whatever is left of our dilapidated, undefined, relationship.

"Hey, Zayne," Mabel lilts when I catch up to her. "Mind if we cut with you?"

Zayne's eyes sweep from Mabel to me, remaining a second too long before looking back at her. "Sure," he says, stepping aside so we have room.

Mabel grins. I hesitate before stepping in front of Zayne and Lenny, who I didn't realize was next to him.

"Hi, Lenny." I wave at him.

He waggles his eyebrows. "Bardot-who-goes-by-Dot." He turns to Mabel. "And Bardot-who-goes-by-Dot's friend."

She looks stunned, like she isn't sure whether to laugh or continue staring at him, dumbfounded. "Uh, hi. You can just call me Mabel."

"Queen." Lenny states the word simply. "That's what I'd call you if Bardot here didn't already own the title."

My lips twitch. Zayne closes his eyes and runs his hand down his face. "Lenny—"

"Lady-in-Waiting will have to do," he continues.

Mabel grins slowly, and Zayne rushes to explain. "You'll have to excuse my brother, he's—"

"A charmer," Mabel finishes for him. "He's a charmer. I love it."

Lenny takes Mabel's hand, brushes his lips across the top, and bows without breaking their gaze. Mabel covers her mouth with her other hand and giggles.

I bite my smile away and turn to Zayne. "We should run lines." It just comes out. But it's true, nonetheless.

He looks around at the cafeteria, at the people in line surrounding us. "Now?"

I blush. "No. Obviously not now. But after school, maybe?" Even though spending extra time with Zayne is the last thing I need to be doing, I know it's the right thing to suggest. Otherwise, me standing in the lunch line with Zayne looks to everyone else, including Carlton, like us hanging out. But if people think I'm only here to talk business with Zayne, especially theater business—the only business I have with him—there won't be any basis for more rumors and Carlton can't stay mad.

Zayne searches my face like he's looking for the truth, or maybe a lie. "After school works. We can meet at my house again if you wan—"

"Actually," I cut him off, because meeting at his house again isn't an option. Not after the field day Little Birdie had last time. "I'd rather not give you-know-who anything to talk about. Is there a...public place you know of that won't make it look like we're sneaking around or something?"

Zayne scoffs out a laugh. "Yeah. I know a place. There's a park not too far. I can text you the address."

"Perfect."

Mabel furrows her delicately arched brows. "You aren't going to invite Carlton, too?"

I didn't realize she'd been listening, but it's not like she and Lenny are far away.

"Yeah." I tug on the sleeve of my sweater. "I guess I could invite him." Zayne frowns at my words. But I meet his gaze and add, "The three of us do have scenes together."

Zayne wrinkles his nose, and as if by magic, Carton brushes past us, lunch tray in hand and a stony expression on his face. He's still ignoring me, but I can tell by the bunching of his shoulders that he sees me standing here. With Zayne.

"Carlton." I grab his arm.

He stops walking and pulls his arm out of my grasp, but finally, *finally*, turns to look at me. "What?"

It takes me a moment to speak because I can't believe he's acknowledging me, let alone actually talking to me. "Oh. Um. We're—I mean, Zayne and I are going to run lines after school." I pause, letting the uncertainty of my own statement ring in my ears.

"That's great, Dot," he seethes. "I'm really happy for

you." Glaring at Zayne, he starts to walk away again, but I stop him.

"Want to come? You know, since we all have scenes together?"

He blinks several times, like he never considered the fact that the three of us would eventually be forced together into an interaction like rehearsal, due to the play. "Sure." Carlton shifts his weight from one foot to the other. "Sure, I guess that makes sense."

"Boston Public Garden. Four o' clock." Zayne's tone is clipped.

Carlton nods once. He looks at me for less than a full second before brushing past us to his lunch table.

Mabel cringes. "Well, that was awkward."

But her words don't register. I stare after Carlton as he walks away, a bud of hope beginning to blossom in my chest. He actually talked to me. And not only that, but he agreed to meet with me and Zayne. Together!

This is probably my last chance to prove to Carlton I care more about him than the play, than the lead role. That there's nothing going on between me and Zayne. Once he sees us together and notices my interactions with Zayne are purely limited to running lines and responding sarcastically to his dry personality, he'll be convinced. And then it won't matter what Little Birdie writes about me anymore. It won't matter what anyone thinks, in fact.

Because I will fix this. I will fix all of it.

Chapter Ten

The rest of the day passes uneventfully. When I get home from school, I change into a sweater dress, tights, and boots and work on my homework until it's time to meet Carlton and Zayne.

I send Carlton a text before I leave the house.

ME

Want to ride together?

I know I'm probably pushing my luck, but maybe his willingness to run lines with me and Zayne isn't the only concession he'll offer me today.

CARLTON

No. I'll meet you there. Have some errands to run first.

Errands? What could he possibly have to do *right now*? *It doesn't matter, Dot,* I remind myself. *You're not his keeper, or even his girlfriend.* I throw my script in my bag, along with a water bottle, and try to push my annoyance away as I open the front door.

Beau frowns from the kitchen table. "Where are you going?"

"Nowhere."

"You're going on a date, aren't you?" He takes in my outfit, which is perhaps a bit more formal than necessary.

I tug on the hem in discomfort. "No. I'm just going to meet Carlton. And Zayne." When his expression shifts from mild curiosity to bafflement, I add, "We have to rehearse."

"Uh huh."

"Shut up, Beau." I glare at him before storming out the door.

Boston Public Garden isn't too far from my house, but then again, nothing in the Boston metro-area is. Everything seems to be highly walkable, which is a nice change from the vastness of Stockbridge.

The park is nestled on the edge of the Charles River, but on the opposite side from my house. As I walk to the entrance, I'm awed by the garden, basked in a glow of soft, afternoon light and surrounding a glittering pond topped with ducks. The colorful green, orange, and yellow trees sprinkled throughout the grass sway in the crisp wind.

I look around, trying to determine if it would be best to sit at one of the picnic tables to rehearse or find a spot under a tree when I hear my name.

"Over here, Dot."

I follow the voice and spot Zayne sitting on the grass by the shallow pond at the center of the park.

"Great," I mutter. "Of course, he would get here before Carlton." I'd been secretly hoping Zayne would arrive last so I'd have a moment to talk to Carlton alone, but that's out of the question now.

"Hey." I set my bag down beside him and take a seat on the blanket he's provided, sprawled out beneath us. "You made it."

"No need to sound so excited." The corner of his mouth lifts.

I toss my braids. "Yeah, well, it's not like homework is exciting."

"Homework?" The way he says it makes it sound stupid. "You know, for some of us, running lines is fun."

I take my script out of my bag. There's no way I'm going to tell him how fun it's becoming for me, too. Admitting it would feel like straying from the plan my parents are working so hard to help me accomplish.

"Not for me," I lie, and then add a small truth to my statement. "So far, this play has done nothing but cause me trouble." I flip through the pages, pretending to read, when really I'm just trying not to retreat back into despair. I need to stay positive. This outing *will* somehow be my ticket to winning a spot back into Carlton's good graces. After all, this was for him. I'm doing all this—the play, rehearsal, and being mean to Zayne—for him. I am.

"Cake?"

I blink away my thoughts. "Excuse me?"

"Do you want some cake?" Zayne holds out a slice of baked goodness wrapped in paper.

I take it gingerly and peel back the parchment paper, salivating as soon as I smell it.

Strawberry.

My favorite.

I hold the base of it by the plastic and take a bite. Zayne studies me, his head tilted sideways. "Why didn't you and your boyfriend come together?"

"Again, he's not my boyfriend," I say around a mouthful. "And he had to run an errand first, so he told me to meet him here."

"An *errand?*" He grins, like the concept is ridiculous. "What is he, forty? What kind of errand?"

Irritation bites me like a bug. "I don't know. An errand. What does it matter?"

He shrugs and looks away. I watch him while he's not looking, study the sharp angles of his face, the fullness of his smooth lips. The graceful way his dreads fall around his forehead.

He glances at me and my gaze jumps back to my cake. I scramble for a way to fill the silence that begins to stretch out. "This is delicious, by the way."

"Thanks." He half-grins. "It's from my family's restaurant. My grandma, Mimi does all the cooking, and Mom does everything else."

"Do you like working there?"

"No. I really don't. And once I get into Underwood Academy, I'll get to move out and never work there again. Lenny on the other hand is stuck till he's a senior."

"How old is Lenny exactly?" It's something I've been wondering since I met him.

"He's fourteen. Young for a sophomore, I know. He skipped first grade around the same time my mom realized he was on the spectrum."

"Oh." I blink. "He's autistic?"

"He has Asperger's, actually. Ever since he was little, he's had a fascination with learning. It's an obsession, really. But he has trouble with social situations sometimes. Like, stuff is often very black and white to him. He doesn't really understand sarcasm or when certain things he says are inappropriate."

"I think he does just fine." A bud of fondness for Lenny blossoms in my chest. "And he likes working at the restaurant?"

Zayne simultaneously scoffs and laughs. "Oh, he loves it. Pretty sure he'll be running the place before Mom and Mimi are even ready to stop working." Zayne's eyes are far away as he stares at the water, the remnants of his earlier smile still lingering on his lips.

He has a really nice smile. Looking at it makes me feel light and airy inside, like nothing can go wrong. Funny, considering Zayne tends to be serious more often than not.

He looks at me then, catching me watching him for the second time now, and I blush furiously.

"You have cake on your mouth," he tells me. He reaches over and wipes at my cheek with his thumb in careful strokes. Zayne squints at my face as he works, as if it's very important the cake be wiped away. It makes me smile. "Hold still," he reprimands.

I do as he says, frozen by his proximity. I notice again how he smells. Like coffee and...*cake.* Now it makes sense why.

When he seems satisfied, he pulls his hand away. Neither of us says anything. I pretend to study the still, glistening pond, and then watch the wind lift and shuffle the leaves of the trees surrounding us and the manicured lawn.

Finally, I can't take the silence anymore. "Have you always liked acting?"

"Yeah. Ever since I was a kid." But I can tell there's more to it than his short statement, so I wait, hoping he'll elaborate, and he does. "There were times I used to wish I could be someone else, especially when I was younger. It wasn't easy going to private school, having this huge expectation for greatness to meet and being unable to read."

"Wait," I interrupt. "You couldn't *read*?"

He shakes his head. "Not for a long time, no. It was a huge problem. It wasn't until I was in, like, fourth grade that I got diagnosed with dyslexia. The other kids in class used to make fun of me during group reading. You know, when the teacher makes everyone take turns reading a story to the class. When it got to my turn, I would just sit in silence, afraid to embarrass myself."

I stare at him. "Honestly, I never would have guessed. The way you read lines now..."

"That took practice." He smiles faintly. "When I was younger, I used to pretend to be different superheroes, because for some reason I thought they didn't need to read." He chuckles. "I totally mastered each different personality, and I'd stay in character for, like, ridiculously long periods of time. It entertained the heck out of Lenny, and it made me feel better about myself. Like I could be anyone else if I wanted to. Like not being able to read well didn't matter much in the grand scheme of things. It wasn't until I got serious about acting that the desire to read better became something I strived toward consistently."

I shake my head. Zayne, who has never, not *once* fumbled during reading lines...dyslexic? "How did you get better?"

He shrugs. "I don't know. Eventually, I learned to manage my disability. It's still a challenge sometimes. It takes me longer to read than most people, probably."

"Well, now I feel like crap. I can't read lines even half as well as you."

"Maybe you should try harder." His teasing tone is back, shattering the serious bubble time just captured us in. I can't help but roll my eyes.

Zayne's laughter cuts off and he stiffens. I follow his line of sight to a stray goose wandering toward us from the pond. "What's wrong?"

He glances at me for half a second before returning his attention to the goose. "What? Nothing. Nothing's wrong." As it gets closer, though, Zayne reaches for his backpack, holding it out in front of him like a shield.

"Are you...?" I can't believe it. It seems too good to be true. The serious, condescending Zayne, afraid? "Do geese scare you?" There's a laugh in my voice, impossible to hide now, and Zayne glares at me.

"I'm not *scared*," he mutters. "But it never hurts to be cautious. Geese can get aggressive."

I lose it at that, hysterical laughter exploding from my mouth. Especially as the goose gets closer and closer, almost as if it can sense his resistance, and he stands up and backs away. "Zayne," I wheeze, "when have you ever in your life encountered an aggressive goose?" Just the thought of it, the imaginary scenario playing out in my head makes me laugh even harder. I fall back against the blanket, holding my stomach to offset the soreness that accompanies my amusement.

As he backs away, still shielding himself from the apparent bloodthirsty monster, some loose papers fall out of his backpack. "Come on," he scowls. "Back away, you—" he shoos the giant bird away, finally dissuading it from pursuing him further.

I take deep breaths to force the smile from my lips, cheeks now burning from laughter, and help Zayne collect his scattered papers. It's the least I can do. I fetch a few, stopping when I grab one that's covered in black sharpie marks. I squint, noticing the way tons of lines have been crossed out in the black marker, while others have been subtly changed with thinner pen strokes. "What is this?" I flip the page over.

"That is nothing." Zayne plucks it from my hand, stuffing it back inside his bag. All traces of humor have vanished between us, and with a dawning horror, I realize what it is.

It's our audition script...and it's ruined.

Although ruined would be putting it lightly. That script would be impossible to read for someone like me, let alone someone with dyslexia. It doesn't make sense why Zayne would do that to his script, not to something that would determine his role in the play. Unless...

"You didn't do that to your script, did you?" It doesn't sound like a question, but a statement, as it leaves my mouth.

"Dot..." He flexes his jaw and stares at the ground. He looks like he's at a complete loss for words.

So, I say the words that we both know are true, that I was too blind to realize from the start when it's been right in front of me all along. "Carlton is the one who sabotaged your audition, not the other way around."

"Just leave it alone, Dot. I had it memorized anyway, so it doesn't matter."

"No. It does matter. It's...it's the principle of the situation. I can't believe this." How could I have been so stupid? Of course, Carlton would be the one to try to cheat his way into the lead role. With all the pressure he's under from his parents, with his desperation to get into Underwood, and knowing Zayne is the better actor between the two of them.

"Why didn't you tell Mr. Saltzman right then and there?"

Zayne frowns. "And given Carlton the satisfaction? No way."

I can't believe how similar his reasoning is to Carlton's when I asked him the same thing.

"Well...why didn't you tell *me* sooner?" My voice is heavy with accusation. Anger. At Zayne, for not telling me. At Carlton, for making me believe the lie in the first place.

Zayne's mouth opens and then closes, like he's

searching for the right thing to say. After a long moment, he asks, "Would you have believed me?"

And I'm silent. Because there's no way I would have believed Zayne's word over Carlton's, until now.

I shake my head, not in an answer to Zayne's question, but in disbelief to this entire situation. I just stand there, feeling like a complete idiot for believing his lie. For altering so much of my life, my mind around him.

And it's at that moment that Carlton chooses to arrive. Zayne and I are still stuck in our face-off when he waltzes up to us, his backpack slung carelessly over one shoulder. "Sorry I'm late. What'd I miss?"

I turn to face him. My mind is still in the moment I'm having with Zayne, so I'm caught completely off guard when Carlton places a very sloppy, very unnecessary kiss on my lips.

Um...what?

I peek over at Zayne, but he's frowning at the grass. I untangle myself from Carlton, cheeks set aflame, and open my mouth to say something. What I plan to say, I'm not sure. I could interrogate him on where he's been all this time. I could ask him why he just kissed me right in front of Zayne when I haven't been able to get him to utter anything more than a few short and reluctant sentences to me the past few days.

But most of all, I want to ask him if it's true. If he really lied to me about what happened at his audition with Zayne. If he was the one who tried to sabotage Zayne's audition so he could get the lead role. Why he would even feel the need to do such a thing in the first place. Carlton knows that lying is a sore spot for me. He knows I was wrecked when Mom lied to me before she went to live with Aunt Lucille.

But I don't say anything to him or ask any questions because I'm too tongue-tied. The opportunity passes when Carlton says, "Are we gonna do this or not?"

Zayne gives me a stern look that says, *don't bring it up yet,* and I know he's probably right. It's not the time.

Zayne picks up his script and he and Carlton start reading a scene together. I'm left open-mouthed, watching dumbly as they rehearse. Watching as Carlton reads his lines, very well, to Zayne. And watching as Zayne reads back, even better.

As I watch them act out the scene, I realize that even after Carlton crossed out as many lines as he could on Zayne's audition script, changed as many phrases as he did, gave his absolute best efforts to sabotage Zayne, it didn't matter. Dyslexia or not, Zayne didn't let Carlton get the best of him. He still got the lead role. And it's very clear why. He's still more talented than his rival.

And perhaps the most jarring revelation of all is not that Carlton isn't the person I thought he was, but that Zayne isn't either.

Chapter Eleven

At school, Carlton acts like everything is back to normal. He's speaking to me again. More than speaking, actually. It's like whatever happened at the park with Zayne has somehow reset everything between us back to normal. Which was exactly what I wanted all along—to go back to how we were at the start of the school year, with everything between us from the summer left untouched. Unchanged. It's been a month since the audition, and now it feels that way, like nothing has changed. Except one thing.

Me.

I can't unsee what I saw at the park. I can't unlearn what I know now.

Carlton is nothing but a really good liar. I don't know how to confront him, and as much as I hate to admit it, I'm afraid of what he'll say. I'm afraid he'll admit it's all true, or even worse, that he'll just lie to me again.

"What do you think?" Carlton asks. His arm is around me as we walk through the corridor after fourth period, and he squeezes my shoulder to bring my attention back to him.

"About what?"

"The movies." He grins like I'm being cute. "We could go tonight. I'm not busy or anything."

It takes me a moment to answer. "Um, yeah. I wish I could, but I have to study for tomorrow's chemistry test." It's a decent excuse. Chemistry is my worst subject.

"Oh." His smile fades. "Alright. Rain check?"

"Sure."

We walk to our lunch table, Carlton's heavy arm still slung over my shoulders. Rue and the twins are already there when we sit down, and Meredith is engrossed in telling Rue about a new boutique she found online.

"Hey, Dot," says Mabel. I smile back at her in response.

The clamoring noise in the cafeteria is a comfortable background for my incessant thoughts. Why did I turn down Carlton's offer to take me on a...dare I say, *date?* Our first real date, in fact. For some reason, us sitting on my roof, or swimming in his backyard, or riding our bikes around Boston all summer didn't feel like dates, but this does.

What is wrong with me?

Everyone tells lies. If I like Carlton as much as I think I do, I should be able to get over this. But for some reason, it feels like my entire image of him has been altered, and no amount of denial will fix it. I feel it—the knowledge that I might not be able to look at Carlton the same way again.

I watch the shrinking lunch line from my seat as Carlton and Mabel discuss ways to spruce up college applications, when my gaze finds its way across the cafeteria to where Zayne is sitting with Lenny and his other friends who look to be a mix of our age and closer to Lenny's. As if by instinct, he glances up. When our eyes meet, a silent communication passes between us. One that, instead of, *I hate you*, or *Stop looking at me*, simply says, *Hi*.

I see you.

And then he breaks away, back to his friends.

Returning me back to mine.

My phone vibrates. It's a text from Mabel, which I find odd, considering she's sitting right across from me.

MABEL

Are you okay?

ME

Yes, why?

MABEL

You seem...out of it. IDK.

ME

I'm fine.

MABEL

K, just checking <3

I try to smile more after I put my phone away. I chip in, offering the name of a few volunteer organizations I know are accepting new recruits that I know will look good on applications. And most of all, I try to ignore the ache in my chest from learning who the true Carlton is.

I kinda wish I hadn't put my phone away just yet. My fingers are itching to pick it back up. To text Zayne.

I need to talk to him.

I need to know if the way I'm feeling toward Carlton—of his nearness feeling practically unbearable—is warranted or if I'm overreacting. I need to know how this rivalry between them started and who's at fault. If there's anyone who will be honest about what kind of person Carlton is, it's Zayne.

I spend the rest of the day thinking about how to casually text him, how to bring up Carlton in a nonchalant manner. In a way that won't seem weird or random or make my newfound disdain for him too obvious.

But there never seems to be a good time.

Before I know it, the final bell rings, signaling the end of the school day, and I still don't do it.

At home, eating dinner, I consider excusing myself early so I can use my phone. Sending the simple message. But I don't.

While I'm reading my lines in front of my mirror before bed, I could easily take a break, grab my phone, and send the stupid message. But of course I don't.

It takes staring up at the ceiling later in the night, trying to sleep for a good two hours for me to grab my phone off the charger and text Zayne.

ME

Are you up?

ZAYNE

I am now.

Why?

Did you have a question about the play?

ME

No.

How long have you and Carlton hated each other?

ZAYNE

LOL

What's this about, Dot?

ME

I just don't understand why he hates you so much

Why you hate him

ZAYNE

Well

I guess it started when we were in middle school

Carlton stole my homework and put his name on it

Turned it in and everything.

The teacher knew it was mine because my letters were facing the wrong direction. You know, with me being dyslexic and all

Anyway, Carlton got detention and somehow it was my fault for ruining his clean record

ME

LOL

Are you kidding me?

ZAYNE

Nope

ME

So that's it?

ZAYNE

Oh heck no

Obviously, I had to get back at him.

I snort aloud at the idea of Zayne plotting revenge.

ME

Oh, no.

What did you do?

ZAYNE

One time in class, Carlton sat in gum

I couldn't help but laugh

And as a result, the whole class joined in

Worse yet, it was the kind of gum you could tell had been chewed all day.

Like, for way too long.

There was no way it was coming off those expensive jeans.

ME

OMG

ZAYNE

Some say I put the gum there in the first place.

ME

Did you?

ZAYNE

You'll never know.

ME

Wow.

Then what?

ZAYNE

Oh, you know. The classics.

Carlton covers my family's restaurant in toilet paper

I egg Carlton's car. It dries and damages the paint.

Typical stuff

ME

You two are terrible

ZAYNE

And then I ran over his childhood cat
while learning how to drive

ME

YOU WHAT?!?!?

ZAYNE

It was an accident

Like I would kill a cat on purpose

ME

ZAYNE

ZAYNE

And what were the odds that the cat
ended up being his

ME

I CAN NEVER LOOK AT YOU THE SAME
WAY AGAIN

ZAYNE

Oh come on. It was an accident.

ME

I think he may be warranted in hating you
after all.

ZAYNE

I said sorry

ME

There is no apology good enough for
such a thing.

Zayne?

Okay fine. It was an accident.

You there?

Great, Dot. You offended him. I bite my lip and sit up in bed. Reaching for my nightstand, I tap my gold, stiletto-shaped nightlight, adjusting it with my touch until my room is basked in a dim, warm glow.

I reread our messages to make sure I wasn't too mean when he finally responds a few minutes later.

ZAYNE

Sorry, Lenny just came in here asking me to silence my phone. He said the sound was carrying over to his room and influencing his dreams

I breathe a sigh of relief. *He's not mad.*

ME

Silence your phone! Don't mess with the poor kid's dreams

ZAYNE

I wouldn't dare

ME

You know, I have a brother too

ZAYNE

I know. I met him when you came to eat at the restaurant, remember?

ME

Oh yeah. Have I told you he used to call me Bar Dot when we were younger, instead of silencing the t at the end? It's how I got my nickname

125

ZAYNE

Really? That's hilarious. How old is he?

ME

13

ZAYNE

Only a year younger than Lenny

ME

Yep. He tries to act like he's older than me sometimes

It's so annoying

He never used to until my mom got sent away.

I inhale sharply as soon as I press send. *Too late to take it back now.* I don't know why I sent it. It's not like Zayne is someone I should be confiding in. But I can't help it—this sudden desire I have to tell him more about me. There's no way I'd ever talk about something like this with him in person. It would feel too vulnerable. But here, in my dimly lit bedroom during the silence of night, there's a safeness I can't explain.

ZAYNE

Your mom got sent away?

ME

Yeah. She was supposed to go to rehab, but she couldn't stand the idea of not being able to communicate with us. To come and go as she pleased.

It's a long story

ZAYNE

If you want to tell me, I have time.

And I did just tell you all about my criminal past, to be fair

The laugh that escapes me is louder than I intend it to be. Every little detail I share with him makes me feel lighter inside. Like there's a stack of textbooks on my back, pinning me to the ground and he's lifting them off me, one at a time.

ME

Okay…fine.

My mom used to be a firefighter

She injured her back on the job a year and a half ago and was granted long-term disability

But the pills she had to take for pain management became a problem. She got addicted to them, and she's had a really hard time ever since. She's just not herself anymore.

She doesn't even want to take them anymore

ZAYNE

So if she's not in rehab, where is she?

ME

Her sister is a drug rehabilitation counselor. She's letting my mom stay with her in upstate New York.

> This way, she can call us and visit more. I miss her a lot.

> I used to be homeschooled before I moved here, you know.

ZAYNE

Really? What was that like?

ME

> It was nice being with my dad, and I got ahead academically, but it got lonely. I was the outsider among everyone else my age, which sucked

ZAYNE

Is that why you moved?

ME

> No. My dad had to go back to work when it was clear my mom couldn't return to her career any time soon, and Boston had the best pay. He also works part-time as a food delivery driver to pay for Fallbrook, so I'll still have an attractive college application.

ZAYNE

Wow.

That's really nice of him.

I swallow the knot in my throat. Thinking about everything Dad does to keep this family thriving makes me emotional sometimes. But worse is the feeling of possibly letting him down. I wipe my eyes and scoot lower into my bed to pull the covers higher.

ME

Can I tell you a secret?

ZAYNE

I'm all ears.

ME

I've never told anyone this, so I'll know it was you if it gets out.

ZAYNE

You have my word, Dot

ME

Sometimes I feel like a fraud.

If it weren't for my dad, I probably wouldn't even want to go to college.

I'm in way too deep now though

I'm worried if I don't get into an Ivy school, all his hard work will be for nothing

ZAYNE

Do you really think your dad would feel that way?

ME

Probably.

ZAYNE

What about your mom?

ME

I have no idea if she's even in her right mind.

I haven't seen her since the summer before school started, when I met Carlton.

ZAYNE

That's when you met him?

ME

Yeah. He was on his way to Rue's house. She lives on my street, and as he was passing by, he saw me crying on the roof.

ZAYNE

You were on the roof?

ME

Yeah. LOL

Silly, I know

But I didn't want my dad or my brother to see me cry.

So I figured the roof was safe

ZAYNE

What were you crying about?

ME

My mom. Her addiction. The unfairness of it all. And then Carlton saw me and came and sat up there to comfort me.

It was really sweet. After that we spent the summer hanging out together

ZAYNE

And that's when you started dating?

ME

Well…we've never been on an official date. And he never technically asked me to be his girlfriend

ZAYNE

That's nuts, Dot.

ME

It's not nuts. We're taking things slow.

ZAYNE

Like, turtle slow. You say you spent the entire summer together, and it's fall now. You still haven't even been on a date?

ME

Whatever

ZAYNE

Don't get defensive.

ME

Don't be accusatory of things you don't understand

ZAYNE

I do understand

I know Carlton really well

ME

But you don't know me

ZAYNE

I'm starting to.

ME

What about you? Are you dating someone?

ZAYNE

Not anymore.

Just didn't really have a connection with
anyone. You know?

ME

I do.

ZAYNE

Dot?

It's 3 a.m.

ME

I know. I'm sorry.

ZAYNE

It's fine. I'm just wondering if you have
any other questions?

ME

None that you can answer for me,
unfortunately. I'll see you tomorrow.
Goodnight, Zayne

ZAYNE

Goodnight, Dot

Chapter Twelve

I skip school the next day.

It's silly, I know. Immature, even, at best. But I do it anyway because it's the only solution that makes me feel better when the problem of Carlton and Zayne comes to mind.

Carlton, because he's suddenly started acting the way I've wanted him to *all year*. Like I belong with him and his friends, like I've somehow earned my way into his group, even though I haven't.

Like he wants me to be his girlfriend. Trouble is, I'm not sure I want to be anymore. But if I'm not a part of Carlton's group, where do I fit in? Without him, I'm not sure if I'd even have any friends at all.

Instead of drumming up an answer to that, I hide in my bed. Pulling the covers over my head, I scroll through social media, liking pictures and posts until my eyes burn.

Beau already left for school, and Dad is at work for his TSA job. I texted Carlton, telling him I wasn't feeling well, and he offered to bring me soup after school. I haven't responded yet. Partly, because I'm worried turning him down will arouse suspicion, and also because soup does sound pretty good. It's been a long time since I've had an appetizing, home-cooked meal, with Mom away and Dad constantly working, and with the exception of Saturday brunch with Beau, we've been living off frozen meals, canned dinners, and Dad's attempts at cooking.

I shut my eyes, numb to the voice in my head telling me I can't just run away from my problems, and then my phone goes off. But it's not just the typical notification sound.

It's Little Birdie's. My stomach clenches as soon as I hear it.

"Please don't be about me," I mumble, even though there's no one else here. I bring my phone to my face, squinting against the brightness after having my eyes closed, and read.

Hello my darling flock!
I've returned with a juicy worm, or two, for you to snack on!
Most of you know Rue Sullivan as the quiet, shy, and sweet drama club girl who tends to mind her own business. Boring, I know. Until recently, I've hardly seen any potential in her when it comes to newsworthy gossip.

But, fledglings, I have discovered Rue's biggest secret! The poor thing has an unrequited crush! Yes! I've heard her discussing it myself, with none other than Meredith Evans! Now the only mystery to solve is who Rue has been pining after. You know I'll find out. And when I do, you will, too!

In other news, our favorite It Girl Bardot has been behaving these days. But a passerby so kindly shared the news with me that she was recently at Boston Public Garden with none other than Zayne Silverman! The pair was huddled near the duck pond, with a blanket to keep them cozy. Who knows exactly what was exchanged between the pair? I would be obliged to any insiders willing to send me the play-by-play through my delightful app.

Until next time!
Yours Truly,
Little Birdie

It doesn't take long for the messages to start pouring in after that.

MABEL

It wasn't me who told her, I swear!

RUE

I'm SO OVER LB!

CARLTON

I can't believe Little Birdie left me out of
the story.

MEREDITH

I bet Little Birdie is Zayne. Who else
would have known about this?

And then a message from Zayne.

ZAYNE

Where are you?

ME

At home.

ZAYNE

Why?

ME

I'm sick.

I sink back into the covers, grateful I decided to stay
home today. The last thing I need is the entire school
staring at me again after they finally stopped. At least
Carlton isn't mad this time.

It's times like this I miss being homeschooled.

I sleep the rest of the afternoon away, waking to make
myself some peanut butter toast and study for tomorrow's
chemistry test. I know I should be more worried about
skipping school possibly jeopardizing my chances to get
into an amazing college, but I just don't have it in me.
Maybe it's self-sabotage at this point.

A little bit after four, someone knocks on the front door. It's probably Carlton with my soup. I take a deep breath. I'm not sure I want to see him. He's the reason I stayed home, after all. But I force myself out of bed, checking my reflection at my vanity table before I answer the door, because I still want to look pretty, even if I'm not excited to see him.

But when I open the door, it's not Carlton waiting outside. It's Zayne, still in his school uniform. He must have come straight from school. I feel an annoying rush of excitement as soon as our gazes collide.

"What are you doing here?" I can't keep the surprise from my voice.

Zayne's expression is stony. Irritated. "You missed rehearsal."

"I know. I'm sick."

"You are not sick," he says, walking in though I didn't invite him. "And not only did you miss rehearsal, but also your boyfriend's little temper tantrum after Little Birdie sent out her latest blast."

"What—Carlton?" I frown. "He was upset? And you *know* he's not my boyfriend."

"Whatever." He crosses his arms, leaning against the entryway wall. "He thought I was the one who shared the story since no one else was there."

I close my eyes. Of course, Carlton would think that. And I have to admit, it makes sense. Zayne and Carlton hate each other. Why wouldn't Zayne try to spin a story to make it look like he's stealing me away from Carlton? It would be decent revenge for what Carlton did to Zayne at the audition. I open my eyes. "Wait, you didn't, though. Did you?"

Zayne gapes at me. "Of course not."

"Well, I don't know. It wouldn't be the first time you've tried to get back at him. You could easily make it look like you're trying to get me to like you."

Zayne lowers his eyelids, giving me a look that sets me on edge. "If I wanted you to like me, I wouldn't have to spread twisted lies to make it happen." His voice sounds low. Husky. "There are much less complicated ways."

I stare at him. Something about the change in his tone, in his demeanor, leaves me speechless.

And then he hands me a folder. "Mr. Saltzman made an amendment to one of our scenes," he says. "We could practice it now if you want since you missed today."

"Thanks. I would, but Carlton is bringing me soup soon." I blush, still not quite back to my normal self. What is wrong with me? "It probably wouldn't be a good idea for you to still be here when he comes."

Zayne searches my face, like he senses it too, that I'm not myself, and says, "Right. Wouldn't want to give him a reason to question your loyalties." The sentence is heavy, filled with a weight of implication I'm not ready to dissect.

"Bye, Zayne."

He looks pointedly at the folder in my hands. "Don't forget to practice. You better bring it, Bennett. I want the performance of a lifetime."

I laugh. "Got it."

I walk him out, exhaling a sigh of relief that he won't be here when Carlton arrives. Relief that I won't have to rehearse today. Relief that I won't have to spend more time under that penetrating gaze Zayne gave me, making me feel things that have me questioning everything.

Chapter Thirteen

I never should have brought my script to brunch. There I was, trying to be a responsible student for the first time in a while, when I saw it. Right there on the page. A scene Mr. Saltzman amended and needed me to read.

And then it was all I could think about until Beau and I got home.

I go straight to my room, mind in a whirl, and take out my phone to text Zayne.

ME

I looked through the amended scene

And…

ARE YOU KIDDING ME?!

ZAYNE

What???

ME

We have to kiss now???

ZAYNE

Is that a problem?

I scoff. "What do you mean, 'Is that a problem?'"

ME

Yes!

ZAYNE

Why? Nervous?

ME

Definitely not

ZAYNE

We're playing the lead roles, Dot. It's only expected that we kiss a time or two

ME

Says who?

ZAYNE

Every storyteller since the beginning of time.

ME

Not true. Pretty sure Catherine and Heathcliff don't even kiss in the novel.

ZAYNE

I thought you only read the summary.

ME

Exactly. There would have been a kiss mentioned in there somewhere.

ZAYNE

Not in a summary

ME

It was a really good summary. Extensive. Detailed.

ZAYNE

I'm sure

I pace back and forth in my room, eyes glued to our conversation. I must have drank too much coffee at brunch because my stomach feels jittery, obnoxiously restless.

ME

The point is that this scene won't work for me

ZAYNE

If you're worried about your first kiss being on stage, just say so.

My mouth falls open.

ME

Please. I've been kissed plenty of times.

ZAYNE

Then I'm failing to see the issue here

ME

The issue is that I'll be kissing you

ZAYNE

And that's an issue because...?

ME

Because.

Because it will make Carlton mad

ZAYNE

It's a play, Dot. We're acting. I think he'll understand.

I force myself to study on Sunday. With my open textbooks sprawled out on my bed, I try to decide which subject will be the least boring to start with. I need to at least try if I'm going to get accepted into one of the schools I claim I so badly want to attend.

I glance at my script, peeking out from my Econ textbook. *Practicing for the play sounds like so much more fun than this.*

But no. I need to focus. I bite my lip.

Or...I could text Zayne. It's not fair that he got the last word on Friday, after all.

ME

Whatcha doing?

It only takes him a few minutes to respond, not that I'm counting or anything.

ZAYNE

Just got home from church. You?

ME

Hey! Same!

ZAYNE

Can I help you with something, Dot?

ME

Upon further reflection, I think I'm okay with the scene

ZAYNE

What a relief.

I can practically hear the sarcasm in his message, but he needs to understand how *not* hung up I am on kissing him.

ME

Because it will mean nothing.

ZAYNE

That's very reassuring.

ME

Like you said, we're only acting

It's the performance of the role in the play

ZAYNE

That is, by definition, what acting is.

ME

Shut up

I'm just trying to clear the air

ZAYNE

I'm not sure what kind of foggy air you're breathing, but mine is clear as crystal

I throw my phone down on my bed. *He's so annoying.* But instead of ignoring him and returning to my studies, I pick it right back up and send him another message.

ME

I mean, would it kill me to get to know you a little better? You practically know everything there is to know about me

ZAYNE

I doubt that's true.

ME

I think you know more about me than I know about you.

ZAYNE

Is there something specific you're trying to figure out?

I ponder for a moment before deciding.

ME

What's your biggest phobia?

Might come in handy to use against him, if necessary.

ZAYNE

Snakes. What's your favorite book?

ME

Probably those magazines they have at the doctor's office

ZAYNE

No. You did not just say that

ME

What's wrong with that?

But instead of just responding to my question like a normal person, he calls me. I stare at my phone, nerves skyrocketing. I've never talked to him on the phone before.

You're being ridiculous, Dot. It's no big deal, just answer.

I lift the phone to my ear. "Hello?"

"That statement was basically an invitation for me to convert you." He sighs dramatically. "I'm going to let you borrow some books."

I try to hide my smile and sound annoyed. "I'm supposed to go to Yale. Or maybe Harvard. I don't have time to read for fun."

"You need to be well-read to get into those schools. Maybe you should start with the classics."

"I've read the classics!" But it's a lie. I can't remember the last classic novel I read. One of the nice things about homeschooling was being allowed to mostly study my areas of interest instead of having to study everything within each subject.

"You haven't even read *Wuthering Heights*," says Zayne. The disapproval in his tone makes me grin.

"That's literally one classic I haven't read. So what?"

"Okay. Name your favorite classic novel then."

I remain silent for too long, my brain scrambling for a title. Any title.

"Hello?" There's a smugness in his voice that irritates me.

"Charlotte's Web," I say with feigned confidence.

Silence.

When he speaks, it sounds like he's trying really hard not to laugh. "When did you last read Charlotte's Web?"

I sigh. "I don't know. Maybe fifth grade?"

"Like I said before...I'll be loaning you some books."

I pick at the yarn on one of my wall tapestries. "I won't enjoy it."

"Oh yeah? What's your favorite movie?"

"Clueless." *Finally, an easy question.* I've probably watched it at least twenty tines, and it never gets old.

"Perfect. I know which classic novel to let you borrow first."

My brows furrow. "Which one?"

"Don't worry about it."

I bite my lip to keep from smiling at the image of Zayne trying to find a book for me to read off that massive shelf of his. He'll probably get distracted in the process and end up lost in a book. I have to admit, I wish I could be like that. I've always envied people who can completely block out what's happening around them and obsess over characters made of ink and paper. "Fine, you nerd."

"A compliment from Dot Bennett? I think I just went into shock."

Chapter Fourteen

Monday morning after homeroom, the smell of pumpkin is in the air. Since it's October, it's only to be expected. But I'm still pleasantly surprised when I see pumpkin loaf on the lunch menu as I pass the serving station on my way to a table to wait for Carlton, Rue, and the twins.

I sit and glance out the cafeteria window, awed by a vast landscape of yellow and orange leaves caressing the stone building of Fallbrook.

"Here."

I jump at the sound of Zayne's voice. Or maybe it's his voice, combined with the giant thud of the enormous text he drops on the table.

"What's this?" I gape at the book, tilting my head to read the upside-down words.

"*Emma*," he states. "Jane Austen. You'll love it."

I frown. "How do you know?"

"I thought you said you were versed in the classics." He

shakes his head. "You love the movie *Clueless*. And *Clueless* is a modern retelling of *Emma*."

My lips part. "You're kidding." I touch the cover with my index finger. "And that was a lie, Zayne. Obviously, I'm not familiar with the classics because I don't like to read." I point to myself. "Phony, remember?"

"Well, that changes here and now. Yale, here you come." He tries not to smile. So serious.

Zayne starts to walk away, but I stand up and shout after him. "Do you really expect me to read this? I haven't even finished reading our script!"

At that, he turns. "Yikes, Dot."

"It's not that I don't want to. But it's not the same, reading it alone. Maybe we should run lines together soon so I can get through it faster." *Because apparently, three rehearsals a week after school aren't enough for me. I just have to torture myself with his presence more than necessary.*

He shakes his head. "Why don't you just come over after school? We can run lines all week if you want. My grandma will be home, so you don't have to worry about whatever it was you were worried about last time."

At that I blush. "Alright."

"Alright." He looks at me pointedly, like I might forget to actually show up even though I just said I would.

After he leaves, I sit back down and glance at the book he left me on the table. *Emma.* I touch the creased paperback cover, then pick up the book so I can read the back. The spine looks like it's been cracked over and over, and the image of Zayne reading this book pops into my head. It makes me smile. Especially because I'm pretty sure Jane Austen strictly writes romance.

Before I can read the summary on the back of the book, Carlton plucks it out of my hand. Where did he even come from?

"Reading this for school?" he asks, scanning the cover as he sits beside me.

"No." Wait, why did I say no? Now I'll have to tell him Zayne gave it to me! "It's—uh," I pause like I'm distracted instead of clamoring for the words that will save me. "My favorite movie is based on it, apparently."

"What movie? *Bridesmaids*?"

"No. *Clueless.*"

"Oh."

An awkward silence falls upon us. I cross my ankles. Uncross them. Recross them again. It's strange sitting here with Carlton after basically texting Zayne all weekend. Even when Carlton came to drop off the soup on Friday, I'd barely uttered a word to him. Just thanked him for the soup and he left. Now, it feels like I've distanced myself from him. Whether intentionally or not, it's practically palpable between us.

A strange, sudden instinct overtakes me—a desperation to see if the connection I had with Carlton at the start of the summer is still here, or beginning to dwindle away, like the leftover sparks from a burnt-out flame. I stand. "Carlton?"

"What?"

"Kiss me." The words sound ridiculous, and Carlton

must think so too because he stares at me with his brows in a deep V.

"Why?"

I huff out a sigh. "Are you seriously questioning a kiss?"

The V melts away and he laughs. "No, I guess not." He stands up, too, until he's right in front of me. Leaning in, he touches his lips to mine, anchoring me in place with his hand on my waist.

I shut my eyes. I await the usual fluttering in my stomach at his affection, the yearning in my veins. Something. *Anything* to prove that I'm overthinking things, that my connection with Carlton isn't disappearing.

But as the kiss stretches out over the painfully awkward, silent seconds, I don't feel anything, other than the metal table bench cutting into my calf.

Nothing.

Not a single butterfly.

When he pulls away, I paste a polite smile on my face to replace the dawning horror surely visible in my expression. "Thanks!" The words come out too loud. Too high-pitched.

Carlton doesn't call me out on it, instead responding with nothing more than a tight-lipped lifting of his mouth.

"Hey guys." Mabel plops several textbooks down on the table. "Today sucks."

Trailing her are Rue and Meredith. All three of them are wearing identically solemn expressions.

"Mabel, stop whining," says Meredith. "Your negativity is starting to bring me down, too."

Rue nods. "I'm with Mere on this one, Mabel."

Mabel sighs. "Sorry."

"What's wrong?" I ask.

She winces. "I failed my calculus test. My mom is going to be pissed."

Carlton says something back to her, but I've stopped listening. Behind Carlton, I catch sight of Zayne walking by. We exchange glances, and I can't help but smile faintly. He returns the grin before he continues walking. Something flutters in my stomach, and at first I ignore it. But then I realize what it is.

Butterflies.

The much coveted butterflies I was anticipating to feel when I kissed Carlton are now fluttering through my stomach.

All because Zayne Silverman smiled at me.

Mom calls after school.

It's the first time she's called in weeks, but it feels more like years. Beau and Dad hover over the phone—on speaker—and talk Mom's ear off about anything and everything. They want her to come back. They hope she's feeling better. This house doesn't feel like home without her. Beau misses her home-cooked meals. Dad is exhausted from working so much, but he can handle it just fine.

She has the perfect response for everything. Of course, she wants to come home. That's why she's away getting better. Aunt Lucille's house doesn't feel like home to her either—not without us. Mom misses making home-cooked meals for Beau, like his favorite vegetable soup and her crispy but tender chicken-pot-pie. She's even learned some new recipes from her sister while she's been away. She can't wait to make them for us. And of course Dad can handle the work. She's had faith in him from the start.

I'm amazed they all manage to talk so much, and even more startled when Mom says, "Dot? I've hardly heard a word from you. What's been going on with you lately, baby?"

"Me? Um. I..." I search for the right words. *I've been struggling big time since you left in May. I have no healthy emotional outlet, other than acting, which I'm not supposed to like as much as I do. I'm caught between my loyalty to the guy who was here for me when you left, and my guilt over thinking the guy who hates his guts isn't so bad. My every move is being reported to the entire school by an anonymous human in disguise as a bird. I committed to getting into an Ivy aloud to impress you and Dad, but my heart has never really been in it and it's starting to show. I haven't been studying and haven't read enough classic novels to be deemed Ivy-worthy. Deep down, I'm not sure I even want to go to college at all, but acting school really doesn't sound too bad.*

But of course I don't say any of those things.

Instead, I tell her, "I got cast as the lead in Fallbrook's upcoming school play."

"Woah. Hang on a minute," she says. "You lost me at play."

I laugh. "I know."

"And you say you got the *lead*? Dot, that's amazing, sweetie. I didn't even know you could act. It's probably going to be a great extra-curricular for your college applications. When is this play?"

"Uh..." I scratch my head. "The first performance is at the beginning of December."

"I've got to come see it."

My heart stutters, but I try not to get my hopes up. "You don't have to do that, Mom."

Her voice is firm. "Yes, honey. Yes, I do. That's the whole point of me being here, so I have more flexibility."

"But what if you're not better by then?" I try not to let the worry in my voice be obvious. "Are you sure it's a good idea so soon into your program?"

"I will be there, Dot. And that's the end of it." She exhales, like we've just finished discussing something pleasant, instead of the possibility of undoing all her hard work and progress with one premature trip home. "Now, tell me about your new friends."

Chapter Fifteen

I almost don't show up at Zayne's. My mind is still whirling after talking to my mom on the phone, so I'm not sure I'm in the right head space to run lines today. She reminded me I'm supposed to be focusing on college. But it's getting harder to live the lie of pretending I want that, especially the more I practice for the play. It's like there's two sides of me that are at war with each other—the good daughter who keeps her promises, and the side of me I've been trying to find. The one that gets excited about something and looks forward to it the same way Beau does when he's learning a new language.

I just wish I could somehow be both.

I knock on Zayne's front door. When it comes down to it, he's my best bet if I want to do *well* in the play. And much as I want to deny it...I like practicing with him.

"Hi, there." An older woman greets me from the other side of the door. She's shorter than me, with chin length dark curls and a wide smile. "You must be Dot! I'm Celia, Zayne's grandma. But you can call me Mimi. Come on in." She swings the door open wider.

"Hi, Mimi." I lift my hand into an awkward wave. "Thanks for letting me come and rehearse with Zayne."

"No problem. He's in his room. Go on up."

I make for the stairs but pause when I see Lenny sitting at the dining table, visible from the entryway. He's hunched over a paperback with his finger against the page, moving as his eyes scan the words.

"Hi, Lenny!" I say. "What are you reading?"

He doesn't glance up but answers me. "I'm trying to determine whether Mary Stuart losing her head was warranted."

I blink. "Oh."

"Did she conspire to steal England from Elizabeth, or should she have been on the throne from the start?" He looks at me over his paperback. "Opinions tend to vary."

I laugh, warmth blossoming in my chest. He looks so serious, like the answer is a matter of life and death. "Let me know what you decide."

He grimaces, turning back to his book, and I take that as my cue to go upstairs. Zayne's door is closed, so I knock softly. He opens it at the same time. I clear my throat and take a step back. "I'm here," I announce.

"I see that." His mouth twitches in amusement.

I brush past him, tossing my backpack onto his bed. "Let's start."

We run through our scenes in chronological order, rehearsing the first few off book until I get through them without fumbling anymore. Half an hour later, Mimi comes in. "I made some ceviche," she says.

Zayne brightens. "Thanks, Mimi." He takes the tray from her, a bowl of fresh shrimp and avocado with a side of tortilla chips on top.

"Is the restaurant closed today?" I ask.

Mimi nods. "Yeah, we close early on Mondays, our least busy day. But still, it seems like I never stop cooking." She shakes her head, her thick hair swinging with her face.

Zayne takes a bite of the food. The crunching of the chips makes my stomach growl, so I have some too. And just as I expect, it's delicious. I also feel a little twinge in my chest because it makes me think of Mom's cooking.

Mimi leaves us and the food, and Zayne and I spend a few minutes scarfing down the chips and shrimp salsa. The room is silent save for us eating, and when the food is all gone, I sigh and pat my tummy. "That was delicious. Your grandma seems nice."

"Yeah, she's great. My dad died when Lenny was a baby, so she's been like a second parent to us all our lives."

"I'm sorry about your dad."

"Thanks." Zayne puts the tray on his dresser top. "You'll probably get to meet my mom, too. She's grocery shopping, but she'll be back soon." He picks up his script off his bed. "In the meantime, let's keep going."

Excitement bubbles inside me. "Now?"

"Yes."

And we do. We begin rehearsing again.

But while the first portion of running lines felt success-ful, something is different now. Maybe it's that my mind is back on my own mom after seeing the easy exchange between Zayne and Mimi. It's a reminder that Mom can't be that for me right now. She can't make snacks for me and my friends on her days off, can't work at all, even. Can barely get out of bed because she's in so much pain. Unless she takes the pills that have made her a slave to them.

"You okay?" Zayne frowns at me.

With a start, I realize I missed my line. "Um, yeah." I pick up my script, looking for where we left off. But all the while, a knot forms in my throat. My eyes blur. And I can't help it. I miss my mom. I miss her so much.

I take way too long, staring at my rehearsal script, swallowing back my tears. Zayne must catch on at some point because his next words come out softer than usual. "Hey, why don't we take a break from all this? Have some fun instead?"

My eyes round as they move from the page to Zayne.

He frowns, his gaze darting around my face. "What? What's wrong?"

"That word you just said. *Fun.* It sounded so strange coming out of your mouth."

His expression clears. "Very funny."

"I wasn't aware you even knew the meaning."

Zayne rolls his eyes. "Do you want to take a break from all this, or not?"

"Fine. Let's go."

I follow him downstairs, and on our way out, someone rounds the corner. Tall and slender, with an angular face and large brown eyes, she looks a lot like Zayne, but with longer eyelashes and a shaved head.

"Oh. Hi, Mom," says Zayne. Over his shoulder, he points to me with his thumb. "This is Dot. We were running lines, but we're going to take a break for a while."

I extend my hand to her. "Hi, Mrs. Silverman."

His mom grins at me. "Hi, Dot." She reaches out and shakes my hand. "You can call me Gwen. Nice to meet you."

"You too." I smile back.

"Alright," Zayne cuts in. "We'll be back soon."

"This is the coolest pumpkin patch I've ever seen," I tell Zayne. "In fact, this may be the king of all pumpkin patches."

He nods. "It really is."

I park and shut off my GPS now that we've reached the destination Zayne typed into my phone. We get out of the car.

I gaze in awe at the corn-maze as tall as a building. The flashing Ferris wheel, the hot apple-cider stand. The pumpkins of various shapes and sizes. Funny, misshapen pumpkins in shades of not only orange, but green, white, and yellow. A group of children laughs as they launch small pumpkins at a target with a sling. A mom leads her toddler into a petting zoo with goats, sheep, and donkeys.

Beau would love this place.

Zayne buys us wristbands at the entrance, and I beam. "What do we do first?"

He nods toward the hot apple cider stand. "We get a hot

drink, of course." Pulling me forward by the hand, he leads me toward the stand. He orders us each a drink and I glance at the spot where his hand touched mine. He probably meant it as a friendly gesture, but I can't help but stare at my skin like he burned it. Like by touching my hand, he marked me as his friend somehow.

He hands me the cider in a to-go mug, oblivious to my whirling thoughts. "This cider is the best money can buy." His voice is serious, like he's warning me about the dangers of sky-diving. "Not even Mimi can make it better."

"Hurry up, then. Give me the cup, Silverman." I take it gingerly. And as soon as the warm contents meet my lips, I realize he's right. My senses cling to the undertone of spices, the creamy foam sitting on top, the sweetness balanced with the most minute tang. I lower the cup from my lips. "Ah."

Zayne's lips quirk into a crooked smile. "Told you." He motions toward the petting zoo with his cup. "Shall we?"

"Actually, I want to launch a pumpkin at that scarecrow target," I say. "Work out some aggression."

He laughs. "What aggression?"

"Oh, you know." I shrug as we make our way across the pumpkin patch toward the launching area and get in line. "Little Birdie constantly lying about me. Getting roped into playing the lead for a play at a new school. Hanging out with *you*."

Zayne smirks. "Come on. I'm not so bad. I introduced you to the world's best pumpkin patch, remember? And this apple cider."

I lift my mug in a toasting motion. "True." When it's

our turn to launch pumpkins, I grab one and situate it atop the sling. "Watch how it's done," I tell Zayne before promptly launching the tiny pumpkin straight onto the ground no more than three feet from us.

Zayne chuckles. I shoot him a death glare, and he tries, unsuccessfully, to make his grin disappear. "Try again," he says.

I put another pumpkin on the sling. Stretching it back as far as I can, I launch it clear past the target altogether this time. "I think this is rigged," I state.

"Step aside, sunshine." Zayne grabs a medium sized pumpkin off the stack of available ones to smash. I briefly wonder who determines what makes a pumpkin worth smashing or selling. Zayne stretches the sling back and aims for the target. When he lets go, I expect his pumpkin to fall on the ground like mine did. Maybe land a few feet from the target. But no. Of course, it smashes right into the bullseye, leaving me gaping in disbelief. He dusts his hands off before picking his mug of cider back up. "Yeah, you're right. Most definitely rigged."

"Not fair. You've probably practiced hitting that target a million times."

He shrugs, a pleased smile still on his mouth. "Maybe. Maybe not. You'll never know."

An employee with a gold smile rakes our smashed pumpkin guts out of the way for the next people. He motions toward a shelf full of stuffed animals. "Go ahead and pick a prize," he tells Zayne.

Zayne plucks a stuffed honeybee off the shelf. As he

walks back, he hands me the bee and says, "Let's ride the Ferris wheel."

"Okay." I stare at the stuffed animal and something in my chest expands. It's a familiar feeling. One I used to experience every time I'd think about Carlton. It's alarming that I'm having it again, but it feels too good to analyze in this moment.

We make our way over, standing in line briefly before stepping up to ride. A short guy with curly hair and glasses marks our wristbands with a black marker.

"Hey, Jude." Zayne cocks his head at the boy.

He nods. "Zayne."

We hop into the next seat and the ride begins. "You know him?"

"He goes to our school. He's in the crew for drama club."

"Ah. I should have known. Because apparently, every high schooler in Massachusetts goes to Fallbrook and cares about theater."

He snorts in amusement at my sarcasm.

As the tiny car we're sitting in rises up, the cool wind stings my cheeks. I stare at the landscape below. The sun is an orange haze, just beginning to dim near the horizon. The inside of the corn maze is visible from this high up, and I spy a few bloody-looking scarecrows tucked precariously throughout its random nooks and crannies.

I point to the maze. "Have you ever done that?"

Zayne blows out an amused laugh. "Oh, yeah. Plenty of times. My mom volunteered me and Lenny to work it one Halloween, even."

"What?" I stifle a laugh. "Zayne and Lenny Silverman, undead brothers?" I grin. "I'm sure Lenny had a *field* day. Ha. Get it?"

Zayne closes his eyes, but a smile spreads across his lips. I can tell he doesn't want to laugh. But my joke is so bad, it's practically impossible. "He kept calling us 'The Salvatore Brothers' actually," he says. "You know. From *The Vampire Diaries*?"

I burst out laughing. "I bet Lenny was Stefan. He's much too nice to be Damon."

"I don't remember who was who."

"That's such a lie!" I point my finger at him. "You're lying."

"I've chosen to forget all about it."

"Well now that I know, I'm going to bring it up as often as I can. Come to think of it, I demand to see photos of this event."

He shakes his head. "That's nothing compared to the time Mom and Mimi made us dress up as cowboys and then forced us into a photo shoot."

"Wait. I think I've seen that photo. It's hanging on your wall."

He nods with his lips pressed together. His shoulders slump. "Yes. Yes, it is."

I turn away to hide my smile. The image comes back to me, of pre-teen Zayne in his cowboy outfit, matching his younger brother. The memory of it makes warmth expand inside my chest. But at the same time, it makes me sad. Because while this entire evening has been, let's face it— amazing—I can't help but acknowledge that it's really nothing more than a distraction, from buckling down and running lines, and inevitably, the play.

Which Mom claims she will be here to see.

"Sorry about earlier," I whisper. "I know I seemed distracted. And that's because I was."

His voice is soft beside me. "What's on your mind?"

"My mom says she's coming home to see the play."

"Oh." Zayne's eyebrows narrow. "But that's a good thing, right?"

"I don't know. Part of me thinks she's not really going to show up. What if I let myself get excited and then she doesn't come? I'll be..." I try to search for the right word. "Devastated."

"That's true," he says. "But if she's set on it, then try to have faith it will work out."

"That's not the only problem though. What if she does come, and I mess up on stage? In front of my mom and my dad and my brother? The entire school? I don't know if *I'm* even ready for all this." I squeeze the poor stuffed bumblebee with agitation.

"Dot." He nudges my shoulder with his. The gesture is innocent. Sweet. "Stop worrying. Nerves are part of the process. You think I'm confident before every performance?"

"Well, you should be," I say. "You're the best actor in the whole school."

He raises his eyebrows. "Was that another compliment I just heard?"

"You know it's true."

"The point is," he continues, "even I get nervous I'm

going to mess up, but I just give it my best effort and try to stay positive. That's all you can do. Besides, you're a much better actress than you think. You're really good, actually."

I try to find any traces of sarcasm in his face, but there are none. "You really think so?"

He nods. "Yep. I bet you even have a shot at getting into Underwood if you keep practicing."

Zayne Silverman himself thinks I'm really good? My entire body feels light and fuzzy as the words float around in my brain. I try to hide how flattered I am by his compliment. "How unlucky for you, since there are only two spots."

"You mean, how unlucky for *Carlton,* since apparently I'm the best actor in the whole school."

I glare at him.

"Your words, not mine," he reminds me, holding up his hands.

"Yeah," I say quietly. I search his face, taking comfort in the teasing confidence I find. "Yeah, I guess that's true."

When we get back to Zayne's house, no one else is home. Zayne tells me that everyone probably went for a nature walk—as Lenny calls it. "We go on them a couple times a week," he explains. "We let Lenny tell us all sorts of random facts about the plants and flowers we see as we walk by. Sometimes he'll pick some and hang them in his room."

"That sounds nice." Picturing the passionate way Lenny would talk about that kind of stuff makes my lips quirk up.

"It's getting late," Zayne says. "We can pick up where we left off tomorrow." We're standing at his front door. He hasn't made a move to go inside, and I haven't made for my car yet either. It feels like there's something left unspoken between us that needs to be addressed before the night can be deemed over. But I'm not sure what it is, and neither, apparently, is Zayne.

"Okay," I say. My feet remain planted on his doorstep despite my brain telling them to move, so I add, "Thank you. For taking me to smash pumpkins and drink apple cider."

His serious expression melts a little as if without his permission, cracking into something warmer. "Anytime."

There doesn't seem to be anything else to say, so I wave. "Bye, Zayne."

I turn and walk to my car. As I go, I hear his voice, so soft it could be mistaken for the wind. "Bye, Dot."

Chapter Sixteen

Zayne and I get through the whole script in two days.

I go to his house after school on Monday and Tuesday, and we run lines like maniacs, scene after scene until we've run out of pages. Mimi's snacks provide us with the fuel we need to get through it, and Lenny provides us with brain breaks, interrupting us now and then to explain why some types of mushrooms are poisonous and others aren't.

I text Carlton back both days when he offers to run lines with me himself, telling him I have too much home-work to catch up on, and Zayne doesn't comment.

When he helps me memorize our last scenes, a wave of triumph hits me so strong, I almost collapse.

We're done.

It feels so good.

When I rehearse at school on Wednesday, it's the first time I'm acting completely off book, like everyone else.

This time, I'm one of them.

"Oh, Nelly," I wail in character as Cathy. I'm lying on three chairs in the rehearsal room set up to temporarily serve as a bed, and Meredith is perched above me with pretend concern etched on her face. She's probably shooting mental daggers at me, but no hint of her disdain is visible, a clear display of her talent. *"I wish I were out of doors,"* I continue. *"I wish I were a girl again, half savage and hardy, and free."* I fan myself, arching my back as I pretend to be feverish in bed, and rest the back of my hand on my forehead.

Out of the corner of my eye, I notice Mr. Saltzman raise his eyebrows and nod from his chair in the center of the classroom. He looks...impressed.

It happens during my scene with Zayne, Carlton, and Rue. Rue, playing Isabella, gestures to Zayne and says. *"Look who I found wandering in the hall."* My character is married to Carlton's here, but when I see Heathcliff, I'm supposed to be filled with a terrible, aching longing. And that's exactly what I try to portray. I stare at Zayne with the same intensity described in the script, hoping my expression fits the scene. Rue says her next line to Carlton. *"Has Mr. Heathcliff not changed beyond all recognition?"*

I can't tell if Carlton's stony expression is acting or not. *"Indeed."*

I let my gaze progress from Zayne's black sneakers all the way up to his face. A heat travels through my body, but I try to focus. *"Heathcliff,"* I say in the tortured way I'd imagine Cathy to speak. *"It's you."*

After the scene, Mr. Saltzman gives us his notes. "Rue, try not to sound quite so eager. I know Isabella is trying to catch Heathcliff's eye, but she must still hold some regard for her brother's negative opinion of the guy. Carlton," he pauses, pressing his lips together in concentration. "Mostly good, but a little dry. Try to give it a bit more *oomf*, if you know what I mean. Remember, this is a show. And Silverman, you were perfect, as usual."

Carlton jerks out of his chair. "I need some air." His steps are loud on the floor as he exits the classroom.

Mr. Saltzman frowns. "Is he alright?" He clears his throat. "Hm. Anywho, Dot. I must say, you're doing amazing. I've actually been really blown away by your scenes today, specifically. Whatever you're doing, don't stop."

I feel a swell of pride. Part of me has been worried I'd let Mr. Saltzman down if my acting didn't prove good enough, that he'd regret taking a chance on me when he chose me to play Cathy.

But that's clearly not the case. Which means my hard work is paying off.

A week later, we get our costumes and Mr. Saltzman tells us we're going to do a dress rehearsal and tech test.

We get to act out the entire play in costume. With mics. On the stage. In the school theater.

I've never been so excited about anything in my life.

"Places, everyone," he calls, ushering the first group of actors onto the stage. Zayne is among them, and I find myself watching from the audience instead of going over my lines backstage for my first scene. Zayne's not in costume or anything, but it's still fun to watch him get into character.

"Hey." Carlton's voice startles me from my reverie.

I smile faintly. "Hey." It seems like rehearsal has taken precedence over everything else this past week. I can't even remember our last real conversation.

He tilts his head. "Why aren't you backstage?"

"Um." I shift in my seat. What am I supposed to say? *I'm enjoying watching Zayne play Heathcliff?* "I was just about to go, actually."

"Cool." His smile is tight. "Let's go, then." He holds out his hand to help me up, and I take it, glancing once more at the stage where Zayne is running his scene with a boy named Owen, who's playing Lockwood.

As soon as we're backstage, some of the tension in Carlton's shoulders eases. "I just can't stand being around that guy."

I bite my lip. "He's really not so bad once you get to know him." I intend for the words to sound reluctant, but my voice sounds much more confident than I want it to. And even a little...dreamy.

Carlton whirls around. His gaze is intense, like I'm a math equation he just can't seem to figure out. "You're kidding, right?"

When I don't say anything, his forehead scrunches together, making the skin buckle into several thin lines. I just shrug, because I'm afraid anything else I say will only make things worse.

"Dot." Carlton shuts his eyes, like he's trying to calm down. "He's the reason I didn't get the role I practiced for all summer. It's because of him I might not even get into Underwood now."

No, I want to say. *It's because of you.* But instead of finally confessing to Carlton that I know the truth, I just purse my lips. Now isn't the time to get into it. I've been wracking my brain to figure out when the right time actually is, but I can't seem to commit. Confronting Carlton and telling him I know he's been lying isn't something I'm looking forward to. I can't imagine he'll handle it well, and who knows how that will affect my friendship with Mabel and Rue?

Meredith approaches us from the other side of the room. She narrows her eyes at me and then at Carlton. "What is going on with you two?"

I cross my arms. "What do you mean?"

"It seems like all you two ever do is bicker lately," she says. "It's getting old."

"We do not bicker," Carlton insists.

Meredith rolls her eyes. "Yes, you do. You're always mad about something, C. And Dot, you're always getting under everyone's skin."

"What?" What is she talking about?

She rolls her eyes as she sighs, then holds up a hand. "Never mind." She struts away and sits back down at a small round table shoved into the corner of our backstage room, which is called the green room, even though there's nothing green about it.

I frown at Carlton. "Do I really do that? Get under everyone's skin?"

"I mean, yeah." Carlton shifts on his feet. "It sometimes

seems that way."

An uncomfortable sensation washes over me. "How?"

"Well, first there was you getting the part of Catherine —which Meredith wanted really bad—and then doing nothing but constantly complain about it at first. And then there's all the time you've been spending with Zayne, who you know I can't stand."

"So, two things then." I raise my eyebrows. "You literally only have two examples. Neither of which were my fault, I might add."

Carlton exhales. "Whatever."

Esme, the student stage manager, appears in the doorway of the green room. "Dot, you're up."

I give Carlton an exasperated look before I follow Esme. My mind is in a whirl. It seems like nothing I do is right, lately. I just can't win.

I'm ushered onto the stage, and I glance up to see none other than Zayne. His eyes meet mine, and his brows inch together as if he can sense my internal stress. But I ignore him, mentally running through our lines. It's a good thing we've been practicing so much. For once, I feel comfortable with my role. Confident. There's still the tiny voice in the back of my mind that whispers, *what if you mess up all your lines?*

But of course that doesn't happen. Thanks to Zayne, the scene flows smoothly as if we're in his bedroom with our books right in front of us. Part of it, I know I owe to his superb acting ability, the way he makes me feel as if we really are these characters and we've been transported right into the pages of the story. Not an ounce of the real Zayne peeks through. When we're acting, he *is* Heathcliff.

I know deep down he carries the brunt of our scenes on his shoulders. But the rest, I realize, is all me. I can hear it in my voice with each line. I can see it on Mr. Saltzman's face with each in-character facial expression I make. Zayne was right about me not being as bad as I think.

And it feels really good. Better than good, actually. It's a rush—one that will be really hard to let go of.

When Zayne and I have our first romantic scene together, I have to admit, I'm caught off guard. Rehearsing it in his bedroom or the classroom is one thing. But the way he looks at me while we're acting it out in front of Mr. Saltzman, the way his eyes tenderly caress my face as if I'm made of delicately spun silver startles me. It seems so real, I almost forget we're acting.

And then it's time for us to kiss. The part we've skipped every time before now.

I step toward Zayne, my heart thundering in my ears. *It's not real,* I remind myself. *It's only a play. You're acting for crying out loud.* "You returned on my wedding day," I whisper into my mic, *"only to punish me."*

His fingers clasp around my waist, gripping me more firmly than I'm prepared for. And then our lips meet.

And that's it.

Or at least, that's all it's supposed to be.

But when we pull apart, Zayne's eyes collide with mine. My stomach dances, the feeling propelling me forward and the next thing I know, we're both kissing again. He reaches for my face, his other arm still around my waist. The taste of his mouth makes my brain feel foggy, but I can't break away. Our tongues touch and then find themselves entangled like wild vines. The only reason my knees don't buckle is because Zayne's hand is still on my waist, holding me up. My teeth graze his bottom lip, my heart pounding in my ears, drowning out all other sounds. The words, *only acting, only acting,* ring through my subconscious, strongly at first, but then begin to dwindle into something less substantial.

This kiss seems to expand into a stretch of time that can't be counted or determined. When our faces finally break apart and Zayne steps away, it feels like a bandage being ripped off a fresh wound. I stare at the ground. *What just happened?*

He doesn't break character, stating his next lines as if we didn't just make out onstage, when we could have just gotten away with a simple kiss. Eyes still round and wide, I glance at Mr. Saltzman. His usually pink cheeks look extra rosy as he watches us with narrowed eyes and low brows. Just past him, Rue is sitting in the audience with her mouth wide open. And Carlton is in the audience, too.

Glaring at me as if I just committed murder.

Fantastic. But instead of running offstage and explaining myself to him like I want to, I remain planted in front of Zayne. I try to stay in character and act out the rest of the scene with him.

I just hope that the guilt isn't written on my face for Zayne, Carlton, Mr. Saltzman, and everyone else who's watching to see.

When the scene cuts, Mr. Saltzman claps his hands

together. "Excellent job, you two." He lowers his glasses to look at me. "Dot, you're really letting your skills shine through lately. I'm impressed."

"Th-thanks." I avoid looking at Carlton and try my best to keep my voice even. Like I meant to kiss Zayne that way. Like it didn't catch me completely off guard. Like I'm not still lost in the way it made me feel, not still reeling from it.

"Carlton," says Mr. Saltzman. "Let's have you up here now in the classic scene with all three of you. This one is my personal favorite and one I know the audience will be looking forward to as fans of the novel."

Carlton drags his feet as if they weigh a ton as he walks onto the stage. This is one of the scenes the three of us practiced at the garden. Zayne and I rehearsed it plenty of times on our own, too, with Zayne reading Carlton's lines in addition to his own.

Carlton takes his place on the stage. His eyes skip over me as he turns to face me. I'm not sure if I prefer this, or his previous glaring, to be honest.

When he finally looks at me, the intensity in his gaze makes me shrink back. *"This is insufferable!"* The words are a snarl. I know his character is supposed to be angry, but I can't help but wonder if he's using his character's bad mood as an excuse to let his own anger show, rather than putting a commendable effort into our rehearsal.

Zayne doesn't react or break character. Crossing his arms, he says, *"That, I echo."* I wonder if he notices the change in Carlton, or cares.

Carlton turns to Zayne and says his next line. *"Your presence is a moral poison that would contaminate the most virtuous. For that cause and to prevent worse consequences, I shall deny you hereafter admission into this house!"* He emphasizes each word.

It's his best performance yet.

So I, too, stay in character. And when the scene is over, Zayne, Carlton, and I exit the stage to the green room.

Carlton makes a beeline for his table, opening his backpack to get a water bottle. "I do not want to talk to you, Dot."

I search for words. Anything to calm him down. Anything to explain my behavior. "It was only acting, Carlton. You know that." But the feeble words, insistent as they are, recycled and repeated from my subconscious, aren't even convincing me.

He starts to say something, but then yelps, pulling his hand out of his bag. He peers inside and yells, "There's a snake in my backpack! I just touched it."

"What?"

"A snake, Dot! *Look.*" He opens his bag and holds it in front of my face. Sure enough, a tan snake with dark brown blotches along its back is coiled atop his sweatshirt.

"That looks like a gopher snake," says Zayne from behind me. "Don't worry. They're harmless."

Carlton points at him. "You put it there, didn't you? I know you did!"

There's a grin on Zayne's lips. "Where would I even get a snake? Grow up, Carlton."

"This is just like the stunts you used to pull when we were kids!" Carlton looks at me for help, like me announcing that I believe him is all the proof he needs.

"I'm terrified of snakes," Zayne states. "Why would I go near one just to put it in your backpack?"

I suppress a laugh, remembering Zayne telling me about snakes being his biggest fear when we were texting. "It's true. Zayne is afraid of snakes. And geese." I fight back a grin as I remember our time in the garden before Carlton arrived. I grin at Zayne and he smiles back, the simple lifting of his lips stirring something in me I can't describe.

"Seriously?" Carlton booms. "You're defending *him?*" He shakes his head, mouth agape. "And stop smiling at him! What's wrong with you?"

"Carlton." I reach to touch his hand, but he yanks it away like I'm holding a hot poker.

"Don't touch me. And don't talk to me." Grabbing his backpack, snake and all, he storms out of the break room. I know I should probably follow him, but I can't seem to find it in me. I'm just so tired of defending myself to him. Of having to explain myself. I know I'll probably kick myself later for not caring more right now, but for the time being, it feels good to just brush it off.

"You think he'll take it to a pet store?" Zayne mutters.

I turn to face him. "What?"

"The snake. Do you think Carlton will take it to a pet store? Or maybe just set it loose somewhere?"

"This isn't funny, Zayne."

"I disagree." He displays a wide grin. "I think it's pretty hilarious, in fact."

"Well that just makes you immature. And how did you even know what kind of snake it was?" I can't deny that his knowledge makes me a little suspicious.

"Lenny. He's obsessed with animals, remember? After a while, hearing about all those different species rubs off on you." He smirks. "But I'm not gonna lie...it's always fun watching Carlton get mad."

I cross my arms. "And like I mentioned before, he wouldn't be so mad if you hadn't kissed me like that."

"Well, like you said, it was only acting. So, there's no reason for him to react."

"Acting." My chest feels like it's gripped in a tight fist. I blink a few times. "Right. I—I'll be right back."

Zayne's smugness dissipates. "Wait, Dot."

"I'm just taking a little walk before my next scene." I don't hide my irritation as I gather my things and leave.

I'm vaguely aware of Mabel and Meredith watching me, and when I exit the theater building, Meredith follows me. I don't speak to her, and she remains silent, too, waiting until we're out of earshot from anyone else. After a few more minutes, she blurts, "Do you have feelings for Zayne?"

It's already enough of a shock that she's speaking to me after all this time, so her question is enough to stop me in my tracks. "What?"

"Zayne Silverman," she repeats. "Do you have feelings for him?"

It takes me a moment longer than it should for the question to register. I can't remember a time when Meredith has ever spoken more than three sentences to me, let alone asked me such a direct question. "I, uh—" I stammer, not even sure why I'm stammering. But then I remember the way I used to hate him. The way even the mention of his name would leave me with a sense of indignation for Carlton. How I felt like Zayne was the reason for everything that was going wrong between me and him. But I can't deny that I don't think that anymore. "Why are you asking me that?"

She narrows her green eyes at me. "I saw the way you kissed him on stage. You've never kissed Carlton like that."

My face burns. "How would you even know?"

"I can tell."

"Sure, Meredith. Whatever you say." I turn to leave, but her voice stops me.

"It's okay if you like Zayne," she calls. "I won't tell Carlton." There's a smile in her voice that leaves me feeling sick.

"I don't know what you're talking about."

Surprise, and maybe even a little disappointment crosses Meredith's face. Disappointment at what, I'm not sure. And I don't care to find out. I walk away at a quicker pace this time. I don't need her following me. Taunting me. Prodding with personal questions. They're completely unwarranted.

Are they, though? The thought is unwelcome, but it enters my mind nonetheless. Carlton is her friend. It's only natural that she'd want to look out for him and make sure the girl he likes isn't leading him on. A few months ago, I wouldn't hear Zayne talk even remotely badly about Carlton, and now here I am defending him without a second thought.

Chapter Seventeen

Hello my sweet fledglings!

It's been a week or two since you've heard from me last but worry not. I've kept busy while I was away.

It appears that Dot Bennett and Zayne Silverman have gotten closer. One might even call them friends! Or at least, that's what I've been hearing whispered throughout the ancient halls of Fallbrook Christian Prep! The scandal. I can't help but wonder how Carlton Peters is handling this change of events. I know I'm not the first to spread the news about the upcoming Halloween party at the house of twins, Meredith and Mabel Evans. A theater party, to be precise. That's right, my dears. A party within the drama club. Which can only mean that there's sure to be drama. Will Carlton choose this event to finally confront Dot?

You know I'll be watching. And if there's a story to be told, you'll hear of it from a little birdie. This one, in fact.

In other news, Rue Sullivan is still fawning over her crush, and I've discovered who it is! That's right, Rue. I've seen the forlorn, unrequited stares. The weight of your hopeful gaze is so heavy, I'm surprised you haven't been crushed by it yet. So, here's some motivation for you, because really, it's becoming pathetic watching you do nothing. Reveal your affections to your crush, or I'll tell the world who it is.

Anywho. That's all.

Yours truly,

Little Birdie

I don't want to go to the party, anyway. Not with all the studying I need to catch up on. Luckily, I'm not falling behind in anything, but to get into an exceptional college, I need to be better than up to par. I need to be *ahead* of the par. And the play has been taking up so much of my time already. That and reading *Emma*, which I actually finished last night. And, of course, Zayne was right. I loved it. It was just as, if not more entertaining than *Clueless*, and so were all the notes he left me in the margins, noting his favorite parts.

The point is, I've been too distracted from my studies. A party is the last thing I need, even if it's Halloween.

Not being invited has nothing to do with it.

But then again, Carlton still isn't speaking to me. It's been days since the run-through rehearsal, and still not a peep. At school, he won't even look at me. The last time I approached him, he turned his back and walked away, leaving me standing all alone. Outside of school, I've tried texting him, calling, and stopped by his house twice. Nothing. Mabel has only been speaking to me over text, too afraid to upset Carlton and her sister by taking my side. Ugh. It's like Carlton is some kind of gatekeeper who determines whether or not I'm worthy of friendship. Luckily, Rue has taken pity on me today, eating lunch at a different table by my side, because it's not like I can go sit with Zayne. That will only make things worse. And I definitely don't want to sit with him anyway. I don't.

"Don't look so sad," says Rue, watching me pick at my lunch for the fourth day in a row.

"You know the twins are throwing that party to exclude me," I point out. "I'm the only person in drama club who didn't receive an invitation."

"It's not like Meredith to do such a thing," she counters. "She must be going through something."

I snort. "Are we talking about the same girl? She's never exactly been warm and fuzzy toward me."

She frowns, bobbing her head from side to side. "She's

not normally like that. Trust me. You haven't known her as long as the rest of us."

"I'm just glad Mabel isn't mad at me, too. At least, not yet." I push my grapes around my lunch tray with my index finger, trying to resist the lump in my throat. I won't let it form. I won't cry over something this silly. "Maybe I should just quit the play." My stomach twists as the words leave my mouth because the idea is horribly unappealing and I don't even mean it.

"Dot, don't you dare." Rue's eyes round in alarm. "You'll ruin the whole production. There won't be enough time to replace you."

"Yeah, right," I mutter. "I bet Meredith's secretly been practicing my lines, lurking in the shadows, eagerly awaiting my failure."

"Okay." Rue slams her hand down on the table. With a start, I look up from my lunch tray at her. Her gaze pins me in place. "You *have* to stop this. Meredith really isn't a bad person once you get to know her. You have to stop talking badly about her. She's my friend."

My heart sinks. *Way to burn all your bridges, Dot.*

But Rue continues. "You're my friend, too. And I don't think it's right for Carlton to be so mad at you. But he does have a right to be frustrated. You keep claiming that you like him, but I can't help but notice you kinda, sorta, might like someone else, too. A little."

My cheeks burn, but I don't say a word in confirmation or denial. I just shrug. "I don't know what you mean."

"I think you do," she mutters. "And I hate to say it, but you need to stop being so wishy-washy. You're in the play, so you need to commit to it once and for all. No more of this back and forth. No more threats. No more pondering. You accepted your role, so it's time to make good on that. And you really should make a decision about Carlton. Either you like him, or you don't. Both are okay, but you need to own your choice either way."

When she finishes talking, she lets out a little sigh of relief. I can't help but wonder how long she's been holding all that in. And I can't help but realize that she's right.

She's completely right.

I've been tossing around my emotions, my thoughts, and my choices so carelessly, I haven't stopped to think of who else might be affected. Carlton isn't the problem, and neither is Zayne. It's me, because I still don't know what the right answer to any of this is. But one thing I do know —I'm grateful Rue had the guts to open my eyes.

"I'm going to talk to Carlton," I decide. Time to rip off the band-aid and be honest about how I've been feeling, no matter the consequences. "Tonight, at the party. I don't care if he and Meredith want me there or not. It's Halloween and I'm playing the lead role, after all. You'd think I'd be allowed to show up."

Rue raises her eyebrows. "Oh. Okay, then."

"Will you come over after school? We could get ready together."

"Sure." Her cheeks lift into a smile.

I take out my phone and send a text because I just can't help it. I have to know.

ME

Are you going to the party tonight?

I wait and notice the guy from the pumpkin patch walking up to Zayne across the cafeteria. It's the first time I've ever noticed him at school before. What was his name again? James? Josh? Jude? *Jude,* I remember. *It was Jude.* I note the way he watches Zayne, like he wants to be noticed, and how Zayne nods at him, and then turns back to one of his other friends. Jude's shoulders sag. How have I never noticed him before?

The bell rings, signaling that lunch is over. I grab my tray, tossing my picked-at lunch in the trash. I walk with Rue down the corridors. And then my phone vibrates. It's a response to my text. I stare at it and can't help the flutters that begin to blossom as a result.

ZAYNE

I'll be there.

"You should wear this." Rue holds up my black jumpsuit, still on the hanger. "You could draw some whiskers on your face with eyeliner and go as a cat. Plus, you'll look hot."

I grin and take it from her. "Thanks. I forgot I had this." And she happens to be right—it's very flattering on me. I gesture to her white dress with wings and the halo headband atop her curly bob. "You look great, by the way. An angel. So cute."

She grins. "Thanks. Now go, get dressed."

I go to the bathroom and put the outfit on. It's tight, hugging me like a second skin, but still comfortable. I love the way the high-quality satin feels against my skin.

I use eyeliner to make whiskers around my nose like Rue suggested, and I twist the front sections of my braids into two buns for ears, leaving the rest down. Rue helps me apply false lashes when I holler at her from the bathroom, and I do the same for her. When we're ready, I take a mirror selfie of us and post it to social media. "I can't remember the last time I got ready with a friend like this," I tell her.

She tilts her head. "Seriously?"

"Yeah, but it's really nice." No need to tell her the woes of being homeschooled in a small town. Of having only a handful of friends, if that. Of not having a reason to dress up like this, because there are no school dances when home is your school.

She smiles, making her dimples show. "It is nice. Just wish Mabel and Meredith could be here, too."

My spirits deflate a little at the mention of Mabel. While Rue stuffs her makeup back into her bag, I send Mabel a quick message:

ME

Miss you.

She responds instantly.

MABEL

Me too :(hope this nonsense is over
soon.

ME

Same here.

Beau knocks on the door. "Hurry up."

I swing the door open, and he takes in our appearance. "Where are you guys going?"

"The theater party," I tell him. "Didn't you read Little Birdie? The whole drama club is invited." *Except me*, I don't add.

"No, I don't read that stupid gossip column. It's not even accurate half the time."

Rue laughs at his bluntness. "True that."

"Alright." I head for the front door. "We gotta go."

"You look nice." Beau wrinkles his nose, an after-affect of complimenting me. "Try not to be a headline tonight."

I give him a thumbs up. "You bet."

Rue and I get in my car, and thankfully, she takes the place of my GPS as she tells me how to get to Meredith and Mabel's house.

"Dot?" She turns the music down.

"Yeah?"

"You know what your brother said? About Little Birdie being inaccurate half the time?"

"Yeah." Something about her tone makes me feel uneasy. "Why?"

"It's just..." She takes a deep breath. "Little Birdie has been writing about me having a crush."

I wave my hand at her. "You should just ignore stupid rumors like that, Rue. Don't let them affect you."

"But they're not stupid rumors," she blurts. "It's true. I do have a crush."

My lips part. "Really? On who?"

Her eyes dart around, and the way she bites her lip makes my stomach feel uneasy. After a long moment, she whispers, "On Carlton."

"Oh." A current of thoughts and emotions whirl through me. *Rue and Carlton?* How long has she been crushing on him? How has her crush affected her friendship with me?

"I'm not going to act on it, so you don't have anything to worry about. He clearly likes you, not me," she explains in a rush. "I just figured it would be better for you to find out from me directly, in case Little Birdie really does tell everyone." She fidgets with her hands.

"Oh, Rue." I sigh. "I'm so sorry." No wonder she's been so frustrated with my inability to settle my feelings toward Carlton.

She offers me a sad smile. "Thanks. What a situation, huh?"

"The worst."

We enter the twins' upscale suburban neighborhood, just outside of Boston, and park on the street near their house. They live in a two-story stucco and stone new-build that looks nearly identical to those surrounding it. It's clear it's their house from the lights and booming music emanating from inside.

I turn to Rue from the driver seat. "You ready?"

"That depends," she says. "Do you have a paper bag I can wear over my head if the truth comes out? Who knows how Carlton would react."

An alert rings on my phone and on Rue's at the same time.

Little Birdie.

"No," she cries. "She wouldn't tell everyone yet, would she?"

I bite my lip. I don't want to give her false hope, because I know there's a good chance Little Birdie *would* spill the beans. "Let's find out."

We both look at the blast. But Rue isn't mentioned at all. Instead, several photos fill the screen, the first one a picture of a boy and a girl drinking from steaming mugs, surrounded by an expanse of orange pumpkins and haystacks.

Rue squints. "Is that...?"

My cheeks burn. "That's me and Zayne." Us together at the pumpkin patch, hot apple cider mugs in hand. In the photo, I'm looking up at him through my lashes, a wry grin on my face. He's laughing hard at whatever I'm saying. I scroll down.

And my heart stops.

"Oh, no." The words escape my lips in a hushed breath. Zayne at my side on the Ferris wheel, the two of us leaning close together in what is unmistakably an intimate conversation.

At the image of the two of us leaning together like I'm a flower and he's the sun, warmth travels up my neck, spreading into my cheeks and hairline.

I remember the way Zayne's cool breath touched my face as he whispered about working the corn maze, as he told me I'm becoming a better actor. Complimenting me, telling me I actually have a chance at getting into Underwood Academy.

The moment replays, spinning in my mind, making me feel things I don't want to feel. So, I shove it all down and focus on what's important.

I never told Carlton about any of this. And I know exactly how he's going to take it. That is, if I don't get in there and explain things myself.

"Come on, Rue." I step out of the car, not checking to see if she's following or not. I need to get inside. Now. Because it's time to fix this mess I created once and for all.

Chapter Eighteen

Rue and I crash through the front door. Not exactly the classy, natural way I envisioned us arriving, but considering the circumstances of tonight, classy and natural will have to wait.

The main entrance of the Evans house opens up to a spacious foyer with high ceilings, chandelier lighting, and a grand staircase. The living room is cozy and inviting, with a plush rug, comfortable-looking sofas, armchairs, and a fireplace. Sprinkled throughout the space are cobwebs, plastic skeletons, bats, and colorful pumpkins.

A few heads turn to look at us, due to our over-the-top entrance. House music blares from the speakers as I push past the thick crowds of costumed students from Fallbrook, half of whom I don't even recognize from the drama club. So much for this party being exclusive to theater students. Apparently, I have nothing to worry about, coming uninvited. Half these people probably weren't invited either.

To my immense relief, hardly anyone is on their phone. I expected Little Birdie's blast to be the conversation point when I walked in. I clasp Rue's hand as we squeeze through a group of freshmen, and relief washes over me when I spy Carlton, Meredith, and Mabel on the staircase a few feet away. Carlton's face is painted green, and he's wearing ripped clothing and a black wig with the hair going in several different directions. Mabel is in a blond wig and a white dress with a name tag on her chest that reads, "Hello, my name is Marilyn." Her sister is wearing a gaudy pearl necklace, with her hair in a French twist and a matching name tag on her black dress that says, "Hello, my name is Audrey."

As if by intuition, Carlton locks eyes with me from across the room. I smile faintly, but his expression seems to transform from neutral into a cold, permanent scowl.

Everything will be fine. You just need to tell the truth. The thought is what propels me toward him, it's what allows me to ignore the warning bells that fire in my mind. Bells that say, *do not approach him while he's angry!*

As Rue and I near the staircase, a gradual hush seems to fall across the room. It feels like a spotlight is suddenly being shined right on us. Unfortunately, this is the only kind of spotlight I'm used to—the kind that alerts others to my personal business and distributes the news as fast as a wildfire.

"What do you want, Dot?" It's Carlton who speaks first. The remaining conversations echoing in the background fade into the booming music, and I resist the urge to look around to see if everyone is watching.

When I answer him, my voice comes out too quiet. "I need to talk to you."

I cringe at how pathetic it sounds. My relationship with Carlton used to be fun. He was there to comfort me when Mom left. But now, it's hard to remember what's left between us now that the majority of our interactions consist of me apologizing to him. Explaining myself to him. Trying to talk him down from blowing up on me.

And I'm tired of it.

"Honestly, Dot," he says. "I don't care what you have to say." The words cut through me, made worse by the dozens of eavesdroppers all around us. "You've been sneaking around behind my back since the school year began," he continues. "All this time, you've been nothing but a liar."

I'm at a loss for words, but I try anyway. "Carlton, I—"

"What's going on?" The voice cuts me off, and it's one I didn't realize I needed to hear until it slices through the room.

Zayne.

Zayne is here.

I scan the room, my eyes flitting over the silent party group huddled on the banisters and stuffed into corners until I find his face in the doorway to the kitchen. It makes me feel braver. Stronger.

"Sneaking around with *him,* no less," Carlton seethes.

"You and I aren't even together. You have no right to be mad." My voice is firmer than any tone I've ever used with him. I'm done trying to be nice to him. For the first time since I met him, I no longer care about his approval, his attention. I don't need him anymore.

I don't want him anymore.

"And we never will be together," he grounds out. "So why don't you take your pathetic acting and go be a nobody in that sad little town again."

My lips part. His words make my face feel like it's on fire. Everyone stares at me as I storm past him, up the staircase. I can feel the weight of all the eyes on the back of my neck as if they're made of stone. I search for an empty room, because I think I might cry. If I do, I want to be alone. It would be just my luck for someone to snap a picture of me. They would probably send it to Little Birdie. I can practically see the headline: *Fledglings! Dot Bennett was spotted crying over Carlton Peters after he insulted her in front of a large crowd of party-goers!*

Not that she would need to post anything at all. Half the school is already here at this party, witnessing it firsthand.

I knock on a door before opening it and find the room empty. *Thank you, Lord.* I sit on the bed. Glancing around, I realize this must be Mabel's room. A mint blue comforter covers her large bed, and accents of what seems like her favorite color are apparent in her pillows, rug, laptop case, and the fluffy robe hanging on the back of her door. She has Polaroid photos and larger prints covering every available space on her walls. Photos of the beach, of sunsets, of herself, and some of her and Meredith as babies. It's easy to see how they became baby models. In every photo, the pair of them are dressed in matching, one-of-a-kind pieces, smiling at the camera like naturals. They look adorable.

A knock on the door startles me. "Who is it?" I wipe away any non-existent tears, just in case.

The door opens, revealing Zayne. I belatedly register his black cape with a tall collar. The fake blood on the corner of his mouth. He's dressed like a vampire.

"Dot." He strides toward me and sits next to me on the bed. "What happened back there?" He searches my face. I'm not sure what he finds, but his frown seems to deepen.

I shrug. "I don't know. I guess Carlton saw the post Little Birdie put out." A pause. "You know. Of us at the pumpkin patch."

"So what?" Zayne narrows his eyes. "What does that matter?"

"It doesn't," I say. "Not really." But I'm lying. And he knows it. I can see it on his face. I can see the intensity in his searching glance, the tautness of his shoulders, like he's afraid to breathe. I can see that he's pretending to be oblivious, probably for my sake.

The scary part is how convincing it is. If I didn't know Zayne better, I'd believe the act.

But I do know him.

So, I take his hand when he stands and offers to help me up. "Let's go back out there," he tells me. But it sounds more like a question.

I nod. "Let's."

We walk back to the staircase, where the groups of party guests have once again dispersed throughout the room. Carlton is still on the stairs, but he's alone now. I have no idea where Mabel, Meredith, and Rue went.

"I see you two had fun together," Carlton spits. "As usual."

My face feels hot. "What's that supposed to mean?"

But Carlton doesn't answer me, instead glaring at Zayne over my shoulder. "You can have her," he says. "I was done with her anyway."

He turns to walk away, but Zayne's voice stops him. "Don't talk about her like that."

"Why not?" Carlton spins around, eyes gleaming in challenge. "What are you going to do?"

"Try it again." Zayne takes a step closer. His gaze is intense on Carlton as he clenches his jaw. "Find out. I dare you."

"Guys, stop," I say with my heart pounding, but they're locked in.

They stare each other down. The moment seems to stretch out, every second leaving me tense. This shouldn't be different from any of their other fights. They've been fighting for years. But now they're fighting about *me*, and it makes my palms sweat.

"We aren't together, Carlton," I repeat, in case he needs the reminder. This is ridiculous. "We never have been."

He looks at me, breaking away from his glaring contest with Zayne. "You're right. We're not together." He reaches out to grab Meredith, who is coming up the stairs with Rue. His arm snakes around her waist, and he pulls her against him, despite the utter confusion on her face. "And we never have been. Which means I can do *this*." And then he plants a long, sloppy kiss on Meredith's lips.

Before I can even react, someone pushes past me to run up the stairs.

Rue.

My heart sinks as she disappears into one of the rooms.

"Oh, no," I whisper. Never mind what Carlton is trying to do to me, getting revenge by kissing Meredith. He has no idea how much he's just hurt Rue, whether she wants to admit it or not. She may not want it to be true, but a crush is a crush, and seeing the boy you like kiss someone else is never fun.

Meredith remains frozen in shock as Carlton releases her, blinking like there's something stuck in her eye.

I frown at him. "Was that supposed to make me jealous? Because it didn't work." And it's true. Other than making me mad at him for hurting Rue, watching him kiss Meredith makes me feel...nothing. I take a deep breath, steadying myself before I say what I came to admit to him. "I haven't felt anything for you in a long time, Carlton."

Something in his eyes changes without his face shifting. "Well, that just makes you stupid."

Zayne snorts, reminding me he's still standing beside me. "What are you? Five?" He crosses his arms. "And what are you dressed as anyway? A zombie?"

Carlton fumes. "I'm Frankenstein."

Zayne laughs. "You mean Frankenstein's *monster.* Frankenstein is the doctor."

Carlton takes a step closer to Zayne. And then he pushes him, hard enough to hurl him backwards, into the railing of the stairs.

"Zayne!" I reach toward him. But he isn't listening. He

tackles Carlton to the ground, and they transform into a tangle of twisted, flying limbs. "Stop it!" I shriek. "Someone stop them!" I glance around, hoping someone is nearby to interfere. And then I spot Jude at the top of the stairs, holding up his phone. He's *recording* this.

"Jude, do something." I wave my hands at him.

He jumps when I use his name. I remember Mom telling me once that asking someone for help directly, by name, is always more effective than yelling aimlessly for anyone who can hear.

Jude looks around, mouth parted and eyes wide. "What am I supposed to do?"

"I don't know. Try to stop them or something. You're friends with Zayne, aren't you?"

He stares after the wrestling forms in front of him, now being recorded by several others near us. The booming music in the house keeps the noise of Zayne and Carlton's fight muffled, but they're starting to attract attention regardless.

"Just forget it." I shoulder past Jude and rush over to the pair of boys, now on the ground. Carlton is pinned beneath Zayne's elbow, and I grab Zayne by his other arm and pull him to his feet. I yank his body in my direction to focus him. A stream of blood trickles from his nose. "Oh, no," I say. I resist the urge to reach up and touch his face, because not only is it covered in blood, but it's probably sore from being punched by Carlton.

Carlton stands up and dusts himself off. "Just wait till I press charges against you, Silverman." He grimaces at me one last time before descending the stairs.

I turn to face the sea of phones filming us. "Enough, already." I use my hands to shield my face. "Stop recording us. Just leave us alone."

"Dot." Zayne touches my shoulder. "Let's just go."

As we walk through the entryway to the front door, I can't help but realize the ridiculousness of it all. It's not like we're celebrities. It shouldn't matter what's going on in our personal lives. Who likes who, who's fighting or angry at someone else. But it does matter. Because Little Birdie says it does.

Beau's words from earlier tonight echo in my mind. *Try not to be a headline tonight.*

I tried, Beau, I think with each defeated step I take to the car. *I really did try.*

Chapter Nineteen

I don't speak to Zayne at first.

I'm not sure if I'm mad at him just yet. He should have never engaged in that fight, even if Carlton did push him first. But then again, I'm not sure I can be mad. He was defending me.

And now his nose is bleeding.

I risk a glance at him. We're standing outside the Evans house, at the end of the driveway. I have no idea what we're supposed to do now. Do we go our separate ways? Should we talk? I should at least offer him a ride home in case he doesn't have one.

Before I can ask, Zayne stuffs his hands in his pockets and sighs. "I don't know what came over me back there. I shouldn't have done that. But hearing him talk about you like that..." He meets my gaze. "I didn't like it. I know it's not an excuse, but it's true."

I shrug, but I feel his words all the way down to my

toes. "At least you're sorry."

"I never said I was sorry. I know it was wrong to hit him, but I'd still do it again."

I inhale sharply. I have no idea what to say to that. So instead, I ask, "Did you drive here?"

He nods. "You?"

"Yeah."

The little puffs of air Zayne is exhaling are visible in the cold night air. "What about your friend?"

"That's right," I say. "I forgot I drove Rue here. I guess I'll wait for her in my car." But I linger in place, not quite ready to walk away. "I think I have a first aid kit in my glove compartment." I wince at his face, where blood is trickling from his nose and mingling with his vampire makeup. "Can I help you clean some of that blood off?"

He swallows, his Adam's apple bobbing, and then he nods. He follows me to my car, and I turn on the engine and crank up the heater as soon as we get in.

Zayne rubs his hands together in front of the vent, and I shuffle through the messy middle console until I find what I'm looking for. I grin and hold it up like a hard-earned prize. "First-aid kit." I place it in his hands. "I'm just grateful all you walked away with is a bloody nose."

"Thanks." He smiles and takes the kit. He grabs an alcohol wipe and begins cleaning the blood off his face.

When he's done, he turns to look at me. I'm still staring. I transfer my gaze to the steering wheel, squeezing it with more force than necessary, and I clear my throat. "You were right, by the way."

"About what?"

"*Emma*. The book." I study my hands. "I loved it."

There's a long pause, and when I look at Zayne again, he's grinning. "You actually read it?"

"Every word. Along with all the notes you left me in the margins."

He chuckles. "Couldn't have you under-appreciating the good parts."

"I wouldn't have."

"You definitely would have, Miss I-only-read-magazines-but-plan-to-get-into-an-Ivy-League."

"Shut up." I bite my grin away and smack his shoulder, but then feel kind of bad, because what if he hurt his shoulder while he and Carlton were fighting? I rub the spot where I just smacked him. "Sorry."

He stares at my hand on his shoulder.

I don't move.

The car is filled with a piercing silence. And then I break it, my voice hardly louder than a whisper. "Why did you defend me, like that?"

He frowns, like my question doesn't make sense. "Why wouldn't I?"

"I guess after the way things started between us...I didn't think you would care."

He gives me a disapproving look. "Come on, Dot. That was a long time ago. You know I care about you now."

The words are casual, and so is his tone. But they settle over me in a way that somehow makes me feel weightless, like I'm floating. "That makes one of you," I say. I try to make it sound funny, like it doesn't bother me that Carlton finally wrote me off. That he tried to make me jealous by kissing Meredith. But deep down, his rejection stings, especially since it was in front of so many others. And I can tell by Zayne's expression that my attempt at hiding the pain is unsuccessful.

"Dot." His voice is low, almost a whisper. "You deserve better than Carlton, and you know it. You deserve better than someone who won't even call you his girlfriend."

There's a deafening pause. I push my rising anxiety aside and then my mouth opens and a whisper escapes it. "Someone like you?" I feel like I'm going to die after I say it.

There they are, Dot. The words you've been thinking, harboring all along.

The words that—now that they've been spoken— change everything between us. Even the shallow air we're breathing.

He inhales sharply.

"Zayne," I mutter, and he glances at my lips. The burning memory of how they felt pressed against his during rehearsal consumes my thoughts.

He pauses, like he's not sure what I want from him. And to be honest, I'm not sure either. All I know is he's nothing like the boy I thought he was when we first met.

He's more.

So much more.

"Zayne," I say again, unable to stop the rush of words that come next. "I think I want you to kiss me."

He blinks a few times, then grins. He reaches up and winds his fingers through my braids until he finds the base of my neck. His skin is warm, and I can't help the nerves, the excitement that spreads through my veins as he pulls me to him, lowers his head, and touches his lips to mine. As soon as our mouths brush together, my heart races like it might escape my chest. I steady myself against my nerves, and Zayne captures my next breath with another kiss. This time, it's more tender, more insistent. It makes my blood feel too hot for my veins, but I don't pull away, because I'm desperate for this moment to stretch out as long as possible. I reach up, hesitate, and touch Zayne's shoulders, letting my palms rest against them.

He pulls back just enough for us to open our eyes, and I meet his gaze. It sends a fresh bundle of nerves through my stomach, and I can't help myself. I grip his shoulders and pull him closer, my nose grazing his and forcing our eyes to fall shut again. My lips part, and when our tongues touch, I taste peppermint and coffee. It's so *Zayne*. And I want more of it.

Someone knocks on the car window, and with a start, we break apart. I blink away the hazy elation of kissing him as I stare at the form on the other side of the car. It's Rue. And she's crying. "I want to go home," she sniffs. "Right now."

Anger sparks in my veins. "I'm going to punch Carlton in his stupid, egotistical—"

"No." Rue shakes her head. "I'd really rather just leave."

"Okay." I nod with a deep sigh. "Of course." I turn back to Zayne, but he's already getting out of the car. My heart sinks. I'm not ready for him to leave. But my friend needs me right now, so I wave at him with my lip in a pout. "I'll text you," I say.

"Okay." The way he stares at my mouth makes me think he's anything but ready to part ways either. "Thanks for the first aid kit, by the way."

"Anytime."

Rue gets in the car, wiping away a fresh tear rolling down her cheek as she shuts the door. When Zayne walks away, I begin the drive back to my house where her car is waiting.

I search for words to comfort Rue, but only manage to settle on, "Carlton is such a jerk."

"I know you're probably wondering why I like him so much after tonight, but there's still such a good side to him." She shakes her head. "It doesn't matter, though. I shouldn't be upset. I should have known he'd go for Mere next instead of me." She takes a long, tired deep breath. The defeated look in her eyes makes me so sad.

"No. He just doesn't know you like him yet, that's all." I squeeze her hand. She doesn't deserve to be burned like this. Especially since she's always there for everyone else. She's the only one of Carlton's friends who didn't turn her back on me when he did, and even still, she remained a good friend to him and Meredith by not letting me talk badly about them. "Everything will work out," I tell her, trying to sound optimistic. But I know what she's thinking, and I can't help but agree—that Little Birdie is going to write about her crush on Carlton.

And then everything else is going to get even more complicated.

"Did you know," she says, "that Meredith used to have really bad social anxiety?"

"No. That's hard to imagine. She seems so confident all the time."

"I know she does," says Rue. "But she's not always confident. When we were younger, I was the only person who knew how hard it was for her to socialize with people. It used to send her into a panic."

"Used to? What changed?"

"I told her that I was scared too. And if I could fake it, so could she." Rue smiles, a faraway look in her eyes. "I told her that anytime she felt like running and hiding, to imagine I was there, standing next to her, holding her hand. Just as scared as she was. That's what started her interest in acting. Pretending all the time. And believe it or not, joining the drama club helped her break out of her shell. But now, I just wish I could take my own advice. I'm so, so scared of what all my friends will think if they find out I like C."

It's weird to think of someone as bold and apologetic as Meredith being afraid of what others think. *Maybe we aren't so different after all.* I trace patterns on the steering wheel with my thumb. "You're a good friend. They'll all understand what you're going through, Rue. But you just need to talk to Carlton. Tell him how you feel and see if he feels the same."

"If Little Birdie doesn't beat me to it." Her voice is laced with bitterness. Out of the corner of my eye, I see her shift toward me, her eyes rounding. "Speaking of which…"

"What?"

"You and Zayne kissing!" she shouts. Her lips form a wide grin. "When did that start happening?"

I laugh. "Just before you came to the car, actually."

Her eyes get round. "You mean I interrupted your first real kiss?"

"Don't worry," I giggle, though she definitely cut our moment off earlier than I would have liked. "It's not like that."

"Ah," she says, like that explains everything. "Got it. It's for the play, then." All traces of excitement seem to melt off her face.

I try to match her words with meaning but fail. "What do you mean?"

"Method acting. You know...how lead couples get together to help improve their onstage chemistry? Zayne's done it before, with that girl Cassidy who played his love interest last year. She ended up getting accepted to Underwood. That's what you guys are doing, right?"

I'm stunned into silence for a long moment. She makes it sound like a common practice among the theater students at Fallbrook. But why am I just now hearing about it?

Because you're stupid and naive, Dot.

Is that what Zayne has been doing? Method acting, so we'd have even better chemistry onstage? A few months ago, I wouldn't put it past him, especially if he thought it would improve his chances at getting accepted to Underwood. But we're closer than that now. He's admitted he cares about me, and I'm going to choose to hold firm to that belief.

Even if it would be the ultimate revenge for the way I

treated him when I first got cast as the lead in the play, Zayne wouldn't do that to me. He wouldn't.

"I like Zayne," I tell her. "And he likes me, too. That's the truth."

She squeals, clapping her hands together. "Oh my gosh! This is crazy. Just wait till Little Birdie finds out."

I smile at her enthusiasm, trying to ignore the sadness her statement makes me feel. Having Little Birdie spread lies about me is one thing, but I'm worried having something this personal put out for the whole school to read will feel like a bit of a loss, dampening the magic of new discovery. "Please don't tell anyone. I want to keep it off her site as long as possible."

She nods. "I won't say a word. Promise."

A surge of relief rushes through me. "Thank you." As I drive us to my house, a bit of my hope is restored. Maybe this will be the first thing I'll get to keep to myself since I became the new girl.

Chapter Twenty

Fledglings!

When a baby bird is born, its mother does not simply feed it an entire worm whole. No!

The mother must chew the food for its fresh hatchling, lest it accidentally choke.

And I, my dearest fledglings, shall do the same for you.

I may have promised to unveil the identity of Rue Sullivan's long pined-after crush, but that, my dears, would be feeding you too much information at once. Instead, allow me to feed you bit by bit.

I have greater news, you see, that I'm almost certain you'll choke on with surprise! It's positively delightful!

Tonight, at the home of twins Mabel and Meredith Evans, Zayne Silverman was caught attacking Carlton Peters! Some say the assault was long overdue, others insist Zayne was out of line.

What we all know for certain?

They were fighting over Dot Bennett.

It's all captured in the video below, thanks to an anonymous party-goer. See for yourself!

Yours Truly,

Little Birdie

I don't see the Little Birdie post until Rue is driving away, leaving me standing at my front door, my hand already turning the knob. As frustrating as it is that Zayne was accused of starting the fight with Carlton—of *assaulting* him, no less—I can't help but feel some relief that Rue has more time to talk to Carlton before her secret is spilled.

I tuck my phone into my pocket and go inside. I set my purse down on the bench in the entryway and round the corner, where Dad is staring at his phone in the kitchen.

I smile at him. "Hey. I didn't know you were home."

His gaze travels up from his phone to look at me. "Dot, have you seen this?" He holds it up.

My spine tingles. "Seen what?" There's no way he could be referring to the blast that was just sent out. Dad doesn't even have social media! He doesn't pay attention to stuff like that. His world consists of jazz music, hard work, and trying his best to be both parents so Mom has nothing to worry about other than getting better. There's no way he knows what happened tonight.

But sure enough, he holds his phone out to me, where the video of Zayne and Carlton fighting is playing. I'm in the video too, standing close to the camera and telling the person holding it to stop them, to do something.

And then my face pales.

Because I know who sent that video in. I know who *filmed* it.

I shake my head. "Dad…"

"What's going on, Bardot?" His voice is serious now. Stern.

"I don't know."

"It looks to me like you do. You're in the video." He points to me standing in the camera's frame, my cat costume unmistakable and my face a mixture of bewilderment and frustration. "Who are these boys?"

"Dad, how did you even find that video?"

"It made its way onto the 'Parents of Fallbrook Christian Prep' group on social media. Now, answer the question, Bardot," he says, and I realize my hopes to dance around the subject are futile. He's not budging on this. And to be honest, if I were him, I wouldn't either.

"Those boys are Zayne Silverman and Carlton Peters," I tell him. "You remember Carlton, right? He's been over here a few times."

He squints. "He the one who came around a few months back during the summer?"

"Yes. And the other one—Zayne Silverman—you don't know. He's the lead actor in the play." I pause, my cheeks warming against my will. "He's my friend."

My father searches my face. I'm not sure what he finds there, but it makes the corners of his mouth lift. "Just your friend?"

"I don't want to talk about this," I say with a laugh. "Zayne is Zayne, Dad."

He looks baffled. "What does that mean?"

"It means..." I search for the words. "It means that I thought I knew what I wanted. I thought I liked Carlton. That auditioning for the play would finally get him to like me back as much as I liked him. But in the process of rehearsing with Zayne, of getting to know him, I've realized Carlton isn't who I thought he was. And neither is Zayne. And it's changed everything." I cover my face with my hands. "I'm so confused."

Dad waits for me to drop my hands. He has a gleam in his eye, like he's happy I've decided to confide in him. "What's there to be confused about, baby? It sounds to me like you like Zayne."

He makes it sound so simple. It would be if that's all there was to it. But there's more, the second part of the truth that I've been suppressing, that I've been hiding in the hopes that it would simply go away with time. "Being in the play has messed up my priorities, Dad. I used to have my head on straight. I used to care about getting into a good college more than anything else in the world. And now I catch myself sometimes fantasizing about *stupid* things."

He frowns. "Stupid things? Like what?"

"I don't know." I wave my hand around in the air. "Stupid things like acting, and going to this really prestigious acting school for select high school and college students instead of going to Yale or Harvard, which is *stupid* and childish and irresponsible, and—"

My dad stops me. "You want to go to acting school, Bardot?"

"No!" My voice jumps an octave. "I don't! I mean, I know it's just a spontaneous urge or something. I know it can't be what I really want, deep down. It *can't* be." I do my best to reassure him, because otherwise, this entire conversation will feel like a slap on the face to him. After how hard he works, after all the time he spent homeschooling me to be ahead of my grade so I'd graduate with a perfect GPA. He's done everything he can to help me get into an Ivy League. *Anything* to help me accomplish my goal. I can't do this to Dad. To Mom. To myself.

I can't.

Dad smiles sadly at me—so sadly it breaks my heart. Because no matter how convincing I try to sound, I know he can see right through me.

"Honey," he says after much too long of a silence. "I will be so proud of you if you get into Yale, or Harvard, or Brown. If you *go* to an Ivy League."

I nod. It's the response I'm expecting, after all. So why does it hurt so bad to hear? "I know," I say. "And I will. I'll—"

"I'm not finished. I will be proud of you if you go to a respectable college. Of course I will. But I will be so much prouder if you make the brave decision to do what you know, deep down will make you happy. Even if that means traditional college is out."

I blink in confusion. I'm certain I misheard him. "What are you saying? I—I can go to Underwood Academy?"

"Do what makes you happy, Bardot. Within reason of course. This Underwood Academy is probably a respectable institution, otherwise I doubt it would even be on your radar. If acting is what you want to pursue...well, who am I to stop you? The last thing I want for you is to be stuck in a life you hate because you thought it would make your old man proud."

I'm stunned into silence. All I can do is stare at him because I can't believe what he just said. "You can't mean that, Daddy. What about all the work we've done to get me this far?"

He shrugs and then does the unthinkable. He smiles. "An education is never a waste. And part of learning is living, Dot. What kind of father would I be if I tried to keep you from living? Tried to force you on the path I thought was best for you? Only you know what path will make you happy."

I can't help it. I start to tear up, and my face splits into a wide grin. I throw my arms around him and hug him. "Thank you," I say around my smile. "Thank you, thank you, thank you!"

Beau comes out of his room. "What's going on?" He rubs his face like he had just been sleeping.

"I'm going to acting school!" I shout and release my dad from my strangling hug.

Beau scrunches his nose. "Since when?"

"Since right now!"

He smirks. "Because of Zayne?"

"No, not because of Zayne. Because of *me!*"

"Uh huh. Right." An antagonistic smirk forms on his mouth.

"Okay. I've officially heard enough out of you," I say.

Dad chuckles. "You both should get to bed. It's getting late."

I kiss him on the cheek. "Goodnight, Dad." I walk down the hall to my room, wondering if Mom will feel the same way he does about my new path. She might not, which definitely worries me, but as soon as I'm face-up on my bed, I grin at the ceiling. There's no way I can sleep. Not after everything that's happened tonight.

Saying out loud that I want to go to acting school.

Kissing Zayne.

Dad's approval.

Kissing Zayne!

I snatch my phone off my pillow. I did promise to text him, didn't I? Just a quick conversation, and then I'll go to sleep.

ME

Hey! Just got home.

ZAYNE

Glad to hear it

ME

Did I wake you up?

ZAYNE

No. I wasn't sleeping. Are you going to
sleep?

I hesitate before responding. Staying awake means texting him. Texting him means discussing *us.* Because how can we not? After all, we did kiss tonight. I don't know what that means.

But I want to find out.

ME

I'm not tired. Guess what?

ZAYNE

What?

ME

Can I call you?

For some reason, the conversation I'm about to have with him feels too important to text. There's too much to say. I answer the phone when it vibrates, my stomach bubbling with nerves. "Hey."

"Hi." His voice is hushed, like mine.

I imagine Beau on the other side of my bedroom door, his ear pressed against the wood. I get off my bed and go sit in my closet because it feels safer, harder for my voice to carry. "I'm guessing you saw what Little Birdie posted."

"Yeah. Can't say I'm surprised."

"Don't worry. No one actually believes you attacked Carlton. And if I have to, I'll be a witness!"

He laughs at my enthusiasm. "Thanks, Dot. I appreciate that."

We're both quiet for a beat, and then I say, "Can you believe the play is two weeks away?"

There's a pause. I can somehow sense his amusement through the phone. "Come on, Dot. I know you want to talk about us. About the kiss."

My mind strays from my conversation with Dad as I remember the burning kisses Zayne rained on my mouth tonight. I blush, grateful that he can't see my face. "We don't have to talk about us. Not if you don't want to."

"I don't mind." His voice is like a caress. "I think it's time we set the record straight, if anything."

My heart speeds up. I press the phone closer to my ear. "What do you mean?"

Another long pause. And then, "I really like you, Dot."

I can't help the smile my lips form. "You mean, you don't kiss all your friends like that?"

"Nope." He laughs. "Definitely not."

I grin again. It's impossible not to. "I like you too, Zayne."

"Do you know what that means?" he asks.

"What?"

"That means you should be my girlfriend and I should be your boyfriend."

I smirk, though he can't see it. "You mean you're not going to string me along? Wait until I join another play and start liking your childhood enemy?"

"Never."

"Good." The butterflies in my stomach rapidly flap their

little wings. My cheeks sting from smiling so much. This moment is perfect. *Perfect.* But still, I can't help but wonder about what Rue said. "Can I ask you something?"

"Of course," he says.

"Is it common for co-stars to date each other at Fallbrook?"

"I'm not sure." His tone sounds wary. It makes my stomach clench. "Why?"

I bite my lip. "Just wondering." I'm dying to ask him about Cassidy, but I don't want to spoil this moment. I don't want the mention of who might have been his ex-girl-friend to taint my memories of this moment. So, I leave it alone for now and add, "By the way, I decided that Ivies might not be all they're cracked up to be."

"What are you talking about?"

I take a deep breath. After all this, what if Zayne doesn't want me to go to Underwood? What if he takes this as me trying to steal his spot? Carlton would. "I finally admitted to my dad that college isn't for me. It felt so good to finally let it out," I breathe.

"Seriously? Dot, that's amazing."

"Thanks. And I've been thinking...you said Nigel Weathers usually offers his two spots to the leads every year. I don't think I would be able to turn down an oppor-tunity like that."

"You mean you wouldn't give your spot up for Carl-ton?" He sounds surprised, and maybe a little too pleased by this idea.

"If I get offered the spot, that means I deserve it more than he does, right?" I try not to sound too hopeful or desperate. I didn't realize until now how much his approval means to me. He's been telling me for months that I'm becoming a better actor. A great one, even. But what if all this time it was just words? "Does it make me a bad person for wanting to steal his dream?" I ask.

"Not if it's your dream, too." His voice is firm. "If you want it, Dot, go and get it. And you better not let someone like Carlton stop you."

Getting into Underwood on scholarship would mean Dad could stop working so hard to pay for Fallbrook. This is my chance to take some of the burden off my family and prove to them that this time, I'm not choosing a path on a whim, or out of envy. It's because of passion. The thing I've finally discovered after so much searching.

"I want it, Zayne. I want to be an actor so bad. I want to go to the best acting school around." I exhale a low breath. Talking about this is making me anxious. Excited.

Terrified.

Because there's nothing in all the world quite as daunting as talk of the future.

"Then Underwood, here you come." There's a smile in his voice.

"Thank you," I whisper.

The future may be out of my control, but right here in the present, things are good. I like them. And nothing—not even Little Birdie herself—can do anything to change that.

Chapter Twenty-One

Fledglings,

As promised, I come bearing more tasty worms in the form of gossip! Our dearest theater darling, Dot Bennett, has caused quite a stir among the drama club with her new boyfriend. That's right—boyfriend. No, your eyes don't deceive you as you read. And you guessed it! It's Zayne Silverman, who was caught last week attacking her previous beau, Carlton Peters. More on that later.

Dot and Zayne haven't left one another's side the past week, during which they've been spotted holding hands, sharing food from their lunches, and—dare I say it—kissing on campus!

None of this has gone unnoticed by Carlton,

who claimed he intends to press charges against Zayne for his assault last week! Hear it for your-self, right in the video! If he's successful with his claims, Zayne can kiss his spot at Underwood Academy goodbye! Best of luck to him. It seems like he'll need it.

In other news, the matter of Rue Sullivan's pathetic crush has not been forgotten. It may seem like old news, but just wait until you hear who she's pining after! It's none other than Carlton himself! But unlucky for Rue, he's already found his rebound in Meredith Evans!

My, what a tangled web of deception and betrayal the theater students' lives have become. And all with Fallbrook's long awaited, upcoming winter production a mere week away!

Lucky for you, I'm here to tell you all about it.
Yours truly,
Little Birdie

"No!" I drop my sandwich onto my lunch tray.

"What?" Zayne looks around. "What's the matter?"

"Little Birdie." I shove my phone in Zayne's face. "That stupid bird told everyone Rue has a crush on Carlton." I know I should be upset that my relationship with Zayne is also out on the dreadful site, but it's not like I've been hiding it well. At least I've had a week of no gossip about me and Zayne. Rue, however, is probably devastated her secret is out.

"She does?" He frowns. "I guess she can come clean now, right?"

"She wanted to talk to him herself. I should go find her. See if she's okay." I stand up and shoulder on my backpack.

"Want me to come?" Zayne starts to push his chair back.

"That's okay. This is girl talk." I lean over and kiss his cheek. But when I start to pull away, he takes my face in his hands and brings me back for another kiss, this time on his mouth. His lips are so soft. I hesitate before pulling away because staying here and kissing him until the bell rings sounds great.

But I need to go find Rue.

So, I untangle myself from Zayne. "Bye," he says. I wave at him, still wearing a hazy half-grin—an after-effect from kissing him.

I walk toward the lockers, hoping to find Rue in one of the corridors along the way. I scour each hall for her, about to text her asking where she is, but I spot Jude from the corner of my eye. My mind flashes to Little Birdie's latest post, to the video of Zayne and Carlton fighting. Thanks to the video, Carlton has proof that he and Zayne fought. His case to press charges is so much stronger because of it. From what Zayne told me, Underwood has strict rules about their students' behavior. Carlton may have started the fight, but from the way in looks in the video, Zayne could be the one attacking Carlton because it doesn't show who started it. If he plans on following through with the threat he made on Halloween, Zayne could lose his dream.

My vision goes red.

I march over to Jude, who is retrieving a textbook from his locker. He doesn't seem to notice that I'm approaching, and when his textbook is in his hand, I slam his locker shut as hard as I can.

He jumps. "Woah!"

"Why would you send that video from the party to Little Birdie? I thought you were Zayne's friend!" I briefly wonder how this outburst of mine will look to anyone who's watching before deciding I don't care. Zayne is more important.

"Video? I didn't send a video." He straightens his glasses and shrugs like he doesn't know what I'm talking about.

I roll my eyes. "Come on. I know it was you. I was there when you recorded it."

"It wasn't me." He arches his brow and shrugs. It makes my blood boil. "And you can't prove that it was. I even cut out the part of the video where you said my name."

"I don't get it. Why?" I drop my hands down to my sides. "I don't understand what you'd gain from doing something like that? Does Little Birdie offer some kind of reward for sending in information? There can't have been a good reason for you to do it, unless..." I squint my eyes at him, recalling how he had been there that day at the pumpkin patch, working the Ferris wheel Zayne and I rode together. He could have easily snapped the pictures that day. He was probably the one to send it in. *Unless...* "Unless you are Little Birdie." My eyes widen. "You're Little Birdie. Aren't you?"

Jude scoffs. "Of course not. Now you're just being ridiculous."

"Am I?" I ask. "It's not like you would admit it. Especially since that would make you responsible for a whole lot of trouble. Do you have any idea what you've done?"

Jude looks taken aback. "You can't be serious."

"I am!" My voice echoes around the wing, bouncing off the lockers and stone walls surrounding us. I don't care that I'm yelling. I don't care that people are starting to look, to stare at the spectacle I'm making. All I care about is finding out the truth. And I can't help but believe that Jude being Little Birdie happens to make perfect sense.

"Dottie!" A voice exclaims. I glance over my shoulder to find Lenny sauntering over, a calm grin on his face.

"Hi, Lenny. I'm kind of in the middle of something right now."

Jude scratches his curly head. "She's completely nuts."

I point at him. "*You,* be quiet. I know you're lying and I'm going to get to the bottom of it." I know I do sound a little crazy at this point, but it feels like uncovering Little Birdie's identity will prevent any more problems from arising. "Zayne could be in legal trouble now, thanks to you."

At that, he frowns. "I thought that was all talk. He isn't really in trouble, is he?"

"Who knows? He might be, if Carlton decides to press charges."

Jude holds his hands up. "Look, Dot, I'm sorry. Is that what you want to hear?"

"I want to hear the truth."

"Hey," Lenny says. "Bardot-Who-Goes-By-Dot? Maybe we should go."

"No, Lenny. I'm dealing with this liar right now."

He stares at Jude with new interest. "Maybe he's a vampire." He takes my arm, pulling me back the way I came. "Come on. Let's go get some vervain in you before he tries to erase your memories."

I take a deep breath, knowing there's no use trying to argue to Lenny that we aren't living in *The Vampire Diaries.* "Okay. Let's go."

But before we walk away, I stare Jude down one last time. In that one glance, I communicate to him everything I want to say. *I'm watching you. I'm onto you. And if you cross me and my friends again, I'll know who it was.*

As I leave with Lenny, I have no choice but to hope my message is received, loud and clear.

"Tell me again what Meredith said. And slow down this time."

Rue's voice cracks as she repeats herself. Her voice buzzes in my ear because of how close I'm pressing the phone against it. "She said she felt *uncomfortable* talking to me." She calms herself with a few breaths. "I asked her if we could talk, and she said things are too awkward now, considering everything. Apparently, she and Carlton are dating now. Mabel had to hug me because I started crying."

I close my eyes. "Wow."

"I don't know what to do."

I wince. "Just give it time, I guess. That's all you can do. I have a feeling if you push too hard it might make things worse."

"Tell me about something else," she says frantically. "Please. I need to take my mind off how much of a fool I feel like right now."

"Rue, it's okay. Meredith will come around, and so will Carlton."

"Please, Dot," she says. "Distract me."

My mind scatters in a thousand directions. "Um, okay. I made a fool of myself today, too. I yelled at Jude in the hallways and accused him of being Little Birdie."

"What? Why?"

"For sending that video from the party in."

"So, you told him you think he's Little Birdie and yelled at him?" She tries to hide a laugh. Relief loosens my joints.

"I just snapped. It's like all this Little Birdie nonsense has gotten to my head." I use the side of my head to hold my phone in place. I change out of my school clothes into a fitted pair of jeans and a tucked in, gray turtleneck. "I shouldn't have done that, though. I don't know what I was thinking."

"Jude will be fine. Whether or not he's Little Birdie, he definitely sent in that video, and probably the picture of you and Zayne on the Ferris wheel, too, now that you mention it. All you did was confront him. I see nothing wrong with that."

"I guess." I try to shove down the heavy guilt in my stomach. "But he's Zayne's friend. I feel kinda bad."

"Speaking of Zayne," she says, jumping on the change of topic. "Where is he taking you for your first date?"

I glance at my reflection in my mirror, biting my lip in anticipation. "I don't know. It's a surprise."

"You better tell me all about it when you get back," she says. "I'm going to need a fresh, new distraction."

"Sure," I mutter. "If you don't hear about it from Little Birdie first."

Beau knocks on my door. "Dot?"

"I'll call you later, Rue," I say into the phone.

"Bye," she says, and I hang up.

Beau opens the door, and I frown when I notice his brows drawn together. His mouth pinched together in worry. "What's up?"

"Have you talked to Aunt Lucille?"

I try to think back to my last conversation with my aunt, but I come up empty. "No. But I've been in contact with Mom. She's supposed to come home tomorrow because the play is next week. I can't believe we get to see her. I know I was worried before about her not being ready to come home, but I think it's been long enough, don't you?"

"I guess," Beau says, waving my chatter away with his hand. "But have you talked to *Aunt Lucille*?"

"I already said no." I feel a prick of irritation at him. Mom is coming home. *Mom.* It's been so long since we've seen her. I don't want anything to ruin it.

"Well, neither have I," he says. "She hasn't returned any of my messages, and I think it's fishy. What are the odds that I can't get ahold of her right before Mom comes home?"

"What does it matter, Beau?" I freshen my mascara with a new coat while he prattles on.

"It matters a lot. What if Mom isn't ready to come home? Shouldn't we talk to Aunt Lucille first? Find out if she's being honest about her progress?"

"I get why you're worried, but I trust Mom. And so should you." The words come out a little harsher than I intend them, especially since I don't fully trust Mom's judgement, but I don't care. I need to see her. I miss her. It's been longer than any of us has wanted, and part of me is worried her coming back is too good to be true. In fact, I'm much more worried about her not showing up at all than lying about her progress. She wouldn't do something like that after all this time.

I refuse to let Beau's cynical suspicions become my worries, too.

"I'm trying to get ready for a date. So, if there's anything else you want to dissect, maybe you should call Dad."

"Whatever," he mutters. He stomps out of my room and slams the door. A pinprick of guilt pokes me, but my desire to see Mom is stronger. Let Beau overthink things. He'll see. Everything will be fine. Mom will come home, she'll see the play, and then she'll return to Aunt Lucille's to continue treatment. If she were in an actual rehabilitation facility, coming home might not be an option yet. He should be grateful.

My phone rings. When I see Zayne's name on the screen, butterflies dance in my stomach. I answer his call, shaking away my irritation with Beau so I don't sound rude when I talk. "Are you here?"

"Yeah, I'm right outside," he says. "You ready?"

"Just about. See you in a minute." I hang up the phone and grab my purse. I add a scarf and leather jacket to my outfit before heading outside. Zayne is sitting in his idle car, parked on the street in front of my house. When I get in the passenger seat, I notice he's wearing a grey shirt with buttons, and jeans. "You look nice."

He tugs on the end of one of my braids. "So do you."

"Now do I get to know where we're going?"

"Nope." He flashes a grin. "But the sooner you put your seatbelt on, the sooner you'll get to find out."

"Fine." A smile tugs at my lips as he starts driving. "I'm so excited to see my mom tomorrow."

"I bet. I can't wait to meet her."

"She'll like you."

"She's okay with you having a boyfriend?"

I laugh. "Oh, yeah. My mom isn't very strict. Never has been. She's supportive to the end. Same with my dad."

"You're lucky to have parents like that," he says. "Not many others do."

"I know." I stare at my lap. I can't help that my mind goes to Carlton. I know how much pressure his parents put on him to lead the life they envisioned for him. I'm not sure if he wants it too, or if everything he does, if all his efforts are exhausted to make his parents proud.

Zayne parks in front of a building with a flashing neon sign in the window that reads *Nickel City.*

"What's this place?" I ask, squinting at the window, trying to peek inside. "I've never heard of it."

"Somehow I knew that would be the case." Zayne offers me a sideways grin. "This, Dot, is the best place in Boston to have some fun."

He gets out of the car, and my stomach somersaults when he walks around to open my door for me. The cold wind stings my cheeks, blowing my scarf around. I step out, blushing as he takes my hand. "Is it made out of nickels or something?"

He shakes his head. "No. It's full of really fun games, and each one only costs a nickel to play."

"Huh."

"Don't judge it until you've played." He taps my nose. "And try not to get attached either. This place is closing down for good in a few months."

"Why?"

He shrugs. "Not enough business, I guess. It's a shame. I've been coming here since I was a kid."

I look at the retro-style building, complete with a giant, illustrated nickel painted on the window, and try to imagine Zayne coming here as a kid, probably with Lenny, excited and holding a bag of nickels. I can't help but smile. "Let's go play!"

He smiles widely and puts his arm around my shoulder. "I'm going to kick your butt at air hockey."

"Probably," I agree. "I suck at air hockey."

"Woah. Don't go doubting yourself already. At least put on a poker face. Make me think the match will be a challenge."

I laugh. "Sorry. Tonight is our break from acting, remember?"

Zayne shakes his head in mock sadness as we walk inside. "But that's the best way to be a good actor. To be acting at all times. Even on your day off."

I know he's joking, but the words bring me back to Rue's statement about Fallbrook actors dating each other to improve their skills. Now that I'm thinking about it again, it's hard to stop. I try to smile, but it feels too forced, so I let it drop from my face.

Zayne doesn't seem to notice. He's inserting his debit card into a vending machine, which sprays out a pile of nickels for us to play games with.

The interior of this place has fun, bright orange carpet with blue accent walls. A variety of arcade-style games are peppered throughout the space, and there's a prize counter along the far back wall. A cluster of younger kids are currently dominating the virtual-reality station. A mom and toddler are trying their hand at a game with a gopher head appearing through one of several holes at random. As soon as it appears through one, the toddler bops it on the head with the attached hammer and laughs. A lone older man is in a concentrated trance as he tries to get his nickel to land on a bullseye slot from its narrow entry point.

Zayne and I make our way to the air hockey table, and he puts a nickel in. "You're going down," he says with a straight face.

I laugh, some of the uneasiness I'm experiencing falling away. "Probably."

I pick up the plastic paddle and ready myself for him to

shoot the puck at my goal. I'm ready to block him, tensed and waiting, but somehow he scores anyway.

"Wow," says Zayne. "You weren't kidding."

I cringe. "Told you."

We play for a grand total of five minutes before victory is his. And when he wins at the next three different games we play, I start to see a pattern form. "You know, I'm not sure this place is what it's cracked up to be after all."

Zayne smirks. "Don't be a sore loser." He pulls me in by the hand and kisses me. I shut my eyes, letting my hands slide out of his and up the front of his shirt until they reach his face. *This is so much better than playing stupid games*, I think, and start to pull away to tell him that, when I see someone staring hard at us over Zayne's shoulder.

My posture goes rigid.

Carlton.

Chapter Twenty-Two

"What are you doing here?" I blurt the words before I can stop myself. Zayne frowns at me before realization makes him turn around and face Carlton.

"This is a public place." Carlton's tone is clipped, his expression cold and stony. "I can be here if I want to."

"You're just...playing games alone at *Nickel City?*" There's a barely contained laugh in Zayne's voice, like he finds the situation hilarious. I squeeze his hand in warning.

"Who says I'm alone?" Carlton arches a brow and nods his head toward the prize counter, where Meredith and Mabel are turning in tickets.

"Oh," Zayne says like it makes perfect sense. "Got it. The thought of being alone with you was so repulsive, your girlfriend had to bring her sister along."

Carlton balls his hand into a fist. "Watch it, Silverman."

I tug on Zayne's hand. "Come on. Let's just go." Carlton's eyes travel from my face to my hand connected to Zayne's, and I swear, I detect a trace of pain in his eyes.

"Fine," Zayne mutters. "Let's go."

"I was hoping I could have a word with you, Dot." Carlton sounds annoyed, like he would rather be doing anything else in the world than asking me to talk to him. But he also sounds kind of desperate.

I can't help the curiosity that takes residence in me. I look at Zayne, trying to gauge what he thinks, and he gives me a look. One that says, *it's up to you, not me.*

I sigh. "Fine."

Zayne lets go of my hand, and I follow Carlton to an empty table. I lower myself into the orange faux leather seat, and Carlton does the same. "Thanks for hearing me out."

"How did you know I was here?"

He purses his lips and takes out his phone, showing me a map on his screen. His contact photo for me hovers over our current location on the map. "You shared your location with me, remember?"

My memory flashes to a moment we shared in my room after he kissed me for the first time. Us exchanging contact info and locations. "Wow," I say. "Thanks for reminding me to fix that." My back is facing Zayne, so I glance over my shoulder to see him leaning against a pillar next to the air hockey game, his arms crossed as he waits for me and Carlton to finish talking.

"I hate him," Carlton says, startling me, and my gaze darts to his face.

"I know. You've told me. What do you want to talk about?"

I can tell by his scowl that he doesn't like that I'm rushing him, that I'm not questioning why he hates Zayne or trying to defend the reasons why I *don't* to him.

But I don't care. My days of adjusting my personality to cater to him are over.

Carlton releases a harsh exhale of breath. "My parents are splitting up."

I stare at him in shocked silence. Some of the tightness in my chest evaporates. "I'm sorry." I may be angry at him, at the way he's treated me, but I'm not going to pretend I don't care about him at all. About his life, or what happens to him. After all, he was there for me during an extremely difficult time of my life.

I wonder if that's why he's telling me this—because he was there for me, and now he expects me to be there for him.

As if he can read my mind, he says, "I'm telling you because I need your advice."

"*My* advice?" I furrow my brow. "For what?"

"I don't know anyone else with a split household that I feel comfortable talking to. I know your parents aren't divorced, but your mom isn't home with you."

Irritation seeps into my bones at the reminder. "Yeah. So what?"

He blinks a long, heavy blink. "I need advice," he repeats, "on how you do it. How you cope without your mom. Because mine is about to move out for good."

"Oh." I lean back in my seat. Turn his words over in my

mind. And then smile sadly at him. "The truth is that I *don't* cope, Carlton. I don't cope at all. I miss my mom more than I can express." I reach over and hesitate before patting his hand. He stares at it like it holds the answers to the world. "But having friends to spend my time with helps."

He meets my gaze, apology and regret written in every line of his face. "Dot…"

"I know." I don't need him to apologize. "It's alright." I stand up and start walking away from the table, but then remember something and turn back. "You know where to find me." I offer the word to him like a white flag. "If you need to talk again. But you better not press charges against Zayne."

His stoic face remains so for a long moment, before cracking into something resembling a smile. "Fine. And thanks."

I nod at him. When I turn around, Mabel and Meredith are standing in front of me. Meredith's face is unreadable, but Mabel beams at me, practically bursting at the seams. "Hi," she mouths, bringing her hand up into a wave.

"Hey." I can't help but smile back.

"See you at school?" she asks. In her voice, I can hear what she's not saying. *Meredith isn't mad at you anymore. We can hang out again.*

"Yeah." I can't hide the hope in my voice. "Sounds good."

She grins, linking her arm through Meredith's, and they pass me to go sit with Carlton.

I walk back over to Zayne, who cocks his head in the direction I came. "Everything okay?"

"Yes," I say, and I mean it. I lace my fingers through his, swinging our hands as we walk. "Everything is great."

Zayne and I spend all our nickels over the course of two hours. We play all the games in the arcade, and I lose every time. Still, there's a giant grin plastered on my face as I get in the car.

That is, until Beau starts calling. He knows I'm out with Zayne so I can't imagine what would be important enough to justify him calling, but I answer the phone. "What's up, Beau?"

"You need to come home."

His words send my mind into a stir. "Why? We're about to go eat."

When he answers, his voice drops, like he's trying to keep our conversation hidden from someone. "Mom is here."

My stomach does a flip. "What?" I must have misheard him. He couldn't have possibly just said what I think he did.

"Mom came home a day early." He annunciates each syllable with emphasis. "She says she wanted it to be a surprise."

I hang up the phone in a complete daze. I stare out the windshield at the fresh dusk, my eyes wide. When I turn to Zayne, my voice sounds like a whisper. "My mom is home."

It takes a moment for the words to sink in. "Seriously?" His curious expression transforms into a huge grin. "Dot, that's awesome!"

"I know, but we were supposed to go eat—"

"Are you kidding?" He shakes his head at me. "It's *your mom*, Dot. This is huge. Hasn't it been like, months since you've seen her?"

"Almost six months," I say, my voice drifting off into a whisper.

"Exactly."

I reach over and grab his hand. "You're the best."

He lifts our joined hands to kiss my fingers.

Time flies by as we drive. My thoughts whirl in my head as Zayne turns onto my street, and when he parks in front of my house, I take a deep breath. He takes my face in his hands, rubbing my cheek with his thumb. His warm eyes stare into mine, filling me with steadiness and determination. "She's going to be so happy to see you," he murmurs.

"I know. Sorry about our date."

"Don't be. We can eat together anytime." He brings my face to his and kisses me. My heart flutters, sending adrenaline surging through my body. I glide my hands along his neck and deepen the kiss until the only audible sound in the car is my pulse hammering in my ears.

We break away at the same time, but our faces are still close, our eyes still partly shut. "You should go," Zayne whispers. I nod but make no move to do so. He laughs softly and lets go of me, grinning and shooing me away with his hand. "Go, Dot."

I open the door and step out. "I'll text you."

And then I run to the front door, my heart leaping with every step that brings me closer to it.

When my hand is hovering over the knob, I wait a few moments, standing there and catching my breath. I'm winded from kissing Zayne and from the anticipation coursing through my veins, wondering if what Beau said could possibly be true.

"You got this," I whisper to myself. "You got—"

The front door swings open and standing on the other side, she's right there—tall and strong, with a bright smile just for me.

"Mom!" I leap over the threshold and wrap my arms around her waist. To my surprise, she feels skinnier. I lean back to get another look at her. She looks the same as she always does, but there's a bead of sweat pooling on her upper brow despite the winter chill.

"Bardot!" She squeezes me back and runs her elegant, calloused fingers along my braids, lifting them and letting them fall against my back. "My baby girl. I missed you so much." She presses her face into my forehead, staying there.

"I missed you, too." I don't even realize I'm crying until the wind hits the moisture on my face. Embarrassed, I wipe it with my sleeve. "I didn't know you were coming home early."

She beams. "Surprise."

Beau catches my eye over her shoulder. His lips are pursed, his expression wary, bordering on a scowl. *What is his problem?*

"Come inside, sweetie." Mom keeps her arm around me, and we walk into the house together. "Let me make you something to eat. You hungry?"

"Yes," I admit. "I skipped eating out with Zayne so I could get here."

She starts up the stove. I can't stop staring at her. It's bizarre to see her in this house, tangible and vibrant, standing right in front of me. She barely spent more than two weeks here before she left for rehabilitation, so this house probably still feels completely new to her. I'm almost scared to blink, lest this turns out to be a hallucination instead of reality. "Zayne," she repeats. "He the boy you're in the play with?"

"Yeah." My face gets warm. I haven't yet filled her in on how much things have changed between me and Carlton. And Zayne.

"He's also her boyfriend now," Beau mutters from the corner of the kitchen. He's leaning against the wall with his arms crossed.

Mom raises her brows at me as she stirs something in a pot. "Is that right? I can't wait to meet him."

"Does Aunt Lucille know you're here?" Beau blurts the question like it's been boiling inside him. Part of me wants to strangle him for being so agitated right now. It's spoiling the moment.

"Beau, come taste this," she says, blowing on the spoon and holding it out to him. It's as if she didn't hear his question. "Tell me if it needs more seasoning."

Beau sighs in frustration before rolling off the wall and

reaching for the spoon. He samples the food and with a shrug mumbles, "It tastes great, Mom."

She smiles and opens the fridge, pulling vegetables out. "That's going to be the perfect base for the soup I'm making."

I brighten. "Soup sounds great." I scoot a chair out from the table and sit. "So, how's it been at Aunt Lucille's? Tell me about what you've been up to the past couple months."

She pushes her short curls away from her face with the back of her hand. "Oh, you know. Just been doing my best. But it's hard out there in the middle of nowhere. It kinda feels like I'm losing touch with reality sometimes." She smiles at me again, but it's a sad smile this time. My stomach feels like it's been wrung out by a pair of hands. "Being here makes me feel human again. I haven't seen anyone but my sister in much too long."

I swallow back the knot in my throat. "I'm happy you're back," I say.

Beau clears his throat. "That's great, Mom. But you still haven't answered my question as to whether she even knows you're here. As to whether you're *okay* being here, yet."

I glare at him. "Beau, stop. Of course she's okay to be here. She wouldn't have come otherwise. Right, Mom?"

But before she can answer, the front door unlocks and opens, producing Dad. The kitchen goes silent as he walks in, taking in Mom standing at the stove, wooden spoon in hand. I have no idea what thoughts are running through his head as he stares at her, but in one swift movement, he lifts her off the ground without a word, hugging her as they spin in a circle.

It's such a beautiful sight.

And I'm crying again. I elbow Beau, who is also watching them with a softer expression than I've seen on his face since I came home. "Come on. Let's let them catch up."

"Yeah." He blinks, lost in the moment we're witnessing, and then nods. He follows me down the hall to my room. I plop down on my bed and Beau sits at the foot. He stares hard at the ground, his guarded and annoyed glare once again present.

I can't take it anymore.

"What's wrong with you?" I demand. "What's with the attitude? The interrogations, when Mom just got here?"

He shakes his head at me. "I have a bad feeling about her being here. I don't think she's ready. If she were in a rehabilitation facility, she wouldn't even be allowed to visit us yet."

"But she's not in a facility!" I throw my hands in the air. "That was the whole point of her staying with her sister. So she could call us when she wants to, and come home for important stuff, like the play."

"I guess." He shrugs. "But what if she..." He trails off, unable to complete the sentence. But I know what he's going to say. *Relapses. What if she relapses?*

I don't blame him for worrying, because the possibility is unthinkable, unfathomable after all this time we've spent apart. After all the effort toward progress she's made thus far.

"She won't." I try to sound firm. Confident. "She'll be fine, Beau. It's a short visit. Everything will be perfect."

"Then why," he asks, his lips forming a pout, "won't she answer any of my questions?"

"Just give her time." I stand up, beckoning him to join me. "Besides, don't you know what this means?"

"What?"

I grin. "No more of Dad's cooking for a while."

Chapter Twenty-Three

It's hard to focus on school when Monday comes. With Mom being home, the last thing I want to do is spend six hours of my day at school. It sucks. I wish I could just take time off while she's here, but there's no way that will fly with Fallbrook or Mr. Saltzman. This week is full of dress rehearsals, and I've been warned against missing a single one of them.

Somehow, I manage to get through homeroom, break, and my first set of classes without too much moping. When the lunch bell finally rings, I make my way to the cafeteria. The smell of lasagna fills my lungs, making my mouth water. I grab a tray and get in line.

"Hey, Dot."

I glance over my shoulder. It's Mabel, wearing a hopeful but subdued expression. The collar of her uniform peeks out from the neckline of her sweater, and her brown hair is in two braids draped gracefully over her shoulders.

I lift my hand. "Hi."

"It was nice seeing you at *Nickel City.*" The words hold a soft note of caution, like she isn't sure if I'm willing to talk to her or not.

"Same here." I hesitate before continuing. It's hard to be mad at her for distancing herself. After all, if she'd ditched Meredith to hang with me and Rue, Meredith wouldn't have had either of them. But that doesn't mean I liked it. "To be honest, Mabel, I've missed hanging out with you."

At that, the corner of her mouth lifts. An invisible, arbitrary barrier between us seems to fall away. "I have too. It seems like forever since we've caught up."

"I know. My mom came back home for a few weeks. She'll be here to see the play."

Her eyes widen. "What? No way." She reaches up and touches my arm. "That's amazing."

Before I can answer, Meredith approaches us, cutting in front of the line that's formed behind us as she stands next to her sister. Her gaze is somehow both accusing and indifferent as it lands on me.

Mabel elbows her. "Dot's mom came home to see the play."

"How nice," says Meredith. "Especially since you're playing the lead."

Mabel claps. "Are you going to the Winter Formal on Saturday? I ordered my dress a while ago, but it's not going to come in time. We should all go dress shopping after school." Her eyes flit to a spot at my right. "You too, Rue!"

My eyes dart up to find Rue hovering next to me. I didn't even see her come over here. Her cheeks flush red, deepening when her gaze flicks to Meredith's before landing on the floor. "Um, I don't know. I already have a dress," she says.

"You should come anyway. It will be fun," Mabel insists. "Just like old times."

I want to tell her how much I doubt that will be the case, and I also don't want to miss out on any time with Mom while she's here. She *just* got back.

But the last thing I want to do is stir the pot when things are finally opening back up between us. So instead, I grin. "I haven't bought mine yet. I'm in."

I set my lunch tray down between Zayne's and Lenny's. Before I can take a seat at our table, Lenny hones in on my side of coleslaw. "Are you going to eat that?"

I remove the bowl of coleslaw from my tray and push it across the table toward him. "I'm going dress shopping with the girls after school," I tell Zayne.

He arches an eyebrow. "Wow. I thought for sure Meredith would try to have you kidnapped if you talked to her again."

"I know right?" I snicker. "She didn't seem pleased but she didn't protest, either."

"Wait, dress shopping?" Zayne's eyes round in feign confusion. "Does this mean we're going to the dance together?"

I suppress a laugh and pretend to look around. "I could always ask Carlton if you're not down."

"Oh, yeah?" He shakes his head, biting back a grin. "That's too bad. Because I already got our tickets and picked out a corsage for you. Guess I'll have to give it to Lenny."

His brother swallows his latest bite of coleslaw and says, "As long as it's not made with daffodils. I'm allergic."

I laugh. "He's kidding, Len. At least, he better be." I lean closer to Zayne. "Because I'm really looking forward to going with you."

A dimpled grin flashes across his lips before he closes the distance between us with a kiss. I shift my body on the bench to face him, hitching my knee up and over the seat so I can wrap my arms around his neck. He parts my lips, and I melt a little. Kissing Zayne feels like the sun hitting my skin for the first time after a rainy day. I tighten my arms around him. His hands travel from my waist up my back before landing on my knee.

Lenny's voice cuts through my senses. "Does kissing with food in your mouth make it taste any better?"

Zayne breaks apart from our embrace to glare across the table at him. "You really know how to kill a moment, man."

I laugh. "Your kisses always taste like coffee and fresh cake." And then I blush, because the words kind of just slipped out.

But he chuckles. "That would be Mimi. She always gives us leftover restaurant sweets for breakfast."

"Did you invite her to Thanksgiving yet?" Lenny asks Zayne.

"Believe it or not, I was getting there."

Lenny pauses and taps his chin. "I believe it."

Zayne turns back to me. "My mom and Mimi are cooking up a storm for Thanksgiving and they would love for you and your family to come." He half smiles. "There will be coffee and fresh cake. You won't even have to kiss me to get a taste of it."

I play with his hand, still resting on my leg. "And what if I want to?"

"I'm not going to stop you."

"I'd love for us to come, but let me double check with my parents," I say. *My parents.* It's the first time in so long I've been able to ask for their permission as a unit, instead of just Dad's.

His half-smile transforms into a full-force grin. My heart thuds a little unsteadily in response.

When we're finished with our lunches, we spend the rest of the break running our lines back and forth, right there at the lunch table. At first it's embarrassing. I don't like the way random pairs of eyes from around the cafeteria seem to watch us, but Zayne makes a good point, stating, "If you can't do it in a noisy cafeteria, it will be even harder once you get onstage and everyone's paying attention."

Lenny chimes in occasionally, disrupting my train of thought, but by the time the bell rings, I feel a sense of accomplishment. Zayne is such a good teacher, it will be impossible to mess up my lines during the play. But even more than that, I feel a sense of freedom. It's crazy how pretending to be someone else can make me feel more myself than ever.

My remaining classes pass in a blur, and dress rehearsal goes smoothly. I ignore Carlton and he ignores me. It's like a civil, mutual understanding between us after our talk. Mr. Saltzman actually claps after one of my scenes with Meredith, and she—dare I say it—cracks a smile at me.

Zayne walks me to my car after rehearsal, and Mabel and Rue walk along with us. "I'm just going to go home and change first," I tell the girls, "and then I'll text you when I'm on my way to the dress place."

"Sounds good." Mabel beams.

After she and Rue leave, Zayne tugs me against him by the hand. "What color dress are you going to pick?"

"I have no idea. Probably yellow, since it's my favorite color."

"I can't wait to see it." He smiles and kisses the end of my nose.

I jerk the lock open in the front door when I get home. I half expect the smell of Mom's cooking to float through the entryway when I step inside, but I'm met with nothing but silence and an empty hallway. "Mom?" I walk through the tidy kitchen to the living room, where she's on her hands and knees. My heart thuds at the sight. "Mom, are you alright?"

She straightens when she hears my voice, standing up like the floor just burned her. "Hey, baby," she says. The words tumble out in a hoarse rush, but she smiles and meets my gaze without effort. "How was school?"

"Fine." I chew my lip as a sinking, unwanted suspicion strikes me. "What were you doing on the ground? You're not...having a hard time, are you?"

Her eyes widen. "No! Of course not, sweetie. I was just looking for my earring. Darn backing came loose. It must have fallen off somewhere around here."

I nod, wanting to believe her. Wanting so badly, but unable to shake my fears away. "Maybe you should get some rest."

"Dot, honey, I'm fine." Her smile wears thin.

"Okay." My brain scrambles for a change of subject. "Guess what? Zayne's family invited us over for Thanksgiving. I told him I'd ask you first."

Her face lights up. "Really? That sounds lovely. Tell him we'd love to come."

I smile faintly. "Okay. And there's a dance at school on Saturday. Zayne's taking me, and my friends want to go dress shopping in a few."

"Dress shopping?" She straightens her spine. "You should let me take you. This is your first school dance, Bardot. This is a big deal."

"Oh." I shift my weight from one foot to the other. "But my friends want to take me. I think they're finally ready to start talking to me again."

She frowns and places her arm on my shoulder, and together we walk to the kitchen. "Honey, those friends of yours sound manipulative. I don't like it."

"What?" My stomach churns with a sense of disappointment I wasn't expecting. My mom's reaction seems off kilter. I thought she would be happy the twins are ready to be friends with me again. "They're not manipulative. It was just a misunderstanding."

"*I'll* take you dress shopping. That's the end of it, okay?"

Her tone and words stun me into silence. Lips parted, I stare at her. Study her. I have no idea what to say. She's never acted like this with me before. Controlling. Unreasonable. I don't recognize her at all.

Mom ushers me toward the front door. "I'll meet you in the car. I just need to grab my purse."

My brows draw together in confusion. "We're going right now? I just got home. I'm not ready. I need to change first." There's no way I'd be caught dead at the mall still wearing my school uniform.

"If we leave now, we'll beat traffic." She all but shoves me out the front door, grabbing my cardigan for me off the coat rack in the entryway. My heart hammers in my chest as the realization sinks in. *She's lying. She is having a hard time.*

Still on the doorstep, I take out my phone and text Beau. Part of me wants to hide her behavior from him, if only so he won't be able to say, *I told you so.*

But there are more important things than being proved wrong, and this is one of them.

ME

Where are you?

BEAU

Just left detention. Texted in class.
Please don't tell Mom or Dad.

Detention? Seriously?

ME

Won't the school tell them anyway?

BEAU

I gave the school your number so you'll probably be getting a call at some point. What do you need?

I resist the urge to roll my eyes, trying to focus on the matter at hand. I hesitate, staring at the screen before typing the message.

ME

Mom is acting strange. What should I do?

BEAU

Just play it cool till I can get ahold of Dad or Aunt Lucille I guess.

ME

Wait, don't tell Dad. He seems so happy that she's back. I don't want to worry him in case it's nothing.

BEAU

K.

The front door opens behind me and Mom comes out with her purse slung across her body. She grins at me and walks past me to get to the car. "Let's go."

I follow her and get in the passenger seat. *Play it cool. Just play it cool.*

"Thanks for taking me." The words come out almost as

light as I intend them. If she detects any traces of unease in my tone, she doesn't show it.

"Absolutely. Do you know what color dress you want? I'm thinking an ice blue or forest green would look lovely on you."

I abandon my ideas of yellow and offer her a weak nod. "That sounds perfect."

We drive toward the mall. I stare out the window, watching the occasional dog and owner walk by, or a kid on a bike as we draw nearer. The day is warm with a cool breeze, and I pull down the sleeves of my mustard cardigan from my elbows to my wrists so I can fiddle with the edge. I send a group text to Mable and Rue.

ME

Not going to make it. Sorry guys. :(

MABEL

What??

RUE

How come?

ME

My mom wants to take me. She wouldn't take no for an answer. I feel bad, I'm sorry.

RUE

Oh. That's okay, Dot.

MABEL

Have fun with your mom and send us pics of your dress!!!

I feel an immense sense of relief that they aren't mad. I release my breath and try to stay positive. There might not be anything wrong with Mom. Maybe she's just in a funk.

When we reach the mall, Mom finds a parking spot near the entrance of her favorite department store. We make our way toward it through the parking lot. Under different circumstances, I'd find this outing exciting. After all, a shopping day with her would have sounded like a dream come true to me yesterday, or last week. Part of me is happy to be spending time with her at all, but the overwhelming worry surging through me right now is much stronger than any positive emotion.

The automatic doors open for us as we step into the brightly lit, colorful store. Special occasion dresses adorn the walls in a seasonal display, and the smell of expensive perfume tickles my nose. The hum of chatter buzzes in my ears as we gravitate toward the nearest cluster of dresses.

"Look at this one, Bardot," Mom says, pulling a ruby red gown off the rack. "You would look exquisite in this dress."

The compliment warms me, but still I'm on edge. "What happened to ice blue or forest green?"

She clicks. "You should at least try it on. I'll hold onto it while we keep looking." She folds the dress over her arm and sucks her lip in concentration as she shifts several garments around on the rack. She shows me a strapless black gown made of a sleek, silky material, and a baby pink dress covered in shimmery sequins. We even find a sparkly yellow one that makes my cheeks lift into a smile. When she finally finds dresses in her coveted color palette, we go to the dressing room. For a moment, it feels like old times, when she'd take me shopping for outfits resembling those I'd find and fall in love with online and in fashion magazines.

Mom hangs up the dresses on the hook in our stall and I slip out of my school uniform. We have the kind of relationship that prevents me from being embarrassed to undress in front of her. *But apparently not the kind that allows her to be honest with me.*

"You can never go wrong with classic red," she tells me as I pull the thick fabric up my body. "It's the ultimate eye-catcher."

I look in the mirror once the zipper is in place. The dress is indeed eye-catching, almost loud in a way that screams, *Look at me!*

"I don't know," I tell her, fiddling with the thin shoulder straps. "It seems like a bit much."

She shakes her head. "No such thing. Bardot, this dress is the one."

"But it's the first one I've tried on." I gesture to the others still hanging on the wall. "Let's at least see the rest."

She sighs, her shoulders drooping on her exhale, but she hands me each dress, and I try them on one-by-one. The black, silky one is "too mature" and apparently the forest green dress washes me out. To my surprise, I'm not a huge fan of the way the yellow dress looks once I'm wearing it. But as soon as the ice blue gown is in place, my insides flood with warmth. "Mom," I whisper, "I love it." I take out my phone and capture this moment on my camera for the girls, hitting *send*.

The dress is the perfect shade of blue, understated in a way that highlights my features, hugging all the right places. It's made in a comfortable, stretchy fabric that also appears to be high quality.

"It's not as good as the red one," she states.

I spin away from my reflection to face her. "What are you talking about? It's perfect!"

But Mom is shaking her head, a troubled expression plain on her face. "No, no, it's no good, Bardot. I'm not letting you go to that dance in anything less than what you deserve." She stands and picks up her purse before reaching for the red dress hanging on the wall. "I'll go pay for this while you change." She rushes from the dressing room before I'm able to process her words.

"Mom!"

But the door closes behind her and as her footsteps retreat, I'm left staring at my stricken face, glossy eyes, and parted lips in the mirror.

Is she for real?

I half expect her to come rushing back to the dressing room, apology fresh on her lips, ready to buy me the dress I'm currently wearing. The dress I actually like. But instead, the silence surrounding me is a presence heavier than the pit in my stomach.

I study the beautiful, ice blue garment on my body as if I can somehow will it to never come off. When I slip out of it, I don't even bother taking it with me. I just leave it hanging on the wall in the dressing room.

I search for Mom once I exit the stall, finding no one except a mother pushing a stroller with a whining, small child in it. I walk around until I catch sight of the back of her red coat near the register in the center of the store. She turns when I approach her, bag in hand and wearing a smile void of guilt. "Ready, sweetie?" She squeezes my shoulder and we walk toward the exit together.

I think about the dance this Saturday. I think about the way Mom is acting, how excited I was for her to be here, and how I now just want the next few weeks to hurry up and pass. Because this woman isn't my mother. At least, not the mother I remember.

"Ready," I say.

I shove the dress in my closet when I get home. I don't even want to look at it. Even worse, when I check my phone I see several texts from Mabel and Rue, gushing over the picture I sent them of me wearing the blue dress.

I call Zayne, speaking into the phone as soon as he answers. "My mom is driving me crazy."

"What do you mean? How is that possible?"

"Something's up with her," I say through the thickness in my throat. "I don't know. She just seems different."

His voice is gentle. "Hey, calm down. Don't worry. She's probably just adjusting to being back, right?"

I nod, though I know he can't tell. "Yeah. What are you doing right now?"

"I was just reading. Do you need me to come over?"

Someone knocks on my door. "It's me," Beau says.

"No, that's alright. Get back to your book, you nerd."

Zayne doesn't mistake the fondness in my voice. He laughs. "Bye."

I open the door. "Please tell me you got ahold of Aunt Lucille."

"Nope," he says. He holds up his phone to show me the massive amounts of messages he's sent her with no response. "Ready to talk to Dad yet?"

I bite my lip. "No. Let's just see how things go from here. Maybe she's just having an off day."

He sighs dramatically. "Fine."

Chapter Twenty-Four

Mom seems fine over the next two days. There's no school because Thanksgiving is on Thursday, so we actually get to spend time together. We cook a stockpile of meals to go in the freezer so we'll have food after she leaves. She paints my nails. I braid her hair and she takes it out because her scalp is sensitive. We play a board game as a family when Dad comes home from work. Beau's pouting is replaced by smiles and laughter for once.

Things feel almost normal again. They're better than I remember them being in a long time. It feels like I'm living life as the old Dot, back in Stockbridge, before our life collapsed.

My parents go on a date the afternoon of Thanksgiving. They're overdue; I can't remember the last time they went out alone. It must have been before Mom became addicted to painkillers. Since we're having dinner at the Silvermans' this evening, they decided to go to the movies. Dad told me and Beau to be ready to leave by the time they get back.

When I get out of the shower, I hang some outfit ideas on my clothing rack and rub apple-scented lotion into my damp skin. I'm about to sit at my vanity to put on makeup, but my phone vibrates on my bed. I pick it up, and the name displayed on the screen makes my eyes widen.

Aunt Lucille. Beau must have finally gotten ahold of her.

I answer the call. "Hello?"

"Thank goodness," she says, through several breathy gasps. "I'm so glad you answered, Bardot."

I'm ready to tell her my concerns about Mom, but my stomach does a flip at her anxious tone. "Everything okay, Aunty?"

"Well, I sure hope so. It's taken me days to find my phone, and your mama didn't even text me to let me know if she made it there safely."

A surge of relief makes its way through me. "So, you know she's here."

"Of course I know." Her voice lowers. "But that doesn't mean I'm okay with it, Bardot. Especially after the argument we had right before she walked out my door. And then my phone *disappeared.*"

My relief vanishes like smoke evaporating into air. "You got in a fight? You didn't want her to come here?" I shut my eyes, not wanting to believe what I'm about to ask next. "Did Mom *hide* your phone, Aunty? So we wouldn't find out you told her no?"

There's a pause of silence. "Is your dad around? I should probably be telling this to him."

"Oh. I'll, uh, pass the message along."

Aunt Lucille sighs. "I can't tell you for sure if she hid my phone, honey. But one thing I do know is that she's not ready. Too late now, but keep a close eye on her. If she starts getting irritable, lying, acting moody, restless, or off, then you know something's up. Also, watch out for signs of your mama vomiting or sweating more than usual."

I squeeze my eyes shut, memories of Mom displaying more than a few of those symptoms flying across my vision. "Okay. Bye." I hang up the phone.

It's one thing to worry about Mom's progress, or have Beau doubt her and insist she's not well enough to take a break from rehabilitation. It's another to have Aunt Lucille flat-out confirm our worries and suspicions. After all, she's the one who's been around Mom twenty-four-seven, tending to her and helping her with the recovery program.

It hurts to hear. And though I know I'd be foolish to deny her words as truth, I can't bear to accept them. Not with the play only a week away.

Mom will be fine until then. And she'll go right back after.

Picking up my phone again, I delete the phone call I just had with my aunt from my call history.

Just in case.

"Opal, do you have my house keys?" Dad asks Mom. He pats his pockets as we get out of the car, parked in front of

Zayne's house. The air is crisp and cool, blowing maple leaves and the scent of pumpkin, coffee, and home-cooked dinner up and around us. The sun is starting to go down, and I grin back at the toothy, rotting jack-o-lantern on Zayne's front porch.

"Honey, your keys are in my purse, remember?" Mom says. She chuckles at my father and links her arm through mine. "I haven't had someone cook *me* Thanksgiving dinner since I was a child. This is going to be so nice."

"I hope they have cranberry sauce," Beau says, a note of hope in his voice. Despite his concerns about Mom, I can tell it's hard for him not to be excited about this evening. I'm trying my best to maintain a positive attitude after talking to Aunt Lucille, because a few months ago the idea of having a family Thanksgiving with Mom home would have seemed unfathomable. Yet, here she is, arm in mine as Beau and Dad follow behind us to the Silverman's front door.

"I'm sure there will be cranberry sauce," I tell Beau. "The Silvermans have a restaurant, after all."

Dad stops walking at our side. He squints at me. "You brought the cider, right Dot?"

"I got it," says Beau.

Mom reaches over and pats Dad's shoulder. "Relax, Paul. You're all wound up."

His joints seem to loosen under her touch. "Sorry. Just hungry."

I knock on the front door, the pinecone wreath hanging on it shuddering. Anticipation flutters in my stomach as I hear footsteps approach.

When Zayne opens the door, our eyes lock, and the flutters in my stomach seem to triple. A grin spreads across his lips. "Hi."

"Hey," I say. My own smile is unavoidable. Our gazes are locked on one another for a long second before he takes in my family standing on the porch with me. If he's nervous to meet them, he's hidden it well behind his friendly smile.

"Please, come in," he tells my parents, moving aside so they can cross the threshold. Mom hangs her coat and bag in the entryway, and Zayne shakes her hand and Dad's. "It's nice to meet you both. I'm Zayne. Thanks for coming."

"Absolutely," Mom says. "I've been so excited to meet you."

Dad nods and adds, "I can smell the food, man. My mouth is watering already."

Zayne laughs. "Thanks. I guess that's what happens when you have a mom and a grandma who cook for a living."

"Here you go." Beau hands Zayne the bottle of cider we brought as a thank you.

He takes it with a surprised smile. "Oh. Thanks."

Mimi rounds the corner from the kitchen into the entryway then, and when she sees us, her entire face lights up. "Oh, you're all here! It's lovely to meet you!" She hurries toward us and tucks a lock of her thick, dark hair behind her ear before hugging my parents, one in each of her arms. They introduce themselves and Mimi glances at Beau. "You must be Dot's brother."

"Yeah, nice to meet you." Beau kicks his shoelaces.

Zayne's hand finds mine, and he tugs, beckoning me to follow him.

Mom is already deep in a conversation with Mimi, and after several lingering moments, Dad and Beau walk to the living room to join Lenny, where a football game is playing.

I follow Zayne to the kitchen. On the island is a line of metal serving trays with closed lids. There are even more resting on the clean, marble countertops. Steam escapes from beneath the lids, and the smell of it is enough to make my stomach rumble.

Zayne lifts one of the lids on the island, a mischievous glint in his eye. "Come taste this." He dips a spoon into the tray, filled to the brim with stuffing. "It's my favorite dish they make."

He holds the full spoon out to me, so I take it. When the bite is in my mouth, my eyes almost roll back in my head. "Wow," I murmur. "That's fantastic."

He nods. "It really is." He sets the spoon down, the metal clanking against the counter just as Lenny rounds the corner to the kitchen.

"Hi." I lift my hand in a wave.

His eyes widen. "I hope that spoon isn't going back into the food, because if you're sick, the whole dish will be infected."

My lips twitch with the effort to hold back a smile. "I'm not sick," I tell him. "I promise."

Zayne shakes his head at his brother and picks up the spoon again, walking to the sink to wash it. Mimi enters the kitchen with my parents and Beau, and Mom sniffs the air. "My word. Everything smells amazing."

A warm blush appears on Mimi's plump cheeks. "Thank you so much."

"Zayne fed Bardot-Who-Goes-By-Dot a bite," Lenny blurts. "But he's washing the spoon now."

A gap of silence follows Lenny's statement, and thankfully, a voice coming from the front door breaks it. "I'm here!"

We all turn our heads as Gwen shuffles into view, her arms full of floral-patterned, reusable grocery bags packed full.

"Here Mom, let us help." Zayne takes several bags from her, passing one to Lenny, and they unload the groceries. My parents reintroduce themselves now that Gwen is here, and Mimi takes a bundle of parsley from her to wash, chop, and add to the salad waiting in a covered bowl.

When Gwen's hands are finally free, she runs them over her smooth head and sighs in relief. Her eyes catch mine, and she crosses the room to pull me into a hug. "Good to see you again, sweetie," she says against the top of my head. For some reason, the warmth in her voice makes my throat burn. She has such a motherly quality to her, and with my own mom being absent so long, I was starting to forget how it felt.

Gwen pulls away, and we all move to the connected dining room to find seats while Mimi sets serving platters on the long wood table. Photos of Zayne and Lenny decorate the walls; some of them old and others more recent. I stifle a laugh as I remember the cowboy photo of them on the stairway.

I sit beside Zayne, and Mom takes the chair on my

other side. I glance at her as she folds her linen napkin across her lap, frowning when I notice a bead of sweat at her temple again. I don't recall her ever sweating so much, especially in autumn. It's not like it's toasty in here, either. Aunt Lucille's warning flashes through my mind. I elbow her gently. "You all right?" I do my best to hide my concern with a polite tone.

Her gaze jumps to mine. "I'm fine, baby." She swallows, hard, and picks up the glass of ice water in front of her but doesn't take a drink.

"Dot, are you excited for the *Wuthering Heights* play?" Gwen asks across the table. "I can't believe it's a week away."

"Me either." I try to sound excited, but a prick of unease crops up in my mind. "And the dance is Saturday."

"Wow." Mimi smiles broadly as she finally takes a seat, now that the last platter is on the table. "So much is happening. Zayne, what color handkerchief are you wearing?"

Zayne blinks a few times, then raises his eyebrows at me. "Dot?"

My shoulders sag. "Red."

Mom clears her throat. "Dot's dress is just divine. Picked it out myself."

Yes. Yes you did, Mom.

Instead of commenting, I pick up my fork and stuff a bite of salad in my mouth. It's probably the best salad I've ever tasted. There are cranberries, walnuts, and apples in it. My stomach grumbles, and I take another bite. We all spend a good half hour eating in quiet satisfaction.

"Zayne, you should bring Dot here before the dance so I can take photos of you!" Mimi says, breaking the silence. "I want to see her dress!"

Zayne catches my gaze and raises his eyebrows in question, but before I can answer, Dad pipes up for what seems like the first time since we sat down. "Y'all better not be out too late." It's meant to be a joke, but because I know him so well, I can tell he's serious.

My cheeks burn in embarrassment. "Dad."

But Mom pats his knee with a chuckle. "Oh, Paul. Stop it!" She scoots her chair back and stands up. "Which way is the restroom?"

Gwen points behind us. "It's the third door down the hall. Would you like me to show you?" She moves to stand, but Mom kindly waves her off.

"No, no. Don't worry. I'll find it." She places her napkin on her empty chair before heading down the hall.

"This salad is really good," says Beau. "What kind of dressing is this?"

Mimi beams. "It's a light poppyseed vinaigrette. Made it from scratch."

Dad's lips form a silent "wow."

The subject shifts to Mimi's cooking, and my dad listens to her and Gwen explain how they started their restaurant. I try to pay attention, but my mind wanders to the play and the dance as Mimi tells us about how she's in physical therapy for a bad case of tendonitis. "I can't chop anything without a flare-up these days." She casts her gaze downward. "It's awful."

There's a beat of silence, and then Gwen makes a face

like she ate something sour. "What—is somebody upstairs?"

Mimi swallows her bite of food. "Probably just that alley cat jumping on the roof again."

"Oh, right. That thing's always causing a ruckus." Gwen blinks away her confusion and resumes the conversation. "Lenny, please eat your turkey."

He shakes his head. "No, thank you."

"It wasn't a request."

"I know. I never would have requested turkey."

She sighs.

But my attention isn't on them. My mind is swirling like a black hole, and it must be obvious, because Zayne reaches over and takes my hand under the table. When I look at him, he mouths, "You good?"

"My mom has been gone for a long time," I say under my breath. I know I don't need to say anything else because the implication is already etched into the tone of my voice.

Ten more minutes pass before Mom returns to the table. I can't help but notice her face has been wiped clean of sweat. An easy smile is in place on her mouth.

"What took you so long?" Beau sets his fork down and stares hard at Mom.

"That's rude, son." Dad frowns at him and shakes his head.

My face heats. *Oh, yeah. That's just great. Get in an argument at my boyfriend's house. Real classy.*

"No, it's fine," Mom says. "I'm just a bit tired tonight. I think it's time we headed home soon."

My brows dart together. What is she talking about? She

spent half of dinner in the bathroom and seemed perfectly well-rested before we got here.

"Oh." Gwen blinks in confusion. "Okay."

The conversation is strained as everyone finishes eating. Nobody speaks as Mimi brings cake to the table. I hope Zayne's family somehow mistakes the awkward silence as us just stuffing our faces too full to speak, but I know it's unlikely. I avert my gaze from everyone at the table, staring only at the remnants of food left on my plate.

When we've all tasted the cake, Mom stands from her seat, indicating it's time to leave.

Mimi hops up. "Please, let me send you home with some leftovers!" She opens her kitchen cupboard and picks up the same takeout containers that I've seen at her restaurant.

Zayne stands too and helps his mom fill the boxes with food for us. I can't help but smile when I see him scoop several slices of cake into a box.

Beau and Dad carry the boxes, and the Silvermans walk us to the door.

"Thank you so much for having us," Mom says. "Dinner was delicious."

How would you know? I almost say. *You barely ate.*

Mom retrieves the keys from her purse as Dad opens the door, but they slip from her hand and clank against the wood floor. She bends to pick them up, and a plastic bottle falls from the pocket of her cardigan, hitting the floor with a thud.

"Oh, sorry." Her hand flies toward it, fingers curling it into her grasp.

Beau squints. "What is that?"

But she doesn't answer, doesn't meet any of our gazes as her fingers wrap around the bottle.

"Are those pills?" Beau demands, his voice increasing in volume. He lunges for the bottle, and we all stare, stunned into place, as he pries it from her hand.

"No, Beau! Stop it!" Mom shouts.

But as soon as he captures it, he reads in a booming voice, "Celia Silverman. Hydrocodone." He drops his hand, still holding the pill bottle to his side.

Silence.

Deafening, unbearable silence, so heavy it could squash every person in this room.

And then Mom runs out the door.

"Stop!" Without a backward glance, I barrel through the front door after her. Behind me, Dad is on my heels and Beau remains shocked in place. Mom gets in the car with more haste than I knew she was capable of. I know I should probably hang back and explain to Zayne and his family, but the shame I feel in this moment is too intense.

I just want to disappear.

She relapsed. She actually relapsed, and Zayne and his family just witnessed it.

When I reach the car, I see Mom sitting in the passenger seat with her head down and her hand covering her eyes.

I wipe an angry tear from the corner of my eye and yank the driver's side car door open. "Unbelievable," I yell. "This—*you*—are unbelievable!" Dad touches my shoulder, but I ignore him.

Mom doesn't react. She doesn't budge from her position in her seat. She just keeps her eyes covered. If it weren't for the trembling of her shoulders, I would think she didn't even hear me.

"I defended you," I continue. "I told Beau to shut up every time he so much as implied you weren't ready to be here. I believed you when you said you were okay. And this is what you do?" I gesture to the crisp evening air around us. "You steal pills from Zayne's house? You relapse on *Thanksgiving?*"

Mom lowers her hands from her face. When she turns in my direction, the look in her eyes makes me clamp my jaw shut. In her gaze, I see the weight of her sorrow, regret, and pain. It's heavier than anything I myself have experienced. Still, I stare back at her.

Beau finally makes it to the car. I risk a glance up at the Silvermans' house, expecting to find the four of them still standing in the doorway, but the front door is closed.

A wave of tears threatens to invade my vision. I didn't say goodbye to Zayne or apologize to his family. Worse yet, they probably don't want to hear a word I have to say. I bet Zayne will text me tonight to let me know he can't take me to the dance tomorrow after all, because what Mom did tonight was unforgivable.

Dad touches my back. "Let's go home."

I move out of the way so he can take his place behind the wheel and get in the back seat next to Beau. My gaze darts to my brother and a look of mutual understanding passes between us. *Mom needs to go back.*

My throat burns again, but I don't cry. I can't let myself fall apart until we figure this out.

"How many did you take, Mom?" I don't know why this is the question that escapes my lips. The fact that she stole the bottle to begin with is bad enough.

"It doesn't matter how many pills she took, Bardot," Dad says. He puts the car in drive and we coast out of Zayne's neighborhood. He glances at my mother before turning back to the road. "This arrangement with Lucille isn't working, Opal. You need to go to a real facility."

In his tone, there is no wiggle room, no bargaining, no room for negotiation. He means it.

Part of me expects Mom to try to plead with him, but instead she just nods. "I know that, Paul."

My lips part. "But Mom..." Going to a real facility means we won't be able to have our weekly phone calls anymore. It means she won't be home for Christmas either, like we planned.

But I also know it might be her only real chance to get better for good. I can feel Beau's eyes on my face so I swallow down my emotion.

Mom's shoulders twitch, and then begin to tremble again. She doesn't turn around to face us. With her head still hung and her hands covering her eyes, she releases a strong sob.

I can't hold back my own tears any longer.

And the thing is, I don't even want to.

Chapter Twenty-Five

24 missed calls from Zayne Silverman.

He's been trying to reach me since last night, and the calls and texts haven't ceased once throughout the day. I shut off my phone screen and toss it onto my bed. I can't talk to him. Not yet. Not after yesterday.

Mom is in her room, packing her suitcase, and Dad is helping her. This time, it's a much bigger suitcase—one that can carry the rest of the belongings we've been storing here for her.

I throw myself onto the bed and cry into my pillow. It's like releasing a tidal wave of emotion I've kept bottled up since the day Mom first admitted she had a problem. I was so angry then, because it wasn't even her fault. She didn't ask to injure her back or give up her hard-earned fire-fighting career. She didn't want to be in so much pain that heavy doses of hydrocodone would be the only mask. She didn't know that by the time her injury healed, she would already be an addict.

She didn't ask to get addicted.

She didn't ask to have her life ruined.

My cries continue to flow freely. I don't know why I'm bothering to smother them with my pillow. I have no pride left after what happened at dinner, so I shouldn't care if anyone hears me.

By morning, Mom will be on an airplane, on her way to a proper facility in Florida with a high recovery success rate. She'll be gone, and I'll be here, unable to talk to her or see her for what seems like an eternity. The worst part is that all I can seem to do is sit in my room and cry.

I'm so mad at her for failing me, Dad, and Beau when she stole those pills. But the other part of me knows I'll regret it if I don't get up and go to her, spend as much time with her as I can before she leaves.

I wipe my nose with my sweater sleeve and get up, walking to my bedroom door and gripping the cool, metal handle. When I swing the door open, Mom is on the other side and she's holding a white rectangular cardboard box. Her eyes widen like she wasn't expecting me to open the door, but the surprise melts into a downturned smile. "Hey, baby. Can I come in?"

I move out of the way so she can enter. I know my eyes are still red and puffy, because her gaze lingers on them before she takes my face in one of her hands and kisses my forehead.

We sit on the bed together. Mom sets the box on the

mattress before turning to face me. "I owe you an apology, Bardot."

I blink in surprise at her words. "For what?" I know it's a stupid question, but what else am I supposed to say?

"I never should have made promises I knew I couldn't keep." Mom sniffs. "I know I should have stayed with my sister. But what you need to understand is that it's just as hard on me to be away from my family as it is for you. When you told me about starring in your play at Fallbrook, it felt like you were growing up and living life without me." She takes my hand, squeezing, and fresh tears appear in both of our eyes. "I just want to be back in your life. But by coming here before I was ready, I've done the worst thing imaginable; I let my baby girl down. And I'm sorry. I'm so sorry, sweetie."

I pull her into a hug. She wraps her arms around my back in response and we sit together in our tight embrace, rocking from side to side like we used to when I was a kid. "Thank you for apologizing," I whisper. "I forgive you." As I speak the words, the tightness in my stomach smooths out, like a hand sliding across bunched up fabric.

We let go of each other, and she turns to pick up the box next to her. "This is for you." She holds it out to me. "Picked it up this evening."

I dab my eyes with my sleeve and take the box. "What is it?" I lift the lid and remove tissue paper from the top.

The ice-blue dress from the department store stares back at me.

My lips part. "Mom."

"You should wear the dress *you* want to wear. That's what you'll truly look your best in, Bardot."

"But... I don't think I'm going to the dance anymore."

She raises her eyebrows. "And why ever not? Because of the mess I caused yesterday?"

I shrug. "Well, yeah."

She pauses, staring at her hands as she takes my words in. "I'm so sorry, honey. But all that was on me, not you. You should still go. I'll personally apologize to Zayne if it helps."

I hold up the dress, and the silky material ripples in front of me like water. She's right—I can't cancel. Just the thought of disappointing Zayne is soul-crushing. My smile turns wobbly. "Thank you, Mom, but you don't have to do that. I'll go."

She smiles, standing to peer into the jewelry box on my dresser. "Will you wear silver or gold accessories?"

"Hmm," I tap my chin. "Silver seems more winter, but gold is more my jam."

We talk accessories while Mom fiddles over me, arranging my braids into various styles for practice until we settle on the perfect updo I'll be able to replicate without her. She even helps me choose makeup, and for the moment, it feels just like old times, before her accident, when she could be my mother, and I could be her daughter. No complications. No fear for the future. It's bittersweet because I want this moment to linger forever, yet I know it's only going to last until she leaves again.

When we've exhausted all possible options for tomorrow's dress-wear, Mom tucks me in like I'm a child. And I don't complain one bit.

When she leaves my room, I check my phone and tap the *off* button next to my morning alarm since tomorrow's Saturday. A twinge of guilt pricks at me because I don't have any new texts from Zayne, no more calls. I open his contact page, my thumb hovering over the call button.

And then a Little Birdie blast explodes in my face.

Fledglings,

Thanksgiving Day is nothing more than a promise for family gossip and drama, and what could tempt a poultry like myself more than a juicy worm of drama over a meal of turkey and potatoes?

That's right! Nothing!

This little birdie has been flying around town, witnessing firsthand the whispers of familial strife and antagonism. And the winner for the juiciest story goes to none other than our favorite girl Dot Bennet!

It appears that, while at an impeccably crafted dinner with Zayne Silverman and his family, Dot's mom transformed into an utter thief before their very eyes! Not even Dot was aware of her mom stealing a bottle of prescription medica-tion from Zayne's house during the holiday meal. That much was clear by the spectacle she caused, yelling at her mom just outside the Silverman brownstone.

Her screams may have scared the other birds away, but this fierce flapper stayed around for the good stuff.

The question is, will our theater darlings split after this unfortunate mishap? Or will the blossom of their young love remain true and with-stand the test of trouble?

You'll know when I do!

Yours Truly,

Little Birdie

My phone feels like dead weight in my hand. A surge of anger blinds me, red and strong and vengeful. I hope everyone in the house, including Mom, is asleep by now because I don't think I'll be able to hide how upset I am and the last thing I want is for Mom to see this.

Who does Little Birdie think she is?

I finally call Zayne back. I need to talk to someone and he's the only one who will understand. I know we'll have to eventually address what happened yesterday, but I need him right now. I can't hold off talking to him another minute.

To my immense relief, he answers on the second ring. "I saw the post." He sighs. "I'm sorry, Dot."

"Little Birdie isn't going to get away with this. This time, she went too far."

"I agree."

My throat feels tight, but I refuse to cry again. I refuse to let her win.

Zayne says in a low tone, "If I ever figure out who's behind this, I'm going to kill them."

For some reason, the comment makes me feel a bit lighter. "Thanks."

There's an awkward pause because this is the first we've spoken since dinner. I'm still ashamed by what happened. "Zayne, I don't even know how to begin to apologize—"

"Stop." His tone is firm. "Do not apologize, Dot."

"But—"

"Nobody's upset. Not me, not Mimi, not Mom. Not even Lenny."

I swallow down a hard knot in my throat. "*I'm* upset, though. I can't believe all this happened. And now my mom is leaving in the morning." My voice wavers.

"I wish I could hug you right now," he whispers in my ear. "I wish I could drive over there right now and just hug you."

The idea alone makes my heart pound. Zayne in here with me, while everyone else is asleep? My voice sounds tiny when I ask, "Can't you?"

A beat of silence. And then, "I'll be right there, Dot."

He hangs up, and my breaths shudder as I look around my room. Is it clean enough? Does it smell nice? I straighten some of the makeup, nail polish, and skincare products scattered across my white vanity.

My gaze snags on the blue dress, still draped across my

bed. I jolt out of bed and gather it up, hanging it in my closet. If he saw it before the dance, it would ruin the surprise. I also collect the earrings and necklace Mom and I picked out and put them back in my jewelry box. I don't know how long it will take Zayne to get here, but I'm sure I have time to change into cuter pajamas.

Ten minutes later, there's blush on my cheeks, and I'm comfy in my champagne jogger lounge set. My braids are in low pigtails and the scent of Chanel no. 4 is just barely noticeable in the air.

My phone vibrates. Zayne's text flashes across the screen.

ZAYNE

I'm here.

ME

Can you come in through my window?
There's a ladder on the side of the house.

ZAYNE

Sure. Which side of the house is your room on?

And why is there a ladder?

ME

If you're facing the house, my room is on the right side. And for your information, I like to sit on the roof sometimes.

I unlock the latch on my bedroom window and slide it open for him. A moment later, his face appears through the darkness of the night, visible from the dim lighting my room is emanating.

"Hi," he whispers, and expertly jumps up onto the window-pane. I reach out to help him, but he doesn't even need it, climbing through and landing on my carpet with a barely audible thud.

"Hi," I giggle. "Welcome to my room." I hold my arms out from my sides.

He blinks, as if just realizing where he is, and takes in our surroundings. "Wow. I really like it. It's so very...*you.*"

I try to see what he's seeing. Fashion magazines stacked on my vanity beside bottles of nail polish and makeup. My clothing rack packed with trendy outfits and my favorite classic pieces. And my favorite color clearly visible in the abundance of yellow hues that radiate warmth and positivity. I smirk. "It's all the yellow, isn't it?"

He nods. "Definitely. That and the lack of books."

We both laugh quietly, hushed, breathy sounds of pure mirth.

Zayne shakes his head. "Have you considered taking that ladder down? Someone could break in, or something."

"I've left against the side of the house since we moved in." I laugh at his troubled expression, but it turns sad. Shaky. I don't even realize I'm crying again until Zayne takes me in his arms, his eyes round. "Hey," he whispers, rubbing circles on my back. "Hey, it's going to be okay."

I bury my face in his chest. Both his arms tighten around me, causing my stomach to dance in circles.

"As promised," he whispers into my hair, "a hug from yours truly."

I smile against his shirt. "Thanks."

We continue to stand in the center of my room,

hugging, when a sink turns on near my parents' room. Zayne pulls back, his eyes wide.

"It's just my dad," I tell him. "He gets up a lot in the middle of the night."

"That's very comforting."

I laugh. "Don't worry. He never comes in here. But if he did, and he saw you, you'd be dead."

Zayne winces. "I figured as much."

"We should lie on the bed. That way if he does come in, you can hide under the covers and he might mistake you for a wall of pillows."

Zayne closes his eyes. "You do realize how ridiculous that sounds, right?" But his lips twist into a reluctant smile. "I guess it's better than standing in the middle of the room, though."

"Or worse," I shrug.

"Not helping."

"Sorry."

He gets on my bed first and scoots against the wall it's pressed against, and I get in on the side closer to the door so I can block him from view. I arrange my many pillows around him to try to hide him a bit, but he just shakes his head. "If I die, I die."

I smother my laugh with my hand. "I hope this is worth the risk."

He touches my cheek, forcing me to meet his gaze. All traces of humor leave his face. "It is."

I search his eyes, level with my own on the pillows and close the distance between us.

The kiss begins softly, like the opening line of a play

whispered between only us, setting the stage for something deeper. It's slow and deliberate.

Until it isn't.

The kiss transforms into something dizzying, something ardent within seconds. Zayne's hands grip my waist, a touch both grounding and electric. When my fingers brush his shoulders to pull him closer, I feel his quiet strength beneath my hands. The air between us is thick with everything unspoken, and as our lips meet again and again, the rest of the world fades away. My heart tangles in my chest when he brushes a stray braid from my face and then softly holds my hand as we kiss.

In this moment, it's not about want—it's about something stronger, something I can't explain. When he pulls back, his eyes are filled with desire and a depth that leaves me breathless. His voice comes out gravelly. "Dot, if we don't stop now, I'm going to rip your clothes off."

"Please don't. This is one of my favorite outfits." I grin, despite the way his words make my cheeks burn.

Amusement flickers in his gaze but he doesn't respond, instead pulling me in for another kiss. This time it's more resigned, less intense, and it only leaves me wanting more. Not fair. Then he kisses my forehead and says, "Goodnight, Dot."

"Are you going to sleep here? I mean, I'm all for it, but my dad will *definitely* find you if you're still here in the morning."

He laughs breathlessly. "No. I'll leave once you're asleep." He trails his fingertips along my cheekbone, and I close my eyes. I try not to think about Mom leaving in the morning, or Little Birdie's nonsense. Part of me wants to ask him how he thinks Little Birdie found out what happened, but the possibilities are so limited, I'm not sure I'm ready to face them right now. Instead, I focus on Zayne's soft, minty breaths caressing my face, and his smooth fingertips against my skin as I drift to sleep.

Chapter Twenty-Six

Zayne is already gone when I wake up the next morning, and so is my mom.

I vaguely remember her pressing a wet kiss against my cheek a few hours ago before disappearing, and I try not to cry as I envision what the next six months are going to look like with her gone again. I check my phone. There's a picture Mom sent me from the plane. She's wearing a hopeful smile and holding one of her thumbs up. Her curly hair is pulled back into a bun, and her face is lit by the sun shining through her window seat on the plane. The message underneath the picture reads:

MOM

Wish me luck, baby. I love you.

I save the picture to my gallery and check Zayne's message next.

ZAYNE

I snuck back out like a pro. But I accidentally lost my balance on the way out and crashed into your neighbor's cans. The whole neighborhood probably hates me.

I laugh, typing back.

ME

Don't worry. I didn't hear a thing.

ZAYNE

You're a really heavy sleeper, though. That's not saying much.

ME

I'm a perfectly average sleeper, for your information.

ZAYNE

If you say so, Bennett.

With a smirk, I toss my phone onto the bed. I slept till noon, which means Zayne will be here to pick me up for the dance in less than six hours. I eye my laptop with a twinge of guilt. I've been procrastinating on homework like crazy. Catching up on all my overdue assignments will be the perfect way to pass the time until it's time to get ready.

I get a bowl of cereal from the kitchen first and spot Beau eating a grilled cheese at the table on my way. "Morning," I say.

He attempts to smile, lifting his lips and then giving up halfway, letting his mouth fall back into a downward curve.

It's the saddest expression I've ever seen on his face, and it makes me do a double-take. "You okay?"

He shrugs. "Are you?"

I close my eyes. I know what he's referring to. Or *who*, rather. "She'll be back, Beau."

"I know." His lips thin. "But why'd I have to be such a jerk to her while she was here, you know? I wish I'd been nicer. I just kept getting so frustrated, thinking she lied about Aunt Lucille knowing she was here."

I pull out the chair across from him. "You acted the way you did because you care about her," I tell him. "And she knows that. She knew it the whole time. You don't need to be so hard on yourself."

He shrugs one shoulder. "I guess." He eyes the pajama set I'm still wearing. "Don't you have the winter formal to go to tonight?" He scrunches his nose. "You're going to shower, right?"

So, this is what I get for trying to have a heart-to-heart? I should have known. "Yes, I'm going to shower. *Duh.*" I get up from the chair, taking my bowl of cereal with me.

Before I disappear down the hall, Beau calls my name quietly. I raise an eyebrow at him.

"Thanks," he mutters.

I hide my grin as I turn away. "No problem."

Six hours later, I've rehearsed for the play and I'm all caught up on my assignments, scrubbed clean, and feeling like a princess in my new blue dress. I had no trouble replicating the elegant twist Mom showed me last night, and my makeup looks fantastic; almost too perfect. I'm afraid to move, in case I somehow ruin or smudge something.

I spray perfume on my pulse points and check the time on my phone. There's a text from Zayne.

ZAYNE

Five minutes away. Can't wait to see you.

I send a pink heart in response and tuck my phone, my lipstick, and a pack of gum into my small, gold clutch. Gold, to match my jewelry.

When Zayne knocks, I make my way to the door. Dad is home from work, doing dishes in the kitchen and he hears the sound of my heels against the wood floor. "Now you wait a minute, Bardot," he calls. "Let me see you before you go."

I pause near the door. The steady ticking of the grandfather clock in the entryway is like a timer, counting down the seconds until I get to open the front door and see Zayne. Until we get to escape to the dance together.

Dad rounds the corner from the kitchen to the entryway where I'm still standing, waiting. When he sees me, he stops in his tracks and blinks a few times. "You look so grown up." He swallows, blinking away the shine on his eyes and clears his throat. "Let me take a picture of you. Zayne can wait one more minute."

"Thanks, Dad." I smile and place my hand on the hip of my gown for the photo.

He snaps several, gazing at each one before taking the next. "Now a few with Zayne," he says. "Go on. Let him in."

A flurry hits the pit of my stomach, but I do as he says, opening the door to find Zayne waiting on the other side.

And my heart beats double its usual pace.

Zayne is dressed in a black suit with a muted yellow handkerchief in his pocket, matching my gold accessories. When he stares down at me, a couple of his dreads fall into his eyes. His gaze doesn't waver from mine. "You look so beautiful," he says in a low voice.

I want to melt at his words, to tell him how hot he looks, but my dad is standing *right there,* watching us. "Zayne, can I get a photo of you two together?" Dad asks.

"Of course." Zayne walks in and stands next to me. He puts his arm around my waist and I try not to blush. I smile at the camera, letting my hands hang awkwardly while Dad takes an unnecessary number of photos.

"Okay, we have to go now!" I take hold of Zayne's arm and half drag him toward the door again. "Bye, Dad."

"Be safe out there, please, Bardot." Dad shakes Zayne's hand, and then finally, *finally,* we're out the door and in his black Camaro. As promised, we stop by his house for photos, too. I'm nervous and embarrassed at first to see his family again, but they put me at ease right away, smiling and complimenting us as they snap photos.

And then we're free again.

Dance, here we come. My first high school dance.

I try to imagine what it's going to be like as we drive to school. The night twinkles, illuminated by the stars and the lights on homes along the way, already decorated for Christmas.

When we find a spot to park in the crowded lot at Fallbrook, Zayne gets out to open the passenger side of his car for me. I smile at him, my insides warming against the chill of the air at the comfort of his hand covering mine. Several other couples are arriving, and Zayne and I follow behind them to the school's giant double doors. The cobbled walkway to the entrance is lined with topiary bushes covered in netted white outdoor lights. When we enter, the main corridor is dark, but there are signs to follow that lead us where we need to go. It's a little eerie, walking through the ancient building at night. There are creaks and echoes that aren't usually noticeable in the day, masked by the hum of voices and footsteps in the crowded corridors.

As we follow the signs, I can't help but acknowledge how much fancier Fallbrook is than what most middle-class Americans get to experience. From what I've seen in movies, most high schools host their school dances in the gymnasium. But apparently, Fallbrook Christian Prep has an official ballroom, and this will be my first time seeing it. The other couples rush inside, but I take each step slowly, wanting to fully soak in every moment of this night.

Zayne pushes the heavy doors open, and I gasp.

Lantern-shaped lights float at the ceiling, like stars sprinkled across the night sky. Each table setting is topped with a seat assignment and bouquet of white roses, fairy lights, and silver tinsel. Heavy, silk runners are draped gracefully across each table in the ballroom. The scent of cinnamon, apple, and glue from the decorations is in the air. There's a silver and white balloon arch at the left side of the room, and a salmon dinner buffet on the right.

It's beautiful.

Zayne takes my hand again, threading his fingers through mine as we walk into the ballroom together. His thumb traces lines on my hand as it strokes back and forth. We find the table with our place settings on it, and I put my clutch on my assigned chair. The cloth napkin at my setting is even embossed with my name, *Bardot Bennett*. I look to the seat at my left, noting the *Zayne Silverman* napkin. Skimming over the rest of the names at our table, I don't recognize anyone else.

Except *Jude Crowe*. Great.

Out of the corner of my vision, Mabel walks over to us with a wide smile on her face. Meredith isn't far behind her, but her gaze hovers around the room, refusing to land in my direction. "Dot!" Mabel exclaims. "You look so gorgeous, it's unreal."

I blush. "Thanks Mabel." I half expected her and Meredith to be in matching dresses tonight, but instead, she has on a crimson, silk gown. Her curly hair is in a twist that lands just above her dress's intricate collarbone cutout. Mabel is donning a simple but elegant chiffon dress in violet, her hair bone straight in a French twist. I gesture to them. "You both look amazing, too."

Mabel beams. "Thanks." But then her smile wavers as she leans in closer to me. "I, uh…saw the Little Birdie post. How are you doing?"

"I'm fine." But it's a lie. My stomach is now twisting at the mere reminder that *everyone* now knows what happened at Zayne's house on Thanksgiving with my mom.

I glance at Meredith. She's studying her nails, but obviously listening, because she looks up and adds, "What a shame. But you two," she juts her chin in Zayne's direction, "still seem cozy regardless."

Zayne wraps his arm around my waist. "Everyone knows Little Birdie is boring," he says. "She's nothing but old news, a fly on the wall with no real source material."

Mabel nods in an overaggressive way that leads me to believe it's only for my benefit.

"I believe her," Meredith lilts with a delicate shrug of her shoulders. Her red lips frame her teeth as she smiles. "Unless you're saying none of it happened."

Zayne and I remain silent, and in this moment I can't help but kind of hate Meredith. Other than technically stealing her part in the play, there's no reason for her to be mad at me.

"I see." She grins when it's clear neither I nor Zayne are going to deny it. "Good luck to you and your mom, Dot. I'm going to go find my date."

Zayne steps in front of her. "None of it happened. Little Birdie lied about the whole thing."

"Hm." She presses her lips together, squinting at the two of us. She spins on her designer heels with soles as red as her dress, leaving Mabel standing with us as she and struts into the center of the dance floor.

I swallow. My throat feels like dry crumbs are stuck in it. "Who's her date?"

Mabel shifts on her feet. "She came with Carlton." She tries to smile but fails. Her eyes land on Zayne's arm still wrapped around my waist. "You two look really adorable together, by the way."

I smile. "Thanks. Who did *you* come with?"

"Me and Rue came together as friends," she explains. "Since neither of us had a date."

I nod. "Nice."

There's an awkward beat of silence, and then she says, "Well...I'll see you later, Dot. I'm going to look for Rue."

I nod as she walks away, less dramatically than her sister.

"Who cares what they think?" Zayne squeezes my hand, so I turn to face him. He leans closer to my face, our foreheads almost touching. "Dance with me."

Excitement bubbles in my chest. "Okay."

We make for the dance floor, hand in hand. I can't help but notice the whispers floating around us, the eyes that flicker from our faces to the ground just as quickly, and then back again. The not-so-subtle pointing and gesturing in our direction. The attention is just as bad as when I first arrived at Fallbrook. It's exhausting. No matter how often this kind of thing keeps happening, I just can't seem to get used to it.

My mind drifts away from the drama at hand as Zayne pulls me to his chest, places his hands on my waist, and gazes at my face.

I reach up and twine my fingers around his neck. A soft melody drifts around us, and we sway back and forth to the tune. Even with all the gossip surrounding us, this isn't so bad. Not with Zayne's intoxicating scent filling my senses, or his lips brushing feather-light across my forehead. Not with him holding me against him, so gently yet so firmly, grounding me to this moment in reality.

Someone taps my shoulder. Zayne and I break apart, and Carlton is standing next to us in a tux similar to Zayne's, save for the red accents instead of yellow. I blink away the spell I'd willingly fallen into a moment before. "Hey."

"Hi." He wets his lips. Swallows. It looks like he wants to say more but doesn't know how.

Zayne arches an eyebrow. "Do you need something?"

"I, uh—" Carlton gestures to me. "I was hoping I could dance with Dot. Just once, for old time's sake?"

My gaze jumps from Carlton's face to Zayne's. He narrows his brows, squeezes my shoulder, then drops his hand. "It's up to you," he murmurs.

The last thing I want is to stop dancing with Zayne, but I'm also curious what Carlton wants to tell me. I know there's something because of the way his eyes keep darting between me and Zayne. "Okay, I guess."

Carlton grins, linking his arm through mine. "Meredith is a great dance partner," he tells Zayne. "You're welcome to have a dance or two with her."

The jealousy that flares inside me at the thought of them dancing together is alarming, but Zayne just rolls his eyes. "That's alright. I'm going to get a drink." He starts to walk away, but then tenses and turns back to Carlton. His gaze narrows in on his arm linked with mine. "Try anything with Dot, and you'll regret it."

And then he's gone, disappearing into the crowd of our classmates.

Carlton scoffs. "A little dramatic, isn't he?"

"Not in the slightest."

Carlton unlinks our arms to face me and puts one hand on my waist. He holds his other out for me to take. My palm hovers in the air, hesitating, before taking his hand. I rest my other on his shoulder, and we sway to the music. There's a new song playing, and it's slow like the last one. A heavy dose of Carlton's expensive cologne tickles my nose.

A few months ago, I would have killed to be here with him, in this moment. To be his girlfriend. To have him look at me the way he is now, like I'm the last piece of gold in the mine. But now, all I can think about is how wrong it feels to be in his arms. How uncomfortable his gaze makes me because the feelings aren't reciprocated. I just want Zayne to come back because I'd much rather be dancing with him.

"He's lying to you, you know," Carlton whispers into my ear. "Zayne."

I roll my eyes. But there's a tiny part of me that reacts to his words. The part of me that can't help but ask, "About what?"

"Zayne isn't who you think he is, Dot. He's a liar. An *actor.* He uses girls. He's been known to get girls to fall in love with him, only to tell them it was all an act. I have a feeling he's doing the same thing to you."

My gut tightens with unease, because he's the second person to say this to me. We stop dancing, and I rip my hand away from his. "Stop it. You don't know anything about Zayne."

He shrugs. Holds both his hands up. "I've known him longer than you have."

My vision turns red. "And what about you? *You* lied to me, Carlton. You lied about Zayne. Why would I believe a word you say?" I try to take a steadying breath to calm myself because the last thing I want to do is make a scene when everyone is already having a hard time keeping my name out of their mouth.

"I'm just looking out for you."

I cross my arms. Like magic, Zayne appears at my side. He looks my face over and frowns. "Are you okay?"

I don't answer, just shrug.

His jaw flexes and he spins to Carlton. His voice is so low, I almost miss what he says. "Don't make me hurt you again."

"Relax," says Carlton. "I was just about to go back to my date." He offers me a last meaningful glance. "Have fun, you two. Thanks for the dance, Dot."

When he walks away, Zayne cups my cheek in his hand. "You look upset. What did he do?"

I shake my head. "No. Nothing, I'm fine." I know telling Zayne what Carlton said would only lead to a confrontation, and I definitely don't want a repeat of them fighting at Halloween.

The song changes to an upbeat club mix, and whoops and cheers explode around us. The dance tempo increases, making me feel claustrophobic.

I need some air.

"Can we go take a photo?" I ask Zayne. The balloon arch photo op looks empty. It will be the perfect break to clear my head.

He smiles, but the V between his eyebrows fails to disappear. "Yeah, let's go."

We make our way to the balloon arch. There's only one couple in line ahead of us, and when it's our turn, we position ourselves in frame under the arch. A short kid with round glasses and curly hair is behind the camera. I squint at him. "Jude?"

He doesn't wave or smile at us and positions himself behind the camera with tense shoulders. "Smile, you two."

I ignore him. "Why are you on camera duty?"

He sighs. "I volunteered, okay? Is that a problem?" Bright red spots appear on his cheeks.

"No, man. Relax," says Zayne. "We'll smile, okay?" He stands behind me. Wraps his arms around my waist.

We both smile.

Jude wordlessly snaps our photo. It's probably going to be a good one. Not to sound conceited, but I know my angles. I know when I see the picture, I'll admire my hair and makeup from tonight. I'll stare with satisfaction at the effortless grin on my full lips, the way Zayne is holding me against him.

But right now, all I can think about is what Carlton said.

"I'll be right back," I tell Zayne. "I'm going to find the bathroom."

"Okay." His voice sounds normal, but I notice the subtle tensing of his body, like he knows something is off. I know I probably should just talk to him about it, but I'm not ready yet. I want to clear my mind, erase the stupid thoughts and suspicions Carlton planted in my brain first.

I find the bathroom near the exit and sit in an empty stall. I take calming breaths and study the pencil markings on the stall door, trying to make sense of the meaningless shapes.

I know I'm being a bit ridiculous. I shouldn't take anything Carlton says seriously. He's nothing but a liar. I should go back out there with Zayne.

I'm about to unlock my stall when my phone vibrates. Probably Zayne checking on me. I turn on the screen and see the familiar, dreaded Little Birdie logo. My stomach drops. "No," I whisper. "Not again."

I read the blast with a thundering heart.

Dearest Fledglings,

It pains me to write words such as these but write them I must.

As it turns out, our theater darlings are not darlings at all, but imposters. From the moment we laid eyes on the pair of Dot and Zayne, we've been enchanted by their undeniable chemistry. Their bonds have strengthened into something not even Dot's old relationship with Carlton Peters could compare to. But now, I must unfortunately shatter the bubble of illusion we've all despairingly fallen under.

According to an insider, this news has escaped from the lips of Zayne himself. He stated, "Dot thinks she's the better actor, but I've had her fooled all along. First, she believed Carlton Peters was a good guy, and now she believes I'm into her. I guess that proves I have more talent. Or maybe she's just plain naive."

Zayne then revealed that dating Dot Bennett has been done with the hopes of creating chemistry between the two of them—chemistry that Zayne will hopefully be able to replicate onstage while the representative from Underwood Academy is watching.

Some will go to drastic measures to get what they want. Apparently, Zayne Silverman is one of those people.

What we've considered a budding romance has really been an act all along. Dot Bennett is no It Girl, but another Cassidy Tucker in disguise. We all remember her, or...do we? I can only hope Underwood is treating her well.

The real question is how Dot will handle this awful truth! Will she collapse under the pressure of it all, or will she prove to Zayne that he cannot get the best of her?

An even more delicious question—how will this leaking news affect their performance?! This little birdie will be sure to watch and find out. And so will anyone who's anyone.

Yours truly,
Little Birdie

Chapter Twenty-Seven

My chest fills with rage and hurt, making it difficult to breathe. If there's one thing I've learned about Little Birdie, it's that there is truth to her words. Of all the things she's written about me, I've only ever detected a bit of embellishment in the content of her writing. Some added effect, for the sake of drama.

But the core of her stories are true.

I think that's why—hidden in the bathroom, phone still in hand—I choose to run.

My heart feels like the strings of a guitar, thrumming at top speed. *Zayne was using me. He was using me all along.* Tears prick in the corners of my eyes, but I wipe them away and duck my head down as I push through the exit to the bathroom.

I half expected there to be a crowd waiting for me on the other side of the door, but luckily that's not the case. Almost everyone is still crowded on the dance floor.

Maybe, since we're at a dance with loud music playing, there's a chance no one read the blast yet. But there's also a chance *everyone* has, including Zayne. I have no intentions of waiting around to find out or hear whatever sorry lie he's cooking up to serve me next. I am so done with the lies. After everything I just went through with Mom, I don't think I can survive another one of this magnitude. I don't want to listen to Zayne try to explain this away.

I keep my gaze on the floor and speed to the doors in the back of the room.

"Dot!" a male voice calls. I have no idea who it is, and I don't care. I run faster, pushing through the exit and down the dark, empty halls. My heels clack rapidly against the ancient stone, and finally, I'm outside.

And then I remember Zayne drove me here. The tears come faster now. Unstoppable. They sting against my cheeks in the cold night air. I let them fall. Somehow, I knew my makeup would be getting ruined tonight.

"Dot!" I turn at the voice. It's Carlton. He stops running once I look at him, bending over to catch his breath. "Dot, wait."

"Are you following me or something?" I hate that he can probably tell from the sound of my voice that I'm fighting tears.

He straightens and holds up his phone. "I saw it. Are you okay?"

"What do you think?" I face the street again. "I just want to go home so I can be alone."

When he speaks again, he's closer. Right at my side. "Let

me drive you." I don't answer, don't even acknowledge him. He tries again. "We don't have to talk. I can drive you home in silence, and then you can get out of the car and leave."

I frown. "What about Meredith?"

"What about her? She has her sister. She'll be great."

I sigh. If it weren't for the fact that I have no other ride home, I wouldn't even consider it. "Fine."

The corner of his lip turns up, but he tries to hide it. I follow him to his car and get in. The familiarity of it, the smell, the feel of the heated leather seats, the dashboard I've stared at as he drove us around all summer, hits me like a brick wall. It feels like flipping through an old album full of unflattering photos.

Carlton keeps his promise. He doesn't try to talk to me, though I can tell he wants to. But I don't care. I stare out the window, watching my own pathetic reflection mirrored back at me.

My phone starts vibrating incessantly, call after call from Zayne. I ignore them all. Texts come through, one after the other, but I don't read any of them.

Carlton makes a little chuckling sound in the back of his throat, and I shoot him a glare. "I know what you're thinking," I say, breaking the silence.

He tilts his head. "Am I allowed to talk now?"

"You're thinking that you were right about Zayne and that I never should have trusted him."

"He's just not a good guy, Dot." He sighs. "I'm sorry you had to find out like this."

"Yeah," I murmur. "So am I."

Carlton drives off when I'm at my front door. It's then that I allow the tears to really fall. The sobs I've been holding in burst from my chest. I let the angry thoughts have their way, shouting in my mind.

Zayne is nothing but a liar.

How could he do this?

I trusted him!

The anger builds inside me until I can't see straight. I unlock the front door and walk in. Dad is on the couch in the living room. A football game has him leaning forward, palms perched on his knees like he's ready to sprint.

I try to walk past him to my room, but he hears my heels on the floor. His gaze darts away from the TV to my face and he stands, a look of confusion crossing his features. "You're back early?" And then he sees my tearstained face, and his own transforms, going from alarmed to murderous. "What happened? Do I need to pay Zayne a visit? Did he hurt you?"

Did he hurt me? I want to laugh. "I guess that depends on your definition of *hurt*. Read this, Dad." I take out my phone and show him the Little Birdie post.

I'm tempted to walk away while he holds my phone and reads so I don't have to see his reaction. But I don't. I watch the redness appear on his cheeks. I watch as the corners of his brows turn down. I can only imagine how similar Mom's reaction would be if she were here.

Dad's eyes flicker to my face. "What's the meaning of

this, Bardot?" He hands me my phone and crosses his arms. "Is this true?"

I shrug. "I don't know. Probably." My voice sounds so small, even to my own ears. I just want to crawl under a rock, hide, and never come out. Everyone at Fallbrook is going to have a field day with this news. My shoulders sag. "I just want to go to bed and forget all about this."

At first, he looks like he wants to argue with me, but then his gaze seems to soften. He nods. "Alright, baby. Let me know if you need anything."

I shuffle down the hall to my room, kicking my heels off once I'm inside and the door is shut. My breathing starts to come in heavier, faster spurts, and my vision blurs once again. *Zayne lied,* my brain screams. *He lied, he lied, he lied.*

I strip out of my dress with harsh, rushed, movements. There's a chance I'll tear the fabric of this beautiful dress if I carry on like this, but I don't care. At least not right now. The sound of a thread snapping does nothing to my heart as the dress falls around my ankles. I kick it to the corner of my room and get into bed wearing nothing but my undergarments.

And then I continue crying.

I don't know how much time passes, but it feels good to let it all out. Really good. In fact, I can't remember the last time I cried like this, and part of me wonders if this is really all because of Zayne, or if my emotion is the product of other, heavier things as well. Either way, I don't stop until I'm all cried out, eyes dry and throat hoarse. My temples are sore from the strain, and my nose is stuffed.

Quietly, I dress into pajamas so I can get a glass of water and some tissues from the kitchen. When I crack my door open, I hear a familiar voice that leaves my heart thundering.

"Please," Zayne begs. "Please, Mr. Bennett. Just let me talk to her." I can't see him, but I imagine him holding up his hands in a praying motion. "This is all a huge misunderstanding."

"Seemed pretty clear to me," Dad growls. "I read the passage that—what was its name—*Little Birdie* put out."

"Little Birdie *lied*." Zayne's voice is strained. "Please. I'm telling you it was a lie. I never said any of that. Not one word."

"Goodnight, young man," Dad says. The door closes in Zayne's face.

I disappear back into my room before Dad can notice my eavesdropping. He trudges down the hall past my cracked door to his own. My heart softens with gratitude for him. It's a good feeling, having someone stand up for me no matter what. But I can't deny my hope that maybe, just maybe, Zayne's being honest.

My phone chimes with a text. I open his message.

ZAYNE

Please talk to me, Dot.

And another.

Please.

I just want to explain

> I know you don't believe me, but Little
> Birdie was lying.

Unable to resist, I respond.

ME

> So there is no Cassidy?

I can practically feel his relief like a palpable thing on the other end of the line.

ZAYNE

> Not exactly...

ME

> That's what I thought.

The knot reappears in my chest as I send one last text.

> Goodbye, Zayne.

And then I block his number.

It feels like cutting off my own arm.

My throat clogs with emotion. *I have to do this. I have to let him go.* And then the realization smacks into me with way too much force. *I love him.*

And along with the love, there's a mix of bitterness and gratitude, because I can't deny that I'm also thankful to Zayne. After all, he introduced me to a different side of acting than Carlton. It's through him that I discovered what makes me feel alive. I finally know what I want to do with my future.

I, Bardot Bennet, want to be an actress, and I want to go to Underwood.

Not to make my parents proud. Not to prove to Zayne that I'm good enough. Not even to steal Carlton's hopes for a spot this year.

I want to go for me.

And all I can do, after everything, is hope that I'm good enough.

Chapter Twenty-Eight

My oh my! Things have taken quite a turn, indeed. With the start of a new week under our wings, the event we've been awaiting is this very Saturday: the winter play! How awkward it will be, indeed!

Our poor little Dot has taken to eating her lunches alone, with not a friend in sight to comfort her. Perhaps one of those Evans twins, or even Rue Sullivan would make an appearance for her if Dot herself would, well, appear anywhere other than an empty classroom. But our It Girl has been M.I.A., hiding from her friends in places only I've noticed.

I do wonder how Zayne Silverman feels about

the tangled web of pain and despair Dot must be
enduring. It will certainly be a spectacle to watch
them star as lovers onstage this weekend for all
to see.

This faithful flapper wouldn't miss it if you
cut off my wings.

Yours truly,
Little Birdie

There's a part of me that wants to skip tech rehearsal to avoid seeing Zayne, but there's simply no way I could do that this close to the production.

It's been two days since I've spoken to Zayne, but I can't hide anymore, not now that we'll be forced to face each other. Now that his true intentions have been revealed, I just want to somehow forget him. I need to get through today's practice without letting my emotions get in the way, but I can't deny how much it hurts.

I get there early so I don't have to endure the eyes of everyone watching me enter the green room. I find a seat at my usual table in the corner and rest my head in my folded arms. A full minute passes before I hear a voice above me.

"Dot?"

I glance up, squinting as my eyes adjust to the fluorescent lighting. "Mr. Saltzman?"

He cocks his head to the side. "Are you all right?"

"Yes." I rub my eyes. "Just waiting for rehearsal to start."

He nods, but there's a frown on his face that only deepens. He lowers himself to sit in the chair beside me. "Well, while you're waiting, I just wanted to let you know I've been very impressed by how much your acting skills have improved since the start of the season."

"Wow. Um..." The compliment warms me. "Thanks, Mr. Saltzman. To be honest, sometimes I wonder why you cast me as the lead in the first place."

He clasps his hands together. "Now, that's one I've never heard before! Usually, students who get the lead expect it. But...you and Zayne make a great team, and an even better Cathy and Heathcliff. I suppose I saw something in your audition I couldn't ignore. "

I want to ask him what it was he saw in me. If it was only my chemistry with Zayne, or if it was *me*. But he stands, motioning toward the door with his hand. The sound of chatter approaches, sending nerves soaring through my stomach. "It looks like your classmates are arriving." He winks at me. "Break a leg."

He leaves to stand at the front of the green room and I'm left staring at the door as everyone else arrives, including Meredith, Mable, and Rue. And Carlton. I wave at them, and Rue nods in my direction, leading the rest of them over to me. They sit at the round table with me, and I'm struck by how much this feels like old times, when I was still trying to win Carlton's affection and fit into his group.

Now I have no idea where I belong. Once upon a time, I thought it was with Zayne.

My throat burns, so I clear it and try to smile at them. "Are you excited for tomorrow?" I ask Mabel.

Her eyes round as she smiles. "Heck yes!"

Carlton watches me, his head propped in his hands, elbows on his knees. He doesn't say anything but studies my face like he's not sure if I'm going to address him or not.

Spoiler alert, I want to tell him, *I'm not.*

Mr. Saltzman claps his hands together at the front of the room. "Welcome to the final round of rehearsals, everyone!" He smiles around the room. "We're almost done! You all should be proud."

The room starts to cheer, but the door flies open with a large slam, startling everyone into silence. Zayne stands in the doorway, his uniform disheveled and wrinkly. Some of his short dreads escape his usually neat bun, and when his eyes meet mine across the room, it feels like a spotlight shines right on us.

"Dot." He pins me with his gaze, oblivious of how crazy he looks with the entire cast and crew staring at us— including Mr. Saltzman. He crosses the room until he's an inch away from me and kneels at my side. "I need to talk to you."

I stare at the ground, cheeks burning. "We're at rehearsal." The words come out in a mumble. It almost sounds like I'm embarrassed, but really, I'm not prepared for the surge of emotions seeing him again makes me feel.

Mabel moves to stand so her body is blocking me from

Zayne's view, and as if by command, Rue and even Meredith follow suit until they block me like a protective wall. Carlton stands so he's towering over still-kneeling Zayne. He crosses his arms. "Not gonna happen, man. We all read Little Birdie. You're a jerk."

Zayne frowns and blinks like Carlton just spoke a foreign language. "I'm talking to *Dot*. Not you."

"No, you're not." Carlton doesn't budge. "Not if I have anything to say about it."

I roll my eyes. "I don't need your help, Carlton."

Zayne stands, shifting the balance so Carlton now has to look up at him instead of the other way around. His penetrating gaze finds me over the heads of my bodyguards. "Dot..." He holds his hands out, palms up. "*Please. Talk to me.*"

Mr. Saltzman removes his glasses to frown at us. "What exactly is going on?"

"Nothing," I say.

"Good. Then if we can all focus on rehearsal, that would be great."

Zayne sighs and sits at a table on the other side of the room.

I try not to meet his gaze as we all get fitted with our mics, but I can feel him looking at me, and I'm forced to endure the sensation through rehearsal.

The whole thing passes much too slowly, and until today, I didn't realize just how many scenes I have with Zayne.

As soon as it's over, I speed-walk out of the green room, but Mabel catches up to me. I'm about to run down the long staircase leading to the parking lot when her hand squeezes my shoulder. "Dot, I think you need the mall."

Rue is right next to Mabel when I spin around. "Yeah. Let's go. This is important." She grabs my hand and yanks me forward.

The mall. Like that's supposed to fix anything. But at the same time, I can't deny it sounds nice.

I follow Mabel and Rue outside to the parking lot, where Rue's silver sedan is parked and waiting. The cold air makes me shiver in my blazer. I rub my arms.

Rue starts her car up with the press of a button on her keys, and the three of us get in, Mabel taking shotgun.

I bite my lip. "Was that rehearsal as awkward as I think it was?"

Mabel turns to wrinkle her nose at me. "Oh, yeah. For sure. You and Zayne were really...stiff with your lines."

"Great," I mutter. The worst part is how guilty I feel knowing Zayne's performance was affected by me. Zayne, who never lets his personal life bleed into his acting.

Rue sighs, shifting the car into reverse. "I'm sure everything will be fine before the show. You just need to de-stress, which is why we're going shopppiinggggg!"

It takes us much longer than it should to arrive at Prudential Center in Boston, thanks to New England traffic. We probably would have gotten here faster if we walked. But when we find a parking spot on the street and step out into the open air, dome-shaped buildings and glass-front stores surrounding us, I breathe out any lingering tension left from seeing Zayne.

I follow my friends along the brick sidewalk. Tall buildings melt into the sky as we make our way to the nearest boutique. A firetruck cuts us off and honks at us as we navigate the packed crosswalk under a glass-walled bridge.

But then we enter sanctuary.

Mabel's mouth curves up into a smile. "Let's look at accessories."

She gravitates to a table full of sunglasses and headbands like a magnet, and we follow her. "Look at this!" She holds up a checkered scarf, eyes practically glowing. "Maybe I'll buy it for Meredith for Christmas."

I glance at Rue to gauge her reaction at the mention of Meredith. "Speaking of her, what's going on with you two?" I can't stop the words from slipping from my mouth.

"Uh..." Rue widens her gaze at Mabel, who just smirks.

"If you're talking about Little Birdie's blast about you having a crush on Carlton, it doesn't matter to me. I always knew something was up."

Rue looks horrified. "What do you mean?"

"Oh, you know." Mabel shrugs, holding a blouse against her chest to guess its sizing. "You're always gazing at him longingly. Being nice to him even when he's a complete jerk. And you seemed so sad when he liked Dot."

"I do not gaze longingly," Rue sputters. "I do not *gaze.*"

"The problem is," Mabel continues, "I think Mere likes him, too, and feels awkward around you now." She sighs. "Apparently, I'm the only one here who isn't obsessed with C."

I arch a brow at Rue. "Has she let you talk to her about what Little Birdie said? It seems like things are somewhat normal between the two of you."

"I haven't said a word to her since she asked me to give her space." Rue sighs. "And she hasn't brought it up either. I have a feeling she's never going to, either. It's just going to be this unspoken, awkward thing between us for the rest of our lives. Carlton hasn't said anything either. I think he's either ignoring it or he thinks none of it is true."

I touch her shoulder. "Just try talking to Meredith again. There are worse things than two best friends liking the same guy."

"Fine." Rue smirks. "I'll talk to her if you talk to Zayne."

I sigh, trudging forward to the boot section of the store. "And this conversation is over."

I hear them both giggle behind me, and though I should probably be irritated, their laughter somehow makes the situation feel lighter. Easier to withstand.

I spin back around to face them. "I love you guys."

Mabel blinks, her lips wobbling up into a smile. "Love you, too."

"Yeah, Dot. You're our girl." Rue reaches over and hugs me.

I close my eyes, a smile forming on my own lips. I missed this. I missed having friends and I forgot how much I needed them until now.

If there's one thing this whole mess with Zayne, Carlton, and Little Birdie has given me to be thankful for, I think silently, *it's them.*

My friends.

Chapter Twenty-Nine

I do my best at the following rehearsals, no matter how much it pains me to see Zayne, to avoid his attempts to speak to me, or listen to him call after me when I run in the other direction between scenes.

I endure his presence over the rest of the week, and on Friday, I tell myself it's almost over. This is the last rehearsal, the last chance to work out any kinks before tomorrow's performance.

Opening night.

I sling my backpack over my shoulder as I walk to the drama room. It's Saturday, and I contemplated not bringing a backpack, full of schoolwork I'll hopefully be able to get to during any downtime I have backstage. Now that I'm no longer dating Zayne, my brain has cleared him out and called my attention to more important things, like my slowly deteriorating GPA.

I try my best not to look in his direction when I open

the door to the green room, but I can't help it. I glance at him, sitting at a table with Jude and some other drama kids I never talk to. As if he can sense my gaze, Zayne glances up, meeting my stare. He looks solemn; resigned. It's like he's given up trying to explain to me what happened. Like he's given up hope on earning my forgiveness, on our relationship.

I ignore the feeling like a knife in my chest and remind myself: *That's exactly what you wanted him to do.*

I set my stuff down on the table my friends are at. Mabel is applying stage makeup with a small, rhinestone compact in her other hand, and Meredith is digging through her purse. "Stupid bag," she mutters. "It's like it *eats* everything important."

"Actually, you're just nervous," says Mabel. "And if you're looking for your falsies, I have them in my bag."

"Oh." Meredith relaxes. "Thanks."

"Hey, D." Rue waves at me from her spot next to Mabel. She's resting her chin on her duffel bag, looking exhausted but done up in her practice look for tonight.

"You look great." I take a seat next to her and gesture to her face. "Can you do mine, too?"

She smiles. "Sure." But her smile falters a bit when I follow her stare, past me, to Zayne and his friends. She touches my hand. "It's going to be okay. You could always still, you know, talk to him."

I shake my head. "I have nothing to say."

Mr. Saltzman claps his hands at the front of the room. "We'll start in about twenty minutes. Be ready to blow my socks off. " He stares around the room. "You're an amazing group of actors. You should be proud of yourselves. *I'm proud to have you all in my production.*"

A collective, murmured, "Aw," floats around the room, and we shuffle out of our seats to put the finishing touches on our costumes.

I'm already dressed in my first look, which is Cathy as a ghost, when Mr. Saltzman approaches me. He lowers his glasses down to the bridge of his nose as he looks me in the eye. "I'm not sure what's going on with you and Zayne, Dot." His mouth curves downward. "But whatever it is, I need you to clear it up before opening night."

Shame burns my face, and I struggle to maintain eye contact with him. "I'm sorry for letting my own business affect the play, Mr. Saltzman."

"I don't want to see it happen again."

The way he looks at me makes me feel like I got onstage and forgot all my lines. "I promise it won't," I say.

"I hope you're right. And I expect you to bring the same chemistry to rehearsal as you would tomorrow's performance. No more miming the romance scenes with Zayne. I don't care if you hate his guts in real life. Onstage, he's the love of your life." He pushes his glasses back up on his face and walks away.

I take a deep breath to recover some of my confidence and swallow down the burning in my throat.

Stages have nothing to do with how I feel about Zayne.

Onstage, he's the love of my life, and offstage, he's no different.

Luckily, I have some time before my first scene. I need to mentally prepare myself to kiss Zayne today instead of miming it like I've done the past few rehearsals. In fact, I'll have to kiss him multiple times, and it's all I can think about because he's no ordinary kisser. I'm pretty sure kissing him for the first time is what pushed my feelings over the edge when I was still trying to fight them.

I shake off the thoughts of his lips against mine. Trailing up my neck, making my knees weak, and...*focus.* Today is about acting. Proving to myself I can give the best performance of my life regardless of the state of my heart.

If Mr. Saltzman wants chemistry, I'll show him chemistry.

We run through the first half of the play in a breeze. We've done this so many times, I can practically recite the whole performance in my sleep. And per Mr. Saltzman's request, I do my best to clear my head and give an amazing performance.

But now, it's time for the moment I've been dreading. I'm standing onstage with Zayne, dressed in a romantic Catherine Earnshaw look—a burgundy silk gown, complete with a corset, laced boots, and white gloves. The backdrops behind us are finally complete and perfectly painted, so detailed I feel like I'm on the set of a period drama TV show. I can't help but be impressed with the set crew's skill in painting the elegantly arched windows, the heavy gold drapes framing them, and the expensive-looking furniture of Wuthering Heights.

I ground out the lines I've said in front of him thousands of times now. "You returned on my wedding day, only to punish me."

But Mr. Saltzman cuts in. "Come on, Dot. Say it like you mean it. I need to feel more emotion from you. *More.*"

I blink in surprise. Am I not giving my best performance? There's no time left for mistakes like this. I should be on my A-Game right now.

I let my eyes bore into Zayne's, returning his intense gaze. And my toes feel numb in response.

In this particular scene, his expression is always intense, but I can't help but notice it's different this time. As if, for once, he's having trouble pushing his real feelings aside to stay in character.

So, instead of shoving mine down, I do the complete opposite. I let myself feel the heartbreak I've been trying to ignore since the dance, allowing it to fully slice through my chest like a knife.. "You returned on my wedding day," I say, "only to punish me."

His eyes fall to my lips. He places his hand on my waist, holding me firmly in place, but there's a subtle tremble in his hand, like he's afraid to break me, and his lips are against mine in the next moment.

The kiss starts as planned. Nothing more than a single, close-mouthed peck. But neither of us breaks apart. His mouth is soft and hot against mine, and when I part my lips for him, I taste mint and the familiar coffee signature of Zayne.

I don't let go right away, gripping his costume shirt in my fists, and he kisses me like it's the last time he'll ever be allowed to, like in a moment, I'll vanish into thin air.

He's an even better kisser than I remembered.

My knees threaten to buckle as I try to find my way out of it, but I can't.

I am lost. And I want to stay lost.

The kiss lasts several more stretched-out moments, and then we finally come up for air, breaking apart but not letting go of one another. I catch Mr. Saltzman's smile from the corner of my eye. Zayne breathes like he just finished running a marathon, and I try to ignore the incessant thudding in my own chest. *Too much. This is too much for me.*

But I finish the scene because I have to. I need to prove that I can do this. That he doesn't affect me the way he thinks he does.

Mr. Saltzman doesn't give us commentary, which means we did a good job, and then Carlton is brought onstage, displaying one of the most generic performances of his I've ever seen. We run through the entire scene, and then the next. After that, the three of us are allowed backstage.

I rush past Zayne without a word.

"Dot!" His voice is as wounded as I feel, but he has no reason to be upset.

I spin around and glare at him. The entire backstage cast is watching us, but I don't care. "You shouldn't have kissed me like that."

"I'm sorry." He holds up his hands. "You're right."

I wipe the corner of my eye, and a strong arm drapes across my shoulder. Carlton.

"It's alright, Dot," he says, making a show of rubbing my shoulder as he stares at Zayne. "Let's go find a seat."

Zayne's eyes harden into ice. "Take your hand off her."

"Both of you, stop it." I shrug out from Carlton's embrace and roll my eyes. "Just leave me alone."

I leave them both standing there and find a chair in the corner of the green room. I sit in it, ignoring the blatant stares and whispers buzzing around the room. Rue and the twins have a scene together right now, so I have no one else to sit with. But I don't even care. I'd rather not talk to anyone. In fact, I can't believe I have to do this all over again tonight.

But if there's one thing I've learned in theater, it's that the show must go on.

After rehearsal, Mr. Saltzman informs us all on what a good job we did today. "I couldn't be prouder," he tells us. We're seated backstage, and he stands at the podium with a proud smile on his face. "It went even better than I expected. Now go home, take a nice long break, and I'll see you all back here tomorrow for opening night."

Applause sounds in the room. I clap along halfheartedly. The room empties then, and Mr. Saltzman goes back to the stage to check the tape placement the actors will use for blocking. I remain seated. I don't have the energy to move just yet. Not after that kiss.

I stare at the ground, but I know there's only one other person in the room with me now. Of course, there is. I lift my head to look at him, standing a few feet away, waiting for the right moment to speak. "Go away, Zayne," I say. "It's over. Accept it."

His shoulders tense. "Not until you let me explain." He approaches my table and sits beside me in a chair. "After that, I'll accept it. I promise."

"What makes you think I'll believe anything you say?"

He opens his mouth to answer, but an alarm goes off on someone's phone. It's too loud and distracting to ignore, so I get up to find and silence it. It's better than sitting here, listening to pathetic excuses anyway.

I find the phone, still blaring, on the podium, and press snooze. "I think this is Mr. Saltzman's," I mutter, swiping at the lock screen. "He must have left it by accident."

Zayne nods, but I squint at the screen when it opens. The phone doesn't have a password, and I can't help but recognize the page our drama teacher has opened on the screen, because it turns my stomach. I hold up the phone. "Even our teacher reads Little Birdie."

Zayne shrugs. "That's great for him. I really think we should—"

"Wait a minute." I scroll, squinting at the page, at the familiar branding of the site, but confused by the unfamiliar formatting of it. At the word in the top corner. "Admin? Why does it say admin?"

Zayne pauses. And then his eyes go round. "*What?*"

In the next moment, his body is next to mine at the podium and we're both staring at Mr. Saltzman's phone. At the *Little Birdie* admin dashboard. We see the unposted drafts in his archive. The already posted blasts along with their analytics. A folder of anonymous tips from classmates, strangers, and even a few from Lenny—*Lenny?!*—all sent in for Little Birdie to post if she wishes.

...If *he* wishes.

Mr. Saltzman rushes into the room. He pauses in the front of the podium, holding his stomach, breathless from running. He stares at me and Zayne with wide, alarmed eyes. Waits for us to speak.

I flip the phone around, showing him what we're seeing. "*You're* Little Birdie?"

"Oh, no." He cringes, and red spots appear on his cheeks. "I was afraid of this."

"You better start talking. *Now.*" Zayne steps in front of me. "Because if you're the one spreading all these lies and meddling with your students' lives, I'm going to need a really good reason not to report you."

His already white face gets a little paler. "I'm your teacher. No one would believe you, Zayne, and I'd have you expelled for trying."

"Before your play?" Zayne crosses his arms. "The one Little Birdie—I mean, *you*—have been urging everyone around here to come watch? I don't think so. Talk."

Mr. Saltzman gazes at me helplessly, but I don't budge. I just stand there, confused and feeling like I'm going to be sick .

"I wasn't always Little Birdie," he whispers. I can't help but notice the way his pulse thrums rapidly in his throat. The way his hands shake as he fiddles with them. "It used to be my daughter. She attended this school nine years ago, and after she graduated, I found the app she developed on her phone. I was extremely impressed, but then again, my little Layla has always been a genius. When I approached her about it, she told me she was done with it, on to bigger and better things. I forgot about it for a while. And then my job was in danger."

I frown. "What do you mean?"

"Fallbrook's drama club wasn't always what it is now," he explains. Without seeming to realize it, he falls back into the seat at his podium. I stay standing, still holding the phone, and Zayne remains at my side. My heart thuds against my ribcage. "Kids used to consider this department very nerdy," Mr. Saltzman continues. "It was like pulling teeth getting anyone to join. Which meant there wasn't a huge need for a drama teacher. I was in danger of being laid off."

"So, you took over your daughter's app," I cut in, "because...?"

He holds up a finger. "I'm getting there."

Zayne glares at him. "Wrap it up."

"I had to find a way to get people to join," he cries. "So, I used Little Birdie's voice to make it sound appealing. And then I used the app as a sort of tabloid for the acting students. To make them sound like celebrities. And it *worked*." In spite of his obvious fear, he holds his chin a little higher. "We had more than enough students after that. I had to turn kids away. And soon enough, Fallbrook's drama department caught the eye of Underwood Academy and earned its prestigious reputation."

I cross my arms. "That doesn't give you the right to meddle in people's lives. It's wrong, Mr. Saltzman. Gossiping is wrong, and this is supposed to be a Christian school."

He offers me a sad, knowing smile. "But it keeps the drama club thriving. It keeps people interested."

"Do you have any idea what you've done to my life?" I shake my head. "You posted about my mom stealing pills on Thanksgiving!"

"Wait a minute," says Zayne. "How did you know about the pills? Were you, like, outside my house on a freaking holiday like a complete psycho?"

Mr. Saltzman utters a nervous laugh. "I *did* say I was flying around the neighborhood, didn't I? Perhaps, I hoped there would be something newsworthy to spread about you two after the holiday. And I was right."

I gape at him. Tears cloud my vision as I imagine him witnessing the events with Mom. It's humiliating.

Zayne shakes his head. "And what about my audition script? Did you already know what Carlton did to it?"

"Carlton?" Mr. Saltzman laughs like we're all good friends sharing a joke. Maybe it's his way of trying to calm us down. "I gave you both a marked up script." At Zayne's murderous scowl, he holds up his hands. "You have to understand how much everyone *loves* your feud with Carlton, Zayne. I was just giving them what they wanted."

"You mean they were both innocent?" I ask. "And you knew they'd both assume the other was sabotaging them?"

Mr. Saltzman shrugs. "Before you two get mad, listen. I already knew who I was going to cast as Edgar and Heathcliff." He turns his gaze on me. "Zayne and Carlton are both talented, qualified actors. It didn't matter if they flubbed their auditions with those scripts. That was all purely to keep the feud going for the column. Same with the snake in Carlton's backpack."

I swallow back my tears so I can ask him the question I've been wondering all along. "Why about me? Why did you really cast me as the lead if you have so many people who want to be in your play?"

He bites away a grin. "Because you were pretty good, but better yet, you're a new actress, and I knew it would make the others angry and jealous. Stir up more drama. I really meant it when I said you two have great chemistry."

My stomach sinks at his words. "So, it wasn't because you saw something special in me?" There's a roaring in my ears I can't ignore. All this time, I thought I had a natural talent Mr. Saltzman couldn't resist. I've been storing that thought in the forefront of my mind to keep myself going. To keep me from quitting. Now that I know he cast me as the lead for the sake of causing drama, I can't help but feel like an imposter who can't act at all.

Zayne sighs. It's like he can sense my disappointment. "You've become the best actress I know, Dot." He touches my arm, sending warmth back into my cold limbs.

"And you're the best liar I know." I pull my arm away from him, but then realize what I just said. I turn to face Little Birdie himself. "Or...is he?

Zayne's lips part. His gaze jumps to Mr. Saltzman, who is watching us with interest. "Tell her," he grounds out. "Tell her the truth about that trash you posted during the dance."

The drama teacher holds up his hands. "I didn't lie. I said I got my information from an insider who claims to have heard you speak those words. I never said I heard them myself."

"Who was your source?" I ask, my eyes narrowing.

But Mr. Saltzman shakes his head. "You'll never get me to talk. Now give me back my phone."

"Who is the insider?" Zayne takes an aggressive step toward Mr. Saltzman. "So help me, I will go to jail over this, and it will be worth it. Don't test me!"

A pathetic squeal escapes Mr. Saltzman's lips, and he shrinks back into his chair. "Carlton! It was Carlton. He sent in a very detailed tip. Please, don't touch me!"

Zayne stiffens. "I should have known."

My face burns like it's on fire. I want to throw something, or yell at someone in frustration. But now is not the time. "Delete the site." I make my voice as firm as possible. "Get rid of Little Birdie. Enough is enough."

"Absolutely not." Mr. Saltzman crosses his arms. "You can't make me."

"I can if you want to keep your job." Zayne balls his hand into a fist, but I grab his arm to keep him from lunging at our teacher.

"It's not worth it," I whisper. By some miracle, he seems to relax his tense form. To Mr. Saltzman, I say, "You've broken so many school rules with this app. We could report you. If you care about your job so much, you'll take this seriously."

He pushes his glasses up his nose. He's wearing a poker face, so I can't tell if my threat makes him nervous or not. "I'll offer you both immunity from the *Little Birdie* platform in exchange for your silence."

"Or we could just get you fired." Zayne crosses his arms. "And you just committed a crime called blackmail. That's grounds for arrest."

Mr. Saltzman shifts in his chair. His cheeks are set aflame, nearly crimson against his round, pale face, and a bead of sweat forms at his temple. "You can't prove anything."

"Actually, I can." Zayne reaches into his pocket and points his phone in the teacher's direction. I started recording when you first ran in, looking all nervous. Say hi to the camera."

"I..." His chin wobbles like a nutcracker. "I'll shut down the app. I promise. No more Little Birdie." He presses his palms together. "I can't lose my job. *Please.*"

The pressure in my chest eases. "You'll have to make one more post, saying goodbye. That way we'll know you're serious."

Mr. Saltzman gravely looks us each in the eye through his glasses. "You have my word." Pain is visible in his gaze. I know he's probably devastated that he'll have to give up this ridiculous legacy he built on the backs of his students, but I don't care. He deserves to feel every ounce of pain he's inflicted on others with this mess.

"Then we have a deal." I hand him back the phone.

Chapter Thirty

My dearest Fledglings,

After months and months of waiting, the event we've all long awaited has finally come to play! Excuse the pun, my darlings, but this fearless flapper is flying on cloud nine after a most unforgettable performance!

Of course, anyone who's anyone was in attendance tonight. You all saw the look of undeniable superiority in Zayne Silverman's eyes as he delivered each flawless, expert line. The way Dot Bennett seemed to melt under his gaze, but still maintain character and composure. Is it safe to assume these delightful darlings have patched up the holes in their relationship? This Little Birdie thinks so!

And who could forget the star guest of the evening? No, your eyes did not deceive you. None other than Nigel Weathers, superintendent of Underwood Academy, was in attendance. And we saw the way he eyed our starring actors. I do wonder...will he choose them to attend his acting school which no other can surpass in esteem?

While this is certainly happy news, it comes with a hint of despair.

It is with heavy wings and a heavier heart that I write this final letter to you, my loyal flock. Yes, you read that right. This is my final farewell to you. I must fly south for the winter, and possibly forever. But take heart—where one birdie leaves, another is sure to arrive.

It has been my finest pleasure to serve you your delicious worms of gossip, straight from my beak to yours. But now my darling fledglings, you must learn to fend for yourselves, retrieve the worm on your own. Your wings are grown and ready.

Yours Truly, always and forever,
Little Birdie

Chapter Thirty-One

The applause echoing around the theater, around *us*, is surreal. It's like all the work we've put into the play, memorizing our lines, dealing with drama and Little Birdie, is worth it right now. All the hard work and effort...paid off. Seeing the audience cheer for us is empowering in a way I never expected.

It's going to be hard to beat this.

Zayne takes my hand, and together, we bow for the audience, earning us a new, louder round of cheers. A few whistles echo around us, too. It's all I see, all I hear, and then we're backstage again, hugging and congratulating one another on the performance. I avoid hugging Zayne even though I don't have a reason to anymore. Now that I know Carlton is the one who claimed he said all those things, I'm not mad at Zayne. I know Carlton, and I know he lied. But still, Zayne did kind of admit to the Cassidy situation being true, so I don't know what to think.

A collective hush falls across the room as Mr. Saltzman enters with a man in a navy blue suit with similar square-framed glasses. He has dark, spiky hair, with a single, purposeful white stripe in the front.

Nigel Weathers.

A few girls in the corner of the room squeal as he walks further into the room, and I hear someone say, "I can't believe it's him."

Mr. Saltzman avoids my gaze. I don't blame him. I tore down his entire safety net, should things go downhill for the drama club ever again. He lingers near the exit, but Nigel continues forward.

"You did amazing," comes a whispered voice from behind me.

I turn around. It's Zayne. He's still in his elegant suit costume, and the look in his eyes is equally proud and resigned.

I swallow. "Thanks. You did, too."

He smiles, and then his eyes widen imperceptibly as he gazes at someone behind me. I turn back around to find Nigel standing in front of us. His smile is wide as he appraises the two of us, teeth blindingly white; almost offensively so. I can't help but stare.

"Zayne Silverman," he says. "I'm Nigel Weathers, a representative from Underwood Academy." As if Zayne, along with everyone else in this room, doesn't already know. As if Zayne hasn't lived and breathed this moment his entire life. Dreamed of it from the moment he knew he loved acting. Nigel reaches out and shakes Zayne's hand. "I was enchanted by your performance tonight," he continues. "I'd love to offer you a spot at Underwood next year."

The floor seems to drop out from underneath me.

Zayne did it. *He did it.* He won.

A swell of pride for him blossoms in my chest, breaking through my defenses. It's strong enough to bring tears to my eyes. *I'm going to miss him so much when he transfers.*

"Wait," Zayne says, holding out his hand. "I don't want to go unless Dot is getting in, too." He places his hand on my shoulder, his eyes pleading with Nigel. "I get that's not really how this works, but if the other spot isn't for her...."

"Zayne." I gape at him like a fish. *What is he doing?* Our gazes meet. His eyes, so fierce on mine like they have a voice of their own, saying *I won't leave without you.*

"I see." Nigel frowns, glancing back and forth between the two of us. "Well, lucky for you, we *do* have two spots available, and the second spot is for her." He checks his clipboard. "Slot number two is Bardot Bennett. We'll be sending you both your official acceptance letters at the beginning of January, so be sure to keep an eye out for them. That is, if it's what *you* want, Dot."

"Yes, please." I try to sound normal, but my nerves are currently somersaulting. I bounce up and down and clap my hands together. A high-pitched squeal escapes me. "Thank you so much!"

Nigel shakes both of our hands and we stare as he turns and walks away. A moment of stunned, absolute silence passes before we're hugging, Zayne lifting me into the air and spinning me. I see Carlton watching us with wide eyes before he storms out of the room, but I don't let it get to me.

"We're going to Underwood!" My voice comes out in a blur of laughter. The rest of the cast is clapping for us, cheering for us.

I'm going to Underwood Academy.

With Zayne.

When he stops spinning me, I frown at him. "You were going to give up your spot if I didn't get in?"

"Of course I was." He takes a deep breath, like he's preparing himself. "Underwood may be my dream, but it would never be the same without you." He touches my face. Swallows, making his Adam's apple bob. "I'm sorry for everything," he whispers, pulling me to the corner of the green room, away from prying eyes and ears. "All of it. I never thought you'd be the one getting hurt."

"It doesn't matter. Carlton's a liar."

Zayne stares at the ground. "Yeah, he is. But he was right about Cassidy. That really happened."

My heart races at his admission, and I can't help but feel a little scared he's going to tell me more of it was true.

"We dated to improve the way our characters interacted onstage. But that was the only time I've ever done that, and it was Cassidy's idea to begin with. You and I, Dot… you're real." He swallows hard, motioning at the air between us. "We're real. I've never loved anyone like I love you."

I nod, taking his hand. I hold it against my chest. My pulse thuds like crazy. "I know. I—I feel the same way about you."

His eyes shine. "Can I please kiss you?"

I try to speak, but there's emotion clogging my throat. Instead, I grab the front of his shirt and pull him to me, kissing him with a ferocity that leaves us both breathless. I don't care if anyone sees us. All I care about is Zayne's lips on mine, and the knowledge that we're taking our next steps together. There's not a thing that anyone else can do to stop us, especially Little Birdie.

I sit on my rooftop when I get home. It feels like a full-circle moment, sitting here, watching the stars, because technically this is where it all started. This is where I met Carlton.

I think about Mom, how when summer began, I was such a mess, unable to see the good in her absence. All I wanted was for her to come back, and I let Carlton fill that void.

Now, I feel so incredibly full, thanks to the closure I got from seeing her again and from forgiving her.

"Mind if I sit with you?"

I jump, startled at the unexpected voice. I squint in the darkness to see Carlton climbing up the ladder propped up against the side of my house. Thankfully, having it there isn't as awkward now that Christmas is coming and people are starting to string lights up on their houses around the neighborhood.

My nerves skyrocket at seeing him. Is he going to yell at me? Tell me I don't deserve to go to Underwood? Or maybe he's just here to plant more seeds of doubt in my mind.

"What are you doing here? You came up way too quietly for my liking," I say.

"Sorry." He smiles tightly and sits down, letting his legs dangle off the edge of the roof. He stares up at the stars, his mouth pressed together.

"You okay?" I nudge him with my shoulder. I know I should be mad at him for spreading those lies about Zayne, for breaking us up, but I can't find it in me. In fact, I feel on top of the world and...kind of sorry for him.

"My parents officially split," he mumbles.

"Oh, Carlton." I shake my head. "I'm so sorry."

He turns to face me. "I owe you an apology, Dot. For—"

"I know. It's okay." I shrug. "I get it, I guess."

"I also wanted to thank you." He frowns at the shingled roof we're sitting on. "All this time I've been so focused on getting into Underwood, I never took the time to figure out if it was what I really wanted. I knew my parents wanted it, but me?" He blinks too quickly. "I couldn't help but feel relieved when I didn't get the spot. It's weird, but it felt like this immense pressure lifted off me."

I purse my lips. "I get it."

He meets my gaze. "I'm happy for you and Zayne," he tells me. His next words are laced with a subtle note of mirth. "But I still hate him."

I roll my eyes, biting back a smile. "Then you should get going, because he'll be here any minute to pick me up."

His brows narrow. "Sneaking out? This late?"

"He wants to celebrate."

Carlton sighs. I can't help but wonder if he regrets how things ended between us, but at the same time, I'm grateful for it. If he hadn't treated me so badly while we were together, I would have missed out on so much later on. Getting to know Zayne. Getting to know myself.

"Goodnight, Carlton."

"Night, Dot."

I get up, leaving him on my roof, and climb down the ladder.

And then Zayne pulls up on the street. *Perfect timing.* I grin and run to the car. When I get in, Carlton is climbing down the ladder.

Zayne tilts his head sideways. "Is that...?"

"Carlton? Yeah." I nod. "He wanted to apologize and say thank you."

"Oh." He frowns and rolls down his window to holler at Carlton. "I still hate you, Peters!"

Carlton freezes and peers at Zayne from across the street. "You too, Silverman," he calls back. I note with amusement that it somehow sounds like a compliment.

As we drive off, I get a text from Rue.

RUE

Talking to Meredith and Carlton tonight.
Wish me luck.

With a smile, I respond to her message.

ME

Good luck. You got this.

I tuck my phone away and watch the starry night unfold above us as Zayne drives. The future feels uncertain, but there's something steady about the way we're moving forward. Underwood Academy will bring its challenges—there's no doubt about that—but we'll take them one at a time, stage by stage.

Zayne's fingers intertwine with mine, his lips brushing my knuckles in a silent promise. I don't need to ask him where we go from here. We've mastered the script, and this is just the beginning of our story—onstage and off.

Want to know who sent what information to Little Birdie? Scan or click the QR code to join my VIP list and gain access to the *Little Birdie Admin Page*!

Thank you so much for reading *Stages*! If you enjoyed this book, I hope you'll consider leaving a review on your favorite platform(s). Every single one helps and it would also make me smile bigger than a sunflower.

Warm hugs and happy wishes,
Whitney

Acknowledgments

I have so many people to thank for helping me along the way with this book.

As always, I'm grateful to God for everything good that comes my way, always and forever.

Michael, thank you for your endless support and for showing me what happens after happily-ever-after. I'm obsessed with you.

Oliver and Phoebe, thank you for sharing your mommy with so many fictional characters and making me smile when I come back to reality.

I'm so very grateful to all my family and friends for always supporting and uplifting me. You all know who you are. Thank you.

Thank you Ashley Seals and Cait Elise for being my ride-or-die besties from the moment I wake up until I fall asleep, and the honest but entertaining voices I always need to hear.

Special thanks to my amazing cover designer, Andra Murarasu, for plucking Dot and Zayne straight out of my imagination and drawing them so accurately, down to every micro-expression. Thank you for giving Stages the most beautiful cover I could imagine.

Thank you to my editor, Wendy Higgins, for rooting so hard for this book and fixing all those rebel commas. Also, thanks for being a mentor to me all these years and for being an all-around wonderful human.

Thank you to the outstanding youths at the Young Editors Project, who read this story in its earliest draft:

Cara from Doncaster, United Kingdom

Isabella from Missoula, Montana

Tamia from Bath, United Kingdom

Lydia from Bath, United Kingdom

Corinne from New York City, New York

Ilaria from Trieste, Italy

Evelyn from Bath, United Kingdom

Ashley from Draper, Utah

Isabelle from Sheffield, United Kingdom

You all are pure gold. I couldn't have done it without you. And Anika Hussain, Young Editors Project Manager, thank you for giving me the invaluable opportunity to participate in your project. Your feedback fueled my enthusiasm and helped shape the bones of my story, and I am forever grateful.

And thank you, reader, holding this book. You're what makes all this worthwhile to me and I love you so very much. <3

Keep in Touch with Whitney Amazeen

Get all my book news, sneak peeks, bonus content, and more exciting stuff by signing up for my newsletter at

WHITNEYAMAZEEN.COM/NEWSLETTER

About the Author

Whitney Amazeen writes cute, cozy love stories with a sprinkle of faith.

Her love for books grew into an obsession in third grade and has been going strong ever since. Before pursuing writing, she studied cosmetology, where she used to hide in the laundry room to read, and work on stories instead of clients.

When she's not writing, Whitney can often be found playing Sims, snuggling with her dogs, and obsessing over Jesus.

Whitney is a California native who now lives in Arizona with her family and expansive tea collection.

Please visit WhitneyAmazeen.com and find her on social media @WhitneyAmazeen!

instagram.com/WhitneyAmazeen

tiktok.com/@whitneyamazeen

facebook.com/WhitneyAmazeenBooks

Also by Whitney Amazeen

Meadow Hills Series

A Summer of Dandelions

Carefree Series

One Carefree Day

One Day Too Late

Something Bright and Burning

9 781961 559868